7/16

DRAGONS REBORN

Suffolk Libraries

AMAZ 7/16

FAN

DRAGONS REBORN

REQUIEM FOR DRAGONS, BOOK II

DANIEL ARENSON

Copyright © 2015 by Daniel Arenson

All rights reserved.

This novel is a work of fiction. Names, characters, places and incidents are either the product of the author's imagination, or, if real, used fictitiously.

No part of this book may be reproduced or transmitted in any form or by an electronic or mechanical means, including photocopying, recording or by any information storage and retrieval system, without the express written permission of the author.

AMITY

She shuffled out of her cell, weak and bleeding, into an arena of fire, death, and the roars of thousands.

Torches blazed around her, filling the chamber with smoke, heat, and dancing shadows. Amity coughed and had to blink a few times, bringing the world into focus. When finally her eyes cleared, her heart sank.

"Bloody shite." She bared her teeth. "Korvin, am I passed out drunk and dreaming again, or are you seeing this too?"

She glanced to her side. Korvin walked there, jaw clenched and eyes dark. His hands balled into fists, and sweat beaded on his brow. Chains hobbled both their ankles.

"Be calm." His voice was low, strained. "Be focused. We can kill it."

Amity spat. "Like an ant can kill a donkey by biting its arse."

Guards of the Horde, bearded men wearing leather and ring mail, knelt to unchain Amity and Korvin. The manacles clattered off their ankles. Amity spun around, wanting to leap back into her prison cell, only to see the guards slam the door shut, sealing her outside. She had spent days banging on that door, trying to break out. Now all she wanted to do was flee back inside. She spun toward the arena again, spitting out every foul curse she knew.

She stood in a vast cave, a cavern larger than any palace or temple, a hollowed-out mountain. All along the craggy walls, alcoves dug into the rock, sealed off with wire mesh. Thousands of these holes spread all around like a honeycomb, spreading hundreds of feet up, and within each burrow, men and women chanted and roared. The crowd--people of the Horde--drank from tankards of ale, sang songs of death, and cried out for blood. High above, in one of the larger alcoves, stood Abina Kahan himself, King of the Horde. The bearded brute roared with the rest of them.

"Behemoth, Behemoth!" the king chanted. "Slay the weredragons!"

Amity gulped and looked back down. A round, rough floor spread before her, and here crouched the creature. The champion of the Horde. Her executioner.

The Behemoth.

"Ugly son of a whore, ain't he?" she muttered.

The creature's back was turned toward her. He lay on his belly, and many chains--the links larger than Amity's head--bound him to the floor. Even like this, lying down and chained, his size made Amity cringe. The monster was massive, several times larger than a dragon. His skin was warty and armored, reminding Amity of a rhinoceros, and many horns rose along his back. With every breath, his body creaked and smoke plumed. Heat emanated from the beast, and his stench wafted, the odor of rotted meat and sulfur.

Tales of Behemoth filled the ancient legends of the Horde. Amity had thought the beast only a myth. Now this myth seemed ready to slay her.

"Release the beast!" roared Abina Kahan from his alcove high above. The king waved a torch. "Unchain Behemoth!"

Along the chamber walls, guards placed keys into padlocks, freeing the chains from their brackets. The men quickly rushed back into their own alcoves, then slammed down iron meshes.

Only Amity and Korvin now remained in the arena. Before them, with a clatter of falling chains, Behemoth began to rise.

Amity gulped. "Spirit's flea-ridden beard, I've seen smaller mountains."

The crowd roared even louder than before, stamping their feet and banging their tankards against the wire meshes protecting them. Behemoth kept unfurling with cracking joints and creaking, thick hide. Smoke and heat rose from the beast, and his grumbles shook the arena. With thumping feet, the monster turned around to face Amity and Korvin.

Behemoth's head was as large as a dragon. A bony plate rose from his brow, lined with horns. His nostrils snorted out smoke, and eight white eyes narrowed above them, swirling like smelters of molten metal. His jaw unhooked, revealing a cavernous maw as large as a prison cell, and let out a roar. The sound blasted against Amity, ruffling her clothes and hair, deafening, shaking the mountain. She cried out in pain.

With blasts of smoke and a grumble that thudded against Amity's chest, Behemoth charged.

Amity and Korvin shifted.

She rose in the cavern, a red dragon, her wings stirring the smoke and stench. Korvin soared at her side, a charcoal dragon with chipped scales. The crowd cheered, and the two dragons blew their flames together.

The two fiery jets blasted forward, spinning and shrieking, white-hot, an inferno that could melt flesh and crumble bones to ash.

Behemoth crashed through the blaze as if charging through a light mist.

"Oh bloody bollocks!" Amity beat her wings, soaring higher.

She was too slow. The charging beast rammed into her like a god's hammer. Amity couldn't even scream. She gasped for breath, unable to inhale. She fell backward and slammed against the chasm wall, cracking the wire mesh protecting one of the alcoves.

Stars floated before her eyes, and through the haze of shadows and light, she saw Behemoth swing his head toward Korvin. The gray dragon was larger than she, the largest dragon Amity had ever seen, yet Behemoth knocked Korvin aside as easily as a bison ramming a deer.

Amity pushed herself off the wall, growled, and charged.

She breathed her dragonfire again. The jet crashed against Behemoth and sprayed off in a fountain, doing the beast no harm. An instant later, Amity slammed against the creature, biting and clawing at his face.

She cried out in pain. Her claws sparked against Behemoth's hide, and her fangs felt close to shattering when she bit. She might as well have attacked a slab of granite. The creature swung his head again, tossing her into the air, then swiped his paw.

Pain blasted through Amity.

Her scales cracked.

She tumbled through the air, hit the wall, and slumped down to the ground. She blinked, dizzy, struggling to cling to her dragon form.

Behemoth bellowed and charged toward her, feet shaking the arena.

Amity growled and ran, tail flicking, to meet him.

An instant before beast and dragon could slam together, Amity released her magic. She shrank and ran in human form, passing between Behemoth's legs and under his belly.

Behemoth slammed into the wall where Amity had lain instants ago. The beast shattered chips of stone and bent the wire meshes across several alcoves. Rock and metal rained. The crowd roared. Amity kept running between the creature's six legs. As she raced, she drew and raised her sword. The blade scraped against Behemoth's underbelly, spraying sparks but not cutting the skin. She might as well have stabbed a stone ceiling.

When she emerged behind the creature, she summoned her magic again and beat her wings, soaring.

"Korvin, the damn thing's harder than your backside!"

The gray dragon growled, flying forward. A gash bled on his head. "Aim for his eyes! Stab them out."

Before she could reply, Behemoth turned toward them, opened his maw wide, and blasted out a jet of raw, red smoke.

The cloud washed over the two dragons.

It felt like falling into the sun.

Amity couldn't breathe, couldn't see. The noxious smoke invaded her nostrils, her mouth, her ears, burning like acid. She tasted blood.

She fell and slammed against the ground. Korvin crashed down beside her, losing his dragon form on impact.

Amity clawed at her throat, coughing blood, struggling for breath. All around her, the people in the alcoves roared, and the chamber swayed. Amity couldn't help it; she gagged, losing what paltry food the jailors had been feeding her.

"Behemoth, Behemoth!" the crowd chanted.

From somewhere far above rose the cry of Abina Kahan. "Slay the weredragons!"

Amity pushed herself onto her knees, realizing she had lost her dragon magic too. Through stinging, watering eyes, she saw Behemoth stomping toward her.

She screamed and rolled aside an instant before his foot slammed down, cracking the ground.

She leaped into the air and shifted again, only for the beast's head to ram into her.

Amity cried out, tumbling through the air, wings flapping uselessly. The cavern spun around her, and blood seeped down her flanks. It was all she could do to maintain her dragon form. Before she could right herself, she slammed into the cavern wall, face-first, cracking the wire mesh protecting one of the alcoves.

Inside the burrow, King Kahan was laughing. He stepped forward and thrust his torch, and the fire burned Amity's cheek.

She cried out and fell, tumbling, wings beating. A heartbeat before she could hit the ground, she managed to steady herself and fly again.

Behemoth was charging toward Korvin now. The gray dragon was blowing fire, but the flames cascaded off Behemoth's face. With a roar, the beast's jaws snapped, crushing Korvin between them.

Amity screamed, swooped, and landed on Behemoth's back.

"Release him!" She clawed and bit, trying to break through the creature's skin. She managed to dig several inches into his leathery armor, but she could not reach the soft flesh and blood that surely lurked within. She snarled, climbed onto Behemoth's head, and drove her claws deep into one of his eyes.

The eyeball, large as a human head, popped and oozed across her paw.

The creature opened his jaws to scream, dropping Korvin to the ground.

Amity snarled and raised her claws again, prepared to pop a second eyeball.

Before she could claw again, the creature bucked madly. She clung on. Roaring, Behemoth leaped through the air, soaring higher and higher, rising hundreds of feet, racing toward the cavern ceiling.

"Oh bloody maggot guts!" Amity scampered off Behemoth's head an instant before the beast could crush her against the ceiling.

The stone cracked above and stones rained. Amity swooped, rocks pounding against her wings and scales. She glimpsed Korvin lying on the ground, bleeding, still in dragon form but unable to rise.

He's still alive. If he's still in dragon form, he's still alive. He--

Behemoth screeched above and blasted out more crimson smoke.

Amity screamed and dodged the noxious cloud. She rose higher, beating her wings madly, as Behemoth slammed back onto the cavern floor. The mountain shook. Rocks still rained from the ceiling, and the crowd cheered madly.

"Slay her, Behemoth!" Kahan cried from his alcove.

The beast charged forward. Amity blasted him with fire, but the flames wouldn't hurt him. She soared, narrowly dodging the assault. Behemoth rammed into the wall, horns driving through an alcove's wire mesh to pierce a cheering man within. Across the cavern, the crowd cheered louder than ever, delighted at the sight of death--even the death of a fellow spectator.

Behemoth tugged back from the alcove, letting his victim slump dead to the floor, then spun toward Amity and charged again.

Amity cursed and flew higher, but she was too slow. Behemoth's horn, still bloody, scraped across her leg. She cried out, and her own blood spilled.

"Korvin, up and fly, damn you!" she shouted down. The gray dragon rose slowly, groaning, bleeding.

Behemoth leaped toward Amity, and his jaws grabbed her wing.

Amity cried out and lost her magic.

She fell and slammed onto the ground, shouting in pain, a human again.

She could barely see, barely breathe, and her blood would not stop falling. She rolled just as the creature's paw slammed down. She rolled again, trying to swing her sword, only to lose the blade under his foot. The sword shattered. Behemoth screamed and blasted down his poisonous breath.

Amity closed her eyes, covered her ears, and knew she was going to die.

I can't beat him, she thought, gagging as the smoke washed over her. She couldn't see. She could hear nothing but the roaring beast, the chanting crowd. *I'm going to die here. I can't beat him.*

"Amity, fly!" Korvin's voice rose. "Fly, damn you!"

She could barely see; her eyes would not stop watering. She thought she could make out Korvin atop the creature, clawing and biting. Above in his alcove, the king laughed.

No, I can't beat this creature, Amity thought. *But maybe I can tame him.*

"Keep him busy, big boy!" she shouted. "I mean you, Korvin!"

She soared as fast as she could.

"Where are you going?" Korvin shouted, clawing at the creature.

"Lady business. Just keep Behemoth busy!"

She growled as she flew, narrowed her eyes, and sneered. Fire and smoke blasted around her, and her wounds dripped, and her eyes and throat still blazed with pain, but she refused to slow down.

I can ram things too.

She flattened her body into a spear and shot across the chamber. Ahead of her, inside his alcove, Abina Kahan cried out and stepped back.

With a roar, Amity drove into the iron mesh, shattering it. Her scaly head thrust into the king's alcove, and she blasted out her fire.

Her inferno filled the alcove like fire in an oven.

Kahan screamed and cowered behind his shield. The flames blasted around him, reaching around the shield to burn his limbs and grab his cloak. His guards screamed and fell, ablaze.

Amity released her magic.

She returned to human form, grabbed the ledge of the alcove, and climbed into the chamber. The fire died down, revealing the corpses of guards and a charred king.

Kahan was still alive. His skin peeled, hanging in sheets, revealing burnt muscles beneath. But still he roared, drew his sword, and raced toward Amity.

She knelt, grabbed a fallen guard's scimitar, and parried. The two blades clanged together.

For an instant, as outside still rose the roars of beast and dragon, Amity and the King of the Horde stared at each other. His beard was burnt, his face blackened, and his eyes blazed with hatred.

"Your son died a hero," Amity said. "You will die like a coward."

The blades pulled apart, then swung again. Showers sparked. Amity sneered and kicked, and her boot drove into the king's stomach. As he doubled over, she swung her scimitar with a scream, putting her entire body into the swipe. Her blade drove deep into the abina's neck.

Blood showered Amity, and she laughed. She tugged the blade free with a fresh gush of blood. The king's head wilted, half-severed, and his body crumpled to the ground.

Hang on a little longer, Korvin, Amity thought, swung her sword again, and cut the head free.

She lifted her gory trophy by the hair, walked back toward the shattered exit, and faced the arena again. Standing on the edge of the alcove, she raised the abina's head.

"Abina Kahan is dead!" she cried. "I claim dominion of the Horde!"

Dozens of guards had been climbing up toward her; they now froze and stared. Even the massive Behemoth gazed at her, blasting out smoke. Korvin slumped to the ground, bleeding from many wounds but still alive.

Amity's limbs shook, her belly ached, and her throat still blazed with pain. She was still bleeding, and poison still coursed through her. But she refused to collapse. She raised the severed head higher, and she let her voice ring across the arena.

"I am Amity of the Horde! I am your queen!" She tossed the head across the chamber. "Kneel before me!"

She ground her teeth, forcing a grin. The abina's son was dead, fallen in Leonis. The man had no other heirs. By the ancient rites of the Horde, it was she--slayer of the monarch--who ruled.

None had ever ascended this way, she knew. Here was a tradition of only the most ancient tribes, an ascension not seen in centuries. Would the people accept it?

"Kneel!" she shouted. "Kneel before your queen! If any dare challenge me, come to me now, and I will burn your flesh to ash. Kneel!"

The guards looked at one another, then back at her . . . and knelt.

Across the cavern, the thousands knelt inside their alcoves.

Even Behemoth, perhaps not as mindless as Amity had thought, grunted and slumped down with a thud, shaking the cavern.

Amity stood on the ledge, dripping blood and sweat, and gazed upon her people. Her grin widened, her jaw clenched, and her fingers tightened around her sword's hilt.

I came here begging for aid, she thought. *I found an empire to lead.*

"And this empire will fly toward you, Beatrix," she whispered. "The might of my Horde will descend upon your Cured Temple. Your head is next."

CADE

He knelt in the chamber, dizzy, as the world collapsed around him.

High Priestess Beatrix, sovereign of the Cured Temple, ruler of the Commonwealth, tyrant and monster . . . my mother. Cade's eyes stung, and he could barely breathe. *Mercy Deus, Paladin of the Spirit, the slayer of thousands . . . my sister.*

He stared up, eyes burning. He knelt in the Holy of Holies, the center of the Cured Temple and the heart of its faith. Marble tiles spread across the floor, and the round walls soared hundreds of feet tall, formed of white bricks. It felt like kneeling in the alabaster well of a god. In the center of this chamber, like a bone inside a hollow limb, soared King's Column, the most ancient artifact of Requiem, the pillar King Aeternum himself had raised thousands of years ago.

Standing above him were those who would see this ancient column fall.

High Priestess Beatrix smiled thinly, and her hand reached out to smooth Cade's hair. Yet there was no warmth to her pale blue eyes, no humanity to her face; it could have been a face carved from the same marble of the column. She was as pale as the chamber around her. Her robes were the purest white, her skin seemed bloodless, and her hair was the color of dry bones.

Beside her stood Mercy Deus, her daughter and heiress to the temple. While her mother was a priestess, Mercy had chosen the life of a paladin, a holy warrior of the Spirit. Rather than robes, she wore armor of white steel plates, a tillvine blossom--sigil of the Temple--engraved upon her breast. Like all paladins and priests, she shaved the left side of her head. On the right side, her hair was white, bleached to mimic the steel plates she wore. But unlike her mother, Mercy showed emotion in her eyes; *her* blue eyes were full of shock and loathing.

"What?" Mercy whispered, turning toward her mother. She seemed barely able to push the words past her lips. "This disease-ridden, pathetic weredragon . . . is my brother?"

Beatrix nodded and stroked Cade's cheek. Her eyes never left Cade, even as she spoke to Mercy. "Your father stole him. He tried to hide him. But Cade's back now. He's back in our family, and we will cure his disease. We will cure him now in the sight of King's Column." The High Priestess turned toward Mercy. "Bring forth tillvine. I will perform the purification myself."

Those words shocked Cade out of his paralysis. He rose to his feet, his chains clattering. He glared at the High Priestess.

"Enough." His chest shook, but he managed to stare steadily into those cold blue eyes. "This is madness. I've heard enough of your lies."

"The truth stands before you," Beatrix said. "Look at your sister. Her face is your face."

Cade turned to stare at Mercy. She stared back, eyes narrowed, lips tight. Cade tried to ignore her bleached hair, the anger in her eyes, to focus on her face alone . . . and he saw his face.

"Oh stars of Requiem," he whispered.

Beatrix nodded. "You are my son, Cade. You have a birthmark, shaped as a bean, on the inside of your left thigh, do you not? You have a little scar on your head, hidden under your hair, right above your ear. How else would I know, if I had not held you as a babe, nursed you, and--"

"Enough," Cade said again. He balled his hands into fists. His voice shook. "Maybe you're right. Maybe you were my mother. Maybe this was my family." His eyes burned and his knees shook. "That doesn't matter. None of it does. Derin and Tisha raised me. They were those who loved me, whom I loved." He spun toward Mercy. "And you murdered them, Mercy." He turned back toward Beatrix. "And you ordered them murdered, no doubt, like the countless others you killed, all those who refused the purification. I refuse it too." He raised his chin and forced himself to keep speaking, though his voice shook. "You're going to have to murder me too then. Your own son."

Beatrix's face changed. It was a subtle change--a deepening of the grooves alongside her mouth, a slight tightening of the lips, a kindling of fire in her eyes.

"Do not think," the High Priestess said softly, "that I would hesitate to slay you. But you would not die easily, boy. You would die screaming. In agony. Have you ever seen my men execute a prisoner? They will slice you open and pull out your entrails, but not before they cut off your manhood and burn it before you.

Emasculated and disemboweled, they will hang you upon the city walls, leaving you to slowly die. It can take hours. Days. If you defy me, that will be your fate, my beloved son."

A chill washed Cade. Only a moment ago, she had stroked his hair, spoken to him as a mother. Now she threatened mutilation and death?

"You're mad," he whispered.

Mercy stepped forth, grabbed Cade's arm, and twisted it behind his back. She drove her foot into the back of his knee, forcing him to kneel.

"I'll force-feed him the tillvine!" Mercy cried. "I'll stuff it into his impudent mouth!"

"No." Beatrix shook her head. "He's not a babe. He has known the magic all his life. He must relinquish it willingly. He must choose to devote himself to the Spirit, to the coming Falling." She knelt before Cade, held his head in her hands, and stared at him. "My son, my precious son . . . I will have you become a great paladin like Mercy, devoted to our cause. This is a fate you must choose for yourself, to abandon the disease inside you, to surrender your will to the Spirit."

"Or die in agony," Cade said, voice dry. "What kind of choice is that?"

"Still a choice. More than what Mercy offers you." Beatrix kissed his forehead. "I will return you to your cell now, where I want you to linger in darkness, in thought. I want you to think about the pain refusing me will bring you. I want you to think about the glory of the Spirit, the only one who can save you from that pain. You have until noon tomorrow to make your decision, son--to lose your magic . . . or to lose your life."

Mercy grabbed his arms, yanked him to his feet, and manhandled him toward the door. They left the Holy of Holies.

Cade's chains dragged and his blood dripped across the jeweled marble floors of the Cured Temple. They walked through halls of splendor--the floors a mosaic of precious metals, the columns gilded, the walls painted with pastel murals, and the ceiling a masterwork of jewels that glittered like stars. Mercy dragged him through these riches, then down into the craggy, dark dungeons, down into the chasm where men screamed in cells, tortured, broken.

"You'll soon break too," Mercy whispered into his ear, teeth clenched. "Look at them, Cade. This will be your fate."

She dragged him along a hallway lined with cells. Inside each cell, Cade saw the prisoners of the Cured Temple. In one cell, a man hung from chains, flayed alive, bleeding and weeping and begging for death. In another cell, a woman prayed feverishly as rats fed upon her, eating her alive. In a third cell, children hung from the wall, whipped and beaten, slowly dying. Aboveground, the Cured Temple displayed its glory; here under the surface beat its rotted heart.

"Don't think for a second that I believe this story," Mercy said, shoving him forward. "You, my brother?" She snorted. "No more than a rat could be my brother. Soon your flesh will be feeding rats."

They passed by another cell, and Cade's heart seemed to freeze. His eyes dampened.

There she was.

Oh stars.

The prisoner knelt inside, chained. Her red hair hid her face, and bruises covered her body. Her green eyes stared at him, shining with tears.

"Domi!" he cried.

He tried to break free from Mercy. He tried to dash toward her cell, to speak to her, to reach inside and touch her hand, comfort her.

"Cade," Domi whispered.

"Move!" Mercy cried and drove her fist into Cade's kidney. He cried out in pain, stumbling forward. Mercy grabbed a fistful of his hair, dragged him the last few feet forward, and tossed him into his own cell.

Cade fell onto the floor, chains rattling, and banged his knees. Mercy stood in the doorway, clad in her priceless armor, a seraph of beauty and light. She stared down at him in disgust and spat on him.

"I hope you choose death," she said. "I'll be the one to torture you. And I'll enjoy it. And I'll make it last a very long time." A mad grin stretched across her face, lurid, inhuman, a grin that tugged at her cheeks as if her face could split in two. It was the grin of a demon. "But not before you watch me do the same to your precious Domi."

With that, Mercy slammed the door shut, sealing Cade in darkness. He heard her footsteps leaving the dungeon, and then he heard nothing but the screams.

ROEN

He stood outside, slamming his axe into the logs again and again, and with every blow he wanted to shatter the world. With every blow, Roen saw her eyes again, saw her walking away, saw her blazing into his life with heat and softness and love, then vanishing, elusive as a sprite.

"Why did you ever come here?" He swung his axe down, cleaving the wooden log. He placed another log on the tree stump and swung again. "Just to love me, hurt me, leave again?"

His axe cleaved through the log, drove into the tree stump beneath, and embedded itself there. Roen grunted and tugged on the axe so mightily he couldn't control it. It tore free, flew backward through the air, hit an oak, then thumped to the forest floor.

Roen dropped to his knees with a similar thump, lowered his head, and clenched his fists at his sides. Piles of chopped wood rose around him in the forest, the pieces of his soul, for Fidelity had broken that soul as surely as he had chopped the wood.

He looked around him. The forest was beautiful, a place of peace, of home. Aspens, oaks, and sugar maples rustled around him, their leaves turning yellow, orange, and gold. Moss coated boulders and fallen logs, and the song of birds and rustling leaves filled the canopy. Roen had chosen this life, a life of solitude in the wilderness, a life of forgetting. Of escape. A life away from the Cured Temple, the bustle of cities, the oppression of the priests . . . and away from her.

Roen closed his eyes, the memories resurfacing.

It had been almost four years ago, on a summer dawn, that she had come into his life. From beyond the years, Roen could still hear the shrieks of firedrakes, still see the fire blaze overhead.

"Slay the weredragon!" the paladin had shouted, and the blast of their firedrakes' wings had shaken the forest canopy. "Burn the reptile!"

While his father still slept, Roen had woken before dawn, and he was fishing from a stream as light slowly filled the forest. At first he thought he was still asleep, still dreaming. Yet when he stared up, he saw her: a blue dragon fleeing across the sky, two firedrakes in pursuit.

"Burn the weredragon!"

Roen stared up, chest constricting, fingers shaking.

Weredragon.

His eyes stung.

My father and I are not alone.

He summoned his magic, the magic the Temple called a curse, and he soared as a green dragon. He crashed through the canopy, rose behind the firedrakes, and blasted out his fire.

His flaming jet washed over one paladin, and the man screamed, and his firedrake spun madly. Roen shot forth and lashed his claws, thrust his fangs, tasted blood, roared with rage. The firedrake crashed down to the forest, dead before it hit the trees. The second beast shot toward him, roaring out fire, and its rider shot arrows. Roen bellowed as the weapons slammed against him, but he refused to fall. He beat his wings, soared higher, and swooped. He felt like a mindless beast, like a firedrake himself, as his claws tore the paladin apart, then sank into the firedrake, ripping it open, sending it crashing down dead.

With his enemies slain upon the forest, Roen reared in the sky, stretched out his claws, and roared, a great roar that echoed for miles.

He had fled the Cured Temple to this forest. They had invaded his territory. He had sent them to their deaths, and his cry of rage rang across the land, a warning for all other enemies to hear and fear.

Hovering before him in the sky, the young blue dragon stared at him, eyes wide, wings beating.

The two dragons glided down and landed in the forest. Roen released his magic first and stood before her, a man again, clad in furs, his boots muddy, his face bearded, his hair strewn with leaves. The blue dragon released her magic next, stood before him as a girl, and pierced his heart with more pain than any arrow or sword could.

She was beautiful. Her blue eyes shone with tears behind her thick, round spectacles. Her golden braid hung across her shoulder. A gash bled on her thigh, and her lips trembled.

"I . . . I only wanted to fly a little in the night, but they saw me, and . . . oh stars, you're one of us." Her tears streamed down her cheeks. "Another Vir Requis. And you're hurt."

He gazed down at the blood pouring from his chest, then back up at her.

"Hello. I'm Roen."

She blinked away her tears. "I'm Fidelity. Oh stars, let me tend to your wounds."

She bandaged him, tearing off strips of her clothes, and she spoke to him of her life, of her books, of Requiem. He took her back to Old Hollow, his home within the log, to meet his father, to rest, to heal.

She told him she'd been traveling to Lynport in the south, seeking rare books the merchants were said to bring from overseas. He told her she was wounded, that she had to stay with him a few days longer to rest, to heal.

She stayed with him that autumn, an autumn of walking together through the forest, hand in hand, speaking of Requiem. An autumn of secret glances over dinner, of sitting close by the fire, of whispering of their dreams. An autumn of making love under the stars, feeling her naked body against his, holding her close, kissing her, sleeping with her in his arms.

An autumn that ended with snow, with loss.

"Stay," Roen told her. "Stay with us here. With Julian and me. You don't have to leave."

She wept. "I must. I must find the old books of Requiem, collect them, cherish them, hide them." She touched his cheek. "Come with me, Roen. Fight with me to preserve the memory of Requiem. To find our kingdom's old books, to keep them safe. To keep the memory alive."

He only shook his head. "And live in Sanctus, in a city full of priests and paladins? Surround myself with their holy books, pretending to serve them?" He laughed bitterly. "My father and I came into this forest to escape all that. To escape the Temple. How can I now go into that vipers' nest?"

"To be with me," she whispered and kissed him.

Yet he could not, no more than she could abandon her quest. With the first snows falling, she left him. Left his life cold. Empty. Scarred.

Until she returned.

"Until you returned, almost four years later," Roen whispered, kneeling between the piles of chopped wood. "Until you returned with your kisses, with your love, your life, your beauty, your softness . . . all those weapons that shatter me. You came to shatter my heart again, then leave."

A voice rose ahead of him. "That's a lot of firewood. Any trees left in the forest?"

Roen looked up to see his father. Julian wore old fur pelts and a leather belt. His feet were bare and muddy, and dry leaves were strewn through his long white beard. His tufted eyebrows shaded kind eyes.

"Enough are left," Roen said.

Julian walked toward the tree stump and sat down with creaking joints. "She'll be back someday, son. You'll see her again."

Roen nodded, jaw clenched. "In three years. Or four." He found himself digging his fingernails into his palms. "Is this such a bad home, Father? That she'd leave?"

Julian reached out and patted Roen's shoulder. "I like to think that I gave you a good home here, son. I moved to this forest so that I could raise you with your magic, keeping the light of Requiem burning inside you. But Fidelity, well . . . she craves more than solitude. She wants to spread that light. To let others see its glow. She wouldn't be happy here in the forest, shying away from a world she wants to save."

More anger filled Roen. He grabbed a rock and hurled it into the forest. "Save the world?" He snorted. "The world can go to the Abyss. Requiem is gone, Father. Why can't she see that? Is it really so bad to . . . to just want to live? At peace? To find a pocket of light in a world gone to darkness?"

"I don't think so." Julian smiled sadly. "That's why I raised you here. That's why we're sitting here now. But you cannot judge Fidelity for her war. She's brave and strong and willing to sacrifice her life for Requiem. So is her father. There is nobility to that."

"The line between nobility and foolishness is often blurry." Roen stared at an old maple tree which he had once climbed with

Fidelity. "I care about my life. Our life. Not the life of dead heroes, not a dead kingdom. She chose that dead kingdom over me." His voice was hoarse. "She abandoned me."

Julian nodded. "Aye, laddie. And she thinks the same of you. In her eyes, you chose the forest over her."

Roen spun toward his father, eyes red. "I wanted her to live in this forest! With us!"

"And did she not offer you to join her in Sanctus, to live with her father in the library?"

"That library burned." Roen's fists shook. "The paladins made sure to burn it. And now Fidelity and Cade are fighting some war they cannot win." He barked a laugh. "Cade--that foolish boy. I saw how he looked at Fidelity, how his eyes strayed down across her body, how he kept trying to hover around her, how--Father! Why are you laughing?"

The old man sighed. "Julian, do you hear yourself? Jealous of a boy? Fidelity loves you, my son. She'll love you always, even if you two are apart." Julian rose from the stump, walked toward Roen, and clasped his arm. "Now come, let's return to Old Hollow, and I'll cook you some mushroom stew."

Roen nodded, feeling weak, and lifted his axe. The two men turned to walk toward Old Hollow, the grand oak that was their home.

Dry leaves crunched behind them, making them pause.

Roen spun around and gasped.

"Fidelity," he whispered.

She stood in the forest, her clothes tattered, her skin scraped and bruised. Her spectacles hung crookedly on her nose, and her eyes were red.

"It's Cade," she whispered, trembling. "They captured him. Please. I need your help."

GEMINI

His mattress was stuffed with softest down, and his sheets were woven of purest silk, and Gemini would have stayed forever were his bladder not protesting. The damn thing felt ready to burst.

"Ggreehhar!" he called out, voice slurred. That was the name of his servant, was it not? It usually sufficed. "Grerehhuuu. Wherema chamer pot?"

He opened his eyes to slits and instantly regretted it. The damn sunlight was too bright, burning his eyes. Why had the servants not drawn his curtains? Why weren't they answering? Gemini pushed himself up in bed and saw the chamber pot all the way across the room. No servant was in sight.

His heart sank.

He'd have to walk.

"Spirit damn it."

He wanted to sink back into slumber, and for a moment he even tried to let sleep reclaim him, but his bladder wailed in protest. Grudgingly, he left the bed, stumbled nude toward the chamber pot, and proceeded to fill it. The damn thing was ridiculous. Was he the son of the High Priestess, or was he some peasant?

With a groan, he stumbled back into bed, pulled the sheets over him, and reached for the lump at his side.

"Domi," he whispered, stroking her. "Domi, I'm awake. Let's make love."

He reached down to caress her curves and kissed her, then winced.

What the Abyss?

He pulled the silken covers off to reveal not a gloriously nude Domi in the morning light . . . but a pillow. It was a fine pillow, to be sure, embroidered with sunbursts and stars, but it could hardly compare with the wonderful woman who had gone to bed with him last night.

This was not Gemini's morning.

He groaned, grabbed a bathrobe, and shoved his arms into the sleeves. This whole day was torturous so far. It didn't help that the damn palace was a hub of noise. From outside, he heard footsteps thumping, armor clanking, and priests chanting. It was louder than a den of firedrakes.

"Shut the bloody Abyss up!" he shouted.

Think, Gemini, he told himself. *Think. You'll get through this.*

"What do I do now?"

His eyes fell upon his table, specifically the jug of wine that stood on it. Yes. That's what he needed to do first. To drink a little. To clear that damn headache and think clearly. He shuffled forward, grabbed the jug, and drank deeply, letting rivulets of wine flow down his chin and chest. When finally he slammed the jug down, the pain blessedly left his head.

"Domi," he said. "I need to find Domi first."

It was unlike the girl to leave his chamber, not so early in the morning, at least. What time was it, anyway? Gemini frowned at the window. Judging by the position of the sun, it was . . . three in the afternoon, perhaps four. He groaned.

He opened his door, prepared to march outside and scour the Temple, only to knock into Mercy.

"Donkey bollocks!" he shouted. "Bloody Abyss, sister, what are you doing lurking outside my door?" He moaned. "Your armor is damn hard, and I think I bruised my elbow."

She stood before him, a statue of steel. "I've come to wake up your arse." She snorted. "You have no idea what's going on, do you?"

Gemini blinked, struggling to bring Mercy into focus. Spirit damn it, he needed more wine. "I know exactly what's going on. You're being a damn pest who needs to get out of my way. I'm looking for something very important. So move!"

Mercy sighed, refusing to budge. "If you're referring to your little redheaded strumpet, you won't find her."

Gemini was trying to shove past Mercy but froze, stepped back, and stared at her. Rage flared inside him. "What did you do to Domi?"

She laughed. "Does the whore have a name now?"

He swung his arm, prepared to backhand her. Mercy caught his wrist, blocking the blow, and twisted it painfully.

"Where is she?" Gemini hissed, baring his teeth. "Tell me, sister. Tell me, or I swear I'll bring every firedrake in this city down upon you, and their fire will roast you alive. Your precious armor will melt across your flesh as you scream." He shook his arm free and balled his hands into fists. "Where. Is. Domi?"

Mercy sighed. "You poor, piss-drunk fool." She turned to leave, then looked back over her shoulder. "Just make sure you're awake and sober tomorrow, will you? We'll be executing the weredragon at noon. You'll probably want to see it."

With that, she turned and marched away down the hallway.

Gemini stood in his doorway, shock pounding through him. His belly twisted. His fingers trembled. He could barely breathe.

"They know," he whispered. "Oh, Spirit, they know about Domi."

His eyes stung with tears. How could they have found out? How could Mercy and the others have discovered Domi's curse? Tears streamed down his cheeks.

You vowed to keep it secret, Domi! You promised me. You promised you'd hide your magic.

Gemini's knees were trembling now. How could anyone know? Only he had known her secret! Only he had seen Pyre, the great firedrake, shift into a woman named Domi, a woman who had become his servant, his lover. Only he--and Domi herself-- had ever known.

Mercy's words echoed in his mind: *We'll be executing the weredragon at noon.*

Bile rose in Gemini's throat.

"No," he whispered. "No." His voice rose to a howl. "No!"

He began to run down the hall, his robe swaying around him.

I'm going to find you, Domi. And I'm going to save you.

He kept racing through the hall, seeking her. His robe flapped around him, and he wished he had taken the time to don his armor.

"Stop!" he cried to a guard. The man was marching down the jeweled hall, clad in chain mail. Normally only paladins--noble warriors in white steel plates--were allowed within these halls, not the scummy cannon fodder of the lower classes.

"My lord!" The man knelt.

Gemini grabbed his shoulders. "What are you doing here? Since when are common guards allowed into the palace?"

Sweat beaded on the man's brow. "My lord, since the weredragon was captured. The High Priestess commanded us to patrol these halls."

Gemini's heart wrenched to think of such brutish, foul guards grabbing his beloved. "Where is she?" he shouted, shaking the man.

"She? My . . . my lord?"

"The weredragon!" Gemini shoved the guard backward.

"In . . . in the dungeon, my lord. I--"

"Give me your sword."

The guard hesitated, then gulped and handed over the weapon. It was a crude sword, the hilt wrapped in leather, and not a single jewel shone upon it. The blade was a coarse hunk of steel, not engraved or filigreed. It disgusted Gemini, but it would have to do for now, at least until he had time to return to his chambers and grab a proper sword. He marched on, leaving the guard behind.

Gemini had not been to the dungeon in years, not since he'd been a child. His mother used to take him there, force him to stare at the broken, tortured prisoners, force him to hear the screams, to watch the bones shatter, the whips tear into the flesh, the rats feast.

"If you misbehave, Gemini, I'm going to place you in one of these cells," Beatrix would say. "Be a good boy, or you'll scream here among them."

Young Gemini would weep, have nightmares of this place, wake up in terror, unable to move, thinking himself down in the cell, hammers breaking his bones, rats crawling over him. In panic, he would hide the sheets he wet during his nightmares, sure that wetting the bed would doom him to this fate. When he grew older, Beatrix had stopped taking him to the dungeon, but Gemini had never forgotten that place, never forgotten the way there.

Now a grown warrior, he made his way down the staircase . . . and into the underground.

"Please!" the prisoner screamed in his memory. "Please, no, not the pain!"

Gemini winced and froze halfway down a dark staircase. His breath quickened and his heart pounded against his ribs. Cold sweat trickled down his back. He forced himself to take a deep, ragged breath.

Domi is down there. She needs me.

He took another step down. Then another.

It seemed like he descended forever, plunging miles underground, until he reached the Temple's dungeon. The hallway loomed before him, lined with cells. The screams rose. The smell of blood filled his nostrils. The nightmare of his childhood stretched ahead.

Gemini ground his teeth, trembling. His eyes stung. The cold sweat no longer trickled; it now drenched him. Again he saw all those old prisoners, tortured, dying. Did some of the same wretched souls still hang here in their chains, still screaming after all these years?

We'll be executing the weredragon at noon.

Gemini raised his chin, clenched his fists, and stepped into the dungeon.

Several guards patrolled the hall, holding maces. They spun toward Gemini, narrowed their eyes, and raised their clubs.

"Get out of here!" Gemini shouted. "Leave this place." He tightened his housecoat around him. "Don't you recognize a paladin without his armor?"

The guards' eyes widened, and they knelt. "My lord Gemini!" one cried out.

Gemini marched forward and grabbed a heavy ring of keys from a guard.

"Now leave!" Gemini screamed, hating that his voice cracked. "I'm here to inspect the weredragon, and I won't have common scum in my way. You stink more than the prisoners."

The guards rushed out of the dungeon, faces pale. Once they were gone, Gemini squared his shoulders, took a shuddering breath, and began walking down the corridor.

The cells stretched along the corridor, full of the rotting, languishing vestiges of men, women, and children. The screams danced around Gemini, a chorus of nightmares. Gemini wanted to close his eyes, to flee, anything but see these terrors again, the terrors that still haunted his nightmares. But he had to find her. To find Domi. The only woman he had loved since . . . since that horrible day when . . .

He pushed the thought aside. That was a memory he would not conjure here.

I will save you, Domi.

And so he walked, and he looked.

He stared into every cell--at the broken, mocking remains of humans, only half-alive. At the mad eyes. The tears. The blood. The broken bodies. The terror Gemini had seen as a child, that made fresh tears spring to his eyes.

The Spirit never wanted this, he thought. *The Cured Temple is about gold, light, splendor, not this.*

He dug his fingernails into his palms. His thoughts were heresy, he knew. If the Spirit heard him thinking this, the god would doom him to an afterlife in the Abyss, a place even worse than this dungeon. He would not contemplate his faith now. He would focus on finding Domi, on saving a pure light trapped in shadow.

He kept walking and finally, in a cell coated with blood and cobwebs, he saw her.

His heart shattered in his chest.

Domi lay curled up on the rough stone floor, her legs and wrists bound in chains. Her red hair spilled across her face, and bruises and cuts covered her white limbs. She wore nothing but tattered burlap, and welts rose across her.

The guards had beaten her.

Gemini's fists trembled with rage, and the keys jangled in his grasp. He would kill them! He would kill them all--the guards, his sister, his mother, the whole damn Temple! Hot tears burned in his eyes, and a lump filled his throat.

But not before I save you, Domi.

With shaking fingers, he began to test key after key in the lock. He had to hurry, he knew. If his sister found out . . .

Finally one key fit. He tugged the barred door open and entered the cell.

"Domi!"

He rushed forward and knelt above her. She lay on the ground, moaning. Her eyes fluttered open--those huge, green eyes that he had first seen on Pyre, that pierced his heart, that melted his heart, that were forever his beacon. Her cheek was bruised, and she whispered his name.

"I'm going to get you out of here," he said, tasting his own tears. He began testing keys in her chains' padlock.

She stared up at him, and she whispered, "Gemini . . . she hurt me, Gemini. Your sister."

Such rage and pain filled Gemini that he could barely hold the keys. He forced himself to breathe deeply.

Mercy will pay for this, he swore. *She will scream in pain.*

Finally a key fit and the padlock opened. Domi's chains fell to the floor.

"Oh, Domi." He gathered her into his arms. "I'm so sorry, Domi. I'm getting you out of here. We're going to leave the Temple. We'll find a new place to live, a safe place, you and me." He touched her bruised cheek. "I should never have brought you here. We'll find a new home, you and me, I promise. Can you walk? We must hurry."

She nodded.

Gemini's knees shook as he held her hand, as he led her out of the cell. He didn't know where to go. Mercy would hunt them, he knew. The armies of the Cured Temple would scour the world, seeking Domi, a weredragon.

"We'll take the firedrakes," he whispered, walking down the hallway. "We'll build our own army! We'll . . . Domi?"

She had stopped walking, feet planted firmly on the floor. He turned toward her, and he saw her staring into another cell. Inside lay a young man with brown hair, chains binding him.

"Domi?" Gemini whispered. "Who is--"

She turned toward him, tears in her eyes. "I'm sorry, Gemini," she whispered . . . and drove her fist forward.

Pain and white light exploded across Gemini's face.

His keys clattered to the floor.

An instant later, Gemini followed the keys, banging his head, and all went dark around him.

FIDELITY

They walked down the cobbled road, heading toward the city of Nova Vita--a father, a son, and a woman with terror in her heart.

"I swore I would never set foot in a village again," Roen said, eyes dark. "Now we walk toward the greatest city in the world."

Fidelity looked at him. Here on a paved road, no trees around him, the tall, bearded woodsman seemed out of place. His dark eyes glanced around, nervous as a bear stepping into the territory of lions, and his hands were tight around his staff. He wore pelts of fur, not the burlap tunics most city folk wore, and the forest still covered him--soil under his fingernails, fallen leaves in his dark hair, sap on his clothes. He looked and smelled of the woods he had spent his life hiding in, and now she would take him into the streets of the Cured Temple where no flower or blade of grass grew.

"It'll be all right, sonny." Julian reached out to pat Roen's arm. "We're here with you. We'll save that boy and be back in the forest by dinnertime."

Fidelity turned to look at Julian next, and she felt some warmth, some comfort, fill her breast. The old man had always been a comfort in her life. She had never seen Julian mad or nervous, and even now, walking toward the capital and the armies of the Cured Temple, Julian seemed calm as if strolling through a meadow. Beads were strewn through his long white beard and hair, and the lines of many years of laughter crawled across his face. While his son was tall, Julian was short and stocky, and his fingers reminded Fidelity of tangled oak roots. He too wore fur pelts, and large muddy boots held his feet.

"And don't you worry, lassie." He turned to look at Fidelity. He patted her hand. "The boy will be all right. We won't let him come to harm."

Fidelity looked back toward the city ahead. Her belly clenched, and her eyes stung.

You're there somewhere, Cade, she thought. *Imprisoned. Hurting. Waiting for death. You need me.*

Along with the fear, guilt flooded Fidelity's belly. Tears filled her eyes.

"I feel so guilty," she whispered. "I let him enter the paper mill alone, even though we knew Mercy might be inside. And then I just . . . just stood there. Just stood there like a coward as Mercy carried him away."

Roen placed an arm around her and pulled her close to him, silent and warm. Julian, meanwhile, kept patting her hand, and his eyes were soft.

"You did the right thing, lassie," said the old man. "No good would have come from chasing the paladins alone. You came to us for aid, and we're glad to help. Cade's a good lad, and we'll bring him home."

Roen nodded. "Aye, we'll show the paladins a thing or two." His jaw tightened. "We've hidden for too long maybe, my gaffer and I." He allowed himself a smile. "We'll show those paladins how dragons fight."

"They command hundreds of firedrakes," Fidelity said. "How can we stop them, just three?"

"Three of the finest Vir Requis in the land!" Julian said, chin raised. "Well . . . three of the finest among only a handful in the world, but fine nonetheless. We're no mindless beasts like the drakes."

"And we've got the element of surprise," Julian added, gaining confidence with every word. "Beatrix doesn't know of my son and me. The witch's eyes will pop right out of her sockets to see new dragons attack."

Fidelity reached into her pocket and closed her hand around the small metal R she kept there, one of the letters from the printing press.

"Sooner or later," she said, "Beatrix will bring Cade out to the Temple balcony to show him off to the crowd. She'll try to purify him before the multitudes, a sign of his submission. If he refuses the tillvine . . ." Fidelity shuddered. "I want us in the crowd. Close to the balcony. Ready to shift, soar as dragons, and grab Cade, then fly as far and fast as we can."

Roen nodded. "When will they bring him out?"

She lowered her head. "I don't know. It might be tonight. It might not be for months. But I know who will have the answer." She swallowed. "Domi."

Roen raised an eyebrow. "Your sister?"

She nodded. "She serves the Cured Temple as a firedrake. She hears the paladins speak. If we can somehow reach her, Domi can help us."

If she hasn't become a full servant of the Temple, Fidelity added silently. She had not spoken to her sister in years, not since Domi had run off, shouting that she'd rather serve as a dragon than live free as a human. Did Domi still hold Requiem any love, or was she fully a beast of the Temple now?

She sent Cade to me, Fidelity reminded herself. *She told him of Requiem. That means she holds Requiem some love. Oh, Domi . . . perhaps I need to save you as much as Cade.*

As they walked toward Nova Vita, many other people joined them on the road: farmers, shepherds, loggers, and other travelers. All spoke in hushed tones of "the weredragon in the city." Some peasant children held dragon effigies, which they stabbed with wooden swords. A few men proudly proclaimed what they would do to any weredragon they caught slinking around their farms.

It seems word has spread, Fidelity thought with a sigh.

They drew closer to the city. The afternoon sun gilded its walls and guard towers. Beyond them, Fidelity could see only one building soaring in the distance: the Cured Temple. All other buildings in Nova Vita, mere huts for the commoners, were too small to rise above the walls, but the Temple rose as a great edifice. Its base was round and white, and from it grew many curving towers of glass and crystal. From this distance, it looked to Fidelity like a fallen comet, its tail still stretching into the sky.

The crowd thickened along the road as they approached the southern gates. Two towers framed an archway here, and guards stood within the doorway, allowing one traveler at a time into the city. Several firedrakes stood upon the walls around the gatehouse, smoke pluming from their nostrils, their claws clutching the city ramparts.

Roen frowned and grumbled. "Don't like so many people around me."

Fidelity nodded. "Nor do I."

Suddenly she missed her old library in Sanctus, and her eyes stung to think of it. The way Roen had sought sanctuary in the forest, she had found solace in that dusty library. She had spent many hours reading her forbidden books in the cellar, dreaming of the old days of Requiem, even of this very city which had once been Requiem's capital. Yearning for Requiem had always seemed sad to her, yet now, walking here toward the enemy, her friend captive, her old life seemed carefree, a life of daydreaming and peace.

Only Julian seemed to remain calm. "Not to worry, younglings. Not to worry. We're naught but simple foresters, come to pray at the Temple."

Yet as they drew closer to the gatehouse, Fidelity's heart sank down to her pelvis.

"Oh bloody stars," she whispered.

At her side, Roen grumbled and even Julian frowned.

"One by one!" a guard was shouting, waving a bundle of leaves. "You don't enter without touching the leaves. Stand back! One by one!"

The travelers--farmers and shepherds and other commoners--were lining up outside the gates. Each person who stepped forward held out his or her arm. The guards, gruff men in chain mail, pressed ilbane onto their skin, then let the traveler pay a toll and enter.

Ilbane. Fidelity shuddered, already feeling the pain. The plant was harmless to most. It burned Vir Requis like fire.

The companions paused and stepped to the roadside.

"Spirit's blistery feet," Roen cursed. "Since when do they test for Vir Requis at the gates?"

Fidelity sighed, keeping her voice low. "Since they caught one." She glanced back at the guards. "Maybe they don't know us by name, but they know other Vir Requis are out there. They know we're coming for Cade." She grimaced. "I touched ilbane once--a couple years ago. I screamed. My skin was raw for days." She shook her head. "We cannot enter here."

Roen smiled savagely. "I can take pain. I can enter." He made to step back onto the road.

"No!" Fidelity grabbed him. "Not even you, Roen. You'd be unable to withstand that pain. No more than you could grin if I kicked you in the groin."

He grimaced. "Ouch. That bad?"

She nodded. "That bad." She took a deep breath. "There's another way in . . . in darkness. In danger." She gulped and looked at the setting sun. "We wait until tonight . . . and we fly."

DOMI

"I'm sorry," she whispered. She stared down at the unconscious Gemini, and she was surprised to find true guilt coursing through her. "I'm sorry, Gemini, but it's something I must do."

He lay sprawled on the floor, blood trickling from his mouth. Domi was surprised at her own strength. Gemini was quite a bit larger than her, yet she had knocked him out cold. Before he could wake, she knelt and slapped her old manacles around his wrists and ankles, then grabbed him under his arms. She pushed her heels against the floor and grimaced, straining to drag him into her old cell.

I have to hurry. Before the guards return.

Her heart pounded, and she was breathing heavily when she released Gemini. Chained inside her prison cell, he began to wake, mumbling confusedly.

She kissed his forehead. "I'm sorry again, my love."

She drove her fist into his face a second time, then grabbed her aching knuckles and cursed. Gemini thumped back onto the floor, and Domi hurried out of the cell, closed the door, and locked it.

She glanced down the corridor. The guards, which Gemini had sent outside, had not yet returned, but she knew they could be back any second.

"Cade, you foolish boy," she muttered. The keys jangling in her hand, she rushed toward his cell, unlocked the door, and swung it open.

"Up!" she whispered. "I'm here to save your backside--a second time. Up!"

Cade blinked at her in amazement as she unlocked his chains. "Domi!" He rubbed his eyes. "Oh, stars, Domi." His eyes dampened, and he tried to embrace her. "Are you all right? What--"

"Hush!" She glared and tugged him to his feet. "Stand up. Now hurry. We're getting out of here." She gulped. "If you see any guards, kill them."

For a moment he stood still, face pale, eyes wide, and Domi realized how young he was: only a boy, that was all, no older than eighteen. But he quickly came to his senses, tightened his lips, and nodded.

"Let's go."

Both were bruised, bloody, and clad in rags. Both limped as they moved, stumbling down the corridor.

They had crossed only half the distance to the exit when the first guard stepped back into the hall.

The man stared at them. His eyes widened. He cried out to his comrades.

"Prisoners escaping! Prisoners out--"

Domi growled, shoved Cade backward, and shifted.

Scales rose across her, and her tail sprouted, knocking Cade farther back. Her body ballooned, slamming against the ceiling and walls. As guards rushed toward her, Domi blasted out her fire.

The inferno blazed across the hall, leaped into the cells, and roared through this cavern of stone. The guards screamed and fell, blazing, trying to roll and extinguish the fire, only for more flames to crash against them.

When Domi shifted back into human form, they all lay dead before her, charred black. She grabbed one fallen sword, grimacing as the hilt blazed against her palm. She kicked another sword toward Cade.

"Now run, you foolish boy!" she said. "Grab that sword and run!"

She tugged him forward, and they ran.

FIDELITY

They crouched behind the bale of hay as the sun sank beneath the horizon, the stars emerged, and the most dangerous night in their life began.

"Darkness falls," Fidelity whispered, clutching the metal letter--the only charm she had left--so hard it dug into her palm. "It's time."

Julian and Roen knelt beside her behind the hay. Crickets chirped, fireflies glowed, and a cool breeze blew. It was strange, Fidelity thought, that this night of horrors seemed so peaceful. She would have given all the treasure in the Commonwealth for a night of clouds and rain, no starlight to shine upon them.

"Are you sure you want to do this?" Roen whispered. "Let me fly. You and my gaffer will ride me. I'm fast and strong."

"And big," Fidelity said. "I'm the smallest. What we need now is stealth, not speed or strength. Only I'll shift--one dragon, sneaky and silent, with you two on my back." She stared across the darkness toward the city. "We fly high. We fly hidden. We descend inside Nova Vita with the Temple none the wiser."

Roen reached out in the darkness and clasped her hand in both of his. He stared at her, the light of fireflies reflecting in his eyes. He still smelled of the forest--the leaves, clear pools, good soil, comfort, safety. His hands were rough but still soft, the hands that had so often explored her body.

"I hope the boy's worth it," he said.

"He's Vir Requis." She stared into those brown eyes she had gazed into so often in her youth. "There might be no more than us in the world. He's worth it."

"Worth dying for?" Roen said.

"Requiem is worth dying for. I will fight for all her sons and daughters. I will not abandon Cade." She lowered her head. "Roen, I know what this means to you. I know that for years you refused to join this fight of mine. I know that for years you sought only to live in the woods, to forget the Commonwealth, the Temple, even Requiem." She looked back up at him, tears in her eyes, and kissed the corner of his mouth. She whispered to him, her voice choked. "Thank you. I love you."

He winked at her, and a crooked smile tugged at his lips. "With me doing this, you'd better love me."

She stepped away from him, raised her chin, and shifted. She stood in the dark field, a blue dragon, and lowered her wing, forming a ramp. Roen climbed first and straddled her back, and Julian followed. Once son and father were safely seated, Fidelity kicked off the ground, flapped her wings, and rose into the night sky.

She spiraled up and up, careful to keep her wings and scales silent, to keep the fire hidden in her gullet. The land sprawled around her. Many years ago, King's Forest had covered these hills and plains, the fabled woods of Requiem. Today the trees were gone, for the birches had been symbols of Requiem to be cut down.

Fidelity rose higher, so high the air thinned out and chilled her. The stars spread above her, and the Draco constellation, ancient god of Requiem, shone upon her. The celestial dragon's eye, Issari's Star, glowed brighter than all others in the sky. Along with King's Column, the stars were the only symbol of Requiem the Cured Temple had been unable to destroy.

Please, stars of Requiem, Fidelity thought, gazing at their light. *Protect me this night.*

She looked at the city that lay a mile away. In her dreams of Old Requiem, the city of Nova Vita had been a hub of light, its lanterns glowing bright even at night. Nova Vita was the largest city in the Commonwealth, perhaps the world, yet now it was dark, almost as dark as the farmlands. Few lanterns lit the streets. Few lights glowed in windows. There was little oil for lanterns, little firewood for hearths these years, little life on the streets after sundown. The Cured Temple had stamped out the lights of Requiem.

All but one light--a great light like the moon. The Cured Temple shone below, the greatest structure in the Commonwealth, a hub of luminescence and splendor. Its crystal spikes soared to the sky, curling inward like claws, carved of glass and crystal, shining with inner lights. Below them, many windows pierced the round base of the Temple, and white light blazed out from them. Here was a comet fallen onto the world, glowing with the heavens.

Are you in there, Cade? she thought.

The only other lights she saw lined the city walls. Archers stood there, torchlight glinting off their armor. And between them, perched like gargoyles, hulked the firedrakes, flames in their maws.

Fidelity kept flying higher. Soon the air was so thin she could barely breathe. She looked over her shoulder.

"Are you all right?" she whispered.

Julian and Roen clung to her back, shivering in the wind, but they nodded. Flying so high, especially in human form, was grueling, but she'd have to become but a speck in the night sky to avoid the firedrakes' eyes.

She made her way northward until she crossed the city walls below. From up here, even the firedrakes seemed like mere ants. She kept her mouth shut as she flew, knowing that a single, errant flicker of fire would shine for miles. She glided, as silent as she could, barely daring to breathe.

Once she had crossed the walls, she allowed herself a short breath of relief. She now flew directly above the city. On the walls, the firedrakes kept staring into the black horizons. They had not seen her.

She glided high above, scanning the city for a place to land. Thousands of domed clay huts covered the hills, huddled together. The streets were narrow between them. She could see no place to land, and she could not land on a roof without waking up those sleeping beneath it.

An empty black patch spread ahead of her, large as an entire town, leading toward the Cured Temple. The Square of the Spirit, built hundreds of years ago, was large enough for armies to muster on. There were no huts there, no lanterns, only shadows.

That's where we'll land. Fidelity glided forward. *In the very heart of the Commonwealth.*

She looked over her shoulder. "Get ready, boys," she whispered. The two nodded, and Julian even seemed to be grinning.

Fidelity turned to look forward again. She was nearing the square now, getting dangerously close to the light of the Cured Temple. She began to glide down, slowly spiraling closer and closer to the square, praying with every heartbeat that none saw the shadow descending in the night.

She was reaching out her claws, ready to land, when fire blazed, screeches rose, and the night exploded with light and sound and fury.

CADE

Cade's heart pounded and his head spun as they ran upstairs, fleeing the dungeon. He clung to Domi's hand, and his breath rattled in his lungs.

So many thoughts swirled through his mind: *Beatrix is my mother. Mercy is my sister. Domi is alive. I must find Fidelity.*

He tightened his lips. For now, he had to focus on escape.

Gripping his sword, he raced upstairs. His wounds ached, and his limbs felt rubbery, but the excitement and fear pounded through him, propelling him onward. They had climbed dozens of steps when the three guards came clanking down toward them.

Domi and Cade glanced at each other, then looked forward, screamed, and charged.

The stairwell was narrow--too narrow to shift in. Their elbows banged together, but they kept racing upward, swords swinging. One guard cried out and fell back a step. Cade snarled and thrust his blade, hitting the man's armored belly. He could not pierce the chain mail, but it distracted the man long enough for Domi to swing her blade, slicing into the guard's leg.

As he crashed down, the two other guards raced toward them, drawing their swords. Cade parried a blade. Domi fought at his side. As another sword swung toward him, Cade ducked and lashed his own blade, hitting another guard's legs. The man fell, and Cade plunged his sword downward, stabbing his back. Domi finished off the last guard.

Cade flashed her a shaky grin. "Not bad, Doms."

She glared. "Less talking, more running!"

She grabbed his hand and yanked him forward, and they kept racing upward.

They burst out of the stairwell into a lavish, marble hall coated with gold, murals, and jewels.

Dozens of guards, priests, and paladins filled the place.

Oh bloody stars . . .

Cade shouted, leaped forward, and shifted into a dragon. An instant later, Domi shifted at his side.

Two dragons, one gold and one the colors of fire, roared in the jeweled hall of the Temple. Their tails slammed against gilded columns. Their claws tore into the mosaic floor. Their horns hit the ceiling, sending gemstones raining down. Their dragonfire blazed, shrieking across the hall.

Gilt melted. Murals crackled. And everywhere, men burned. Soldiers screamed and fell. Priests fled, robes blazing. A paladin tried to race through the fire, to swing his sword, only for Cade's claws to crash against him, knocking him down. The dragons moved through the hall, roaring, blasting out fire, their tails swinging into men.

Shouts rose behind them. Pain drove into Cade's back, and he yowled. He turned his head to see soldiers aiming crossbows, firing quarrels. Another shard drove into his shoulder, crashing through a scale and punching into his flesh. Cade growled and blasted flame. The jet streamed across the hall and crashed into the crossbowmen. They fell, screaming, their skin peeling off, their armor melting.

"Cade, to the exit!" Domi cried, her claws clattering as she raced forward. "Follow!"

He spun back toward her and lolloped in pursuit, his wings banging against the walls, his horns etching grooves along the ceiling. Doors rose ahead, and more guards shot crossbows. A blast from Domi knocked them down, and an instant later, her horns slammed into the doors. They shattered in a shower of splinters.

The fiery dragon burst out into the night, beat her wings, and soared. Cade leaped after her and soared at her side, laughing, his wings billowing with air. The city sprawled before them, countless huts spreading into the darkness, and beyond them the forest.

We're free.

Screeches rose all around. Dark wings shaded the moon. With flashes of scales and roaring flame, the firedrakes swooped toward them.

DOMI

She beat her wings, soaring toward the firedrakes.

"Fight them, Cade!" she cried and blasted out her flames.

A dozen firedrakes or more flew toward her, and their own dragonfire cascaded down. Paladins sat in their saddles, firing crossbows. Domi screamed as a quarrel slammed into her shoulder, as fire washed her. She bellowed with rage, beat her wings, and soared higher. Cade flew at her side, a golden dragon, blowing his flames. He too bled, and one of his wings burned; he beat it madly, extinguishing the fire against his flank.

More firedrakes kept rising. Archers ran into the square below, and arrows flew. Domi kept soaring, but firedrakes swooped from above, blocking her passage, surrounding her, and she knew she was going to die.

She growled. *So I go down fighting.*

Bleeding, burnt, dying, Domi lashed her claws, snapped her jaws, blazed out her fire. A firedrake screeched above her. Domi's claws tore open its belly, and its entrails spilled. A paladin fired his crossbow. Domi's dragonfire washed over his steel, heating the armor and melting the flesh within. Another drake swooped toward her, and she bit deeply, tearing out its neck, tasting its blood. Cade fought at her side, roaring, blood on his fangs, his fire blasting out. They could not win this fight, Domi knew, but they could make a last stand to be sung of for centuries.

Domi rose higher, crashing through the enemies. Her tail slammed into a rider, knocking him off his saddle. Her fire and claws drove firedrakes aside. She soared into open sky high above the city, opened her jaws wide, and bellowed out only one word, the word that meant everything, the word the city needed to hear, that she needed to shout with all her rage and pain one last time.

"Requiem!"

Cade soared at her side, several scales missing from his back, several quarrels sunken into him, but he too blasted out his fire, and he too roared the cry.

"Requiem!"

The firedrakes screeched all around, and the riders shouted, and more of the beasts kept soaring, but from the east Domi heard it: the cry answered. Again. Again.

"Requiem! Requiem! Requiem!"

Domi gasped, soared higher. *Who--*

She stared toward the east, and her eyes watered.

Three dragons came flying toward the battle, not firedrakes but noble dragons of Requiem.

"Fidelity!" Domi cried out. "Julian! Roen!"

The three charged forth and blasted out their dragonfire.

The firedrakes surrounding Domi and Cade howled and burned. Their riders fell, and hope filled Domi, and her tears streamed down her cheeks.

"Requiem!" Domi cried, weeping, calling out the forbidden name, letting all hear, all see the glory of her fallen kingdom.

The cries echoed in the night. Requiem! Requiem!

The song of dragons in her heart, Domi blew more fire, hitting a drake, and swooped, her claws tearing at another. Her comrades fought around her, four other dragons of Requiem, proud and strong.

A scream shattered the battle.

Flames, blue with heat, showered skyward, and the city shook.

With a deafening cry, with light and heat and roaring sound, the great firedrake Felesar soared up from the Temple--the largest of the beasts--and upon his back rode Mercy.

The paladin's face was white with rage, and her eyes burned, two blue pools of rage. Twenty more firedrakes rose around her, emerging from the tunnels below the Temple, and her voice stormed across the city.

"Slay the weredragons!"

Dozens of flaming jets blazed toward Domi. Dozens of arrows flew, and the firedrakes closed in.

Domi snarled and flew to battle, to blood, to death.

"Domi!" Cade grabbed her tail and tugged her. "Come on!"

The young golden dragon shot eastward, dragging Domi with him across the sky.

"Domi, fly with us!" Fidelity cried ahead, a blue dragon blasting out fire. She, Julian, and Roen were driving forward, breaking through the noose of firedrakes.

"I won't flee from battle!" Domi shouted.

Cade growled and bit right into her haunches. "Yes you will. Now move it!"

Domi yowled and flew, Cade chomping at her backside. They shot forward. Firedrakes charged toward her. The dragons blew their fire and lashed their claws. One firedrake's teeth dug into her shoulder, and Domi yipped and swung her tail, digging its spikes into the creature's flanks. An arrow shot through her wing, and she cried out in pain. Cade flew above her, blasting fire, clearing a path forward.

Domi roared and flew with him, biting and clawing, knocking the enemies aside.

I won't let that damn boy live while I die!

Together, the fiery and golden dragons burst forward, breaking through the ring of firedrakes. The other three dragons flew ahead.

The five dragons, perhaps the last Vir Requis in the world, flew over the dark city of Nova Vita. Behind them, a hundred firedrakes or more roared and flew in pursuit, their flames lighting the night.

KORVIN

The two dragons, gray and red, perched atop the citadel's highest tower and gazed down at the sprawling land of stone and iron.

"Gosh Ha'ar," said Amity, her red scales burning bright in the sunset as if aflame. Her eyes shone. "Thousands of years ago, the ancient civilization of Goshar fell upon this mountainside." Fire flicked between Amity's teeth. "Now Gosh Ha'ar, the Heart of the Horde, is mine to rule."

Korvin grunted, his claws digging into the parapets. "It's one city, Amity, and you're not yet crowned. The Horde is vast and covers much of Terra. Not all will accept your rule, even if you did cut off the old abina's head."

She turned her scaly head toward him, and her jaw opened in a smile. "They will. Gosh Ha'ar will swear its loyalty to me tonight. This city, this mountain, this citadel--they will be mine. And soon all the Horde will swear its allegiance to me, Abini Amity." Smoke blasted out of her nostrils. "And then Beatrix will beg me for mercy . . . mercy I will not grant."

Korvin's belly clenched; it felt full of rocks.

And so Amity, the new woman I love, the woman I made love to in the bowels of the mountains . . . will fight Beatrix, the woman I loved and spurned. His chest felt too tight. *And only one will survive this.*

He gazed across the landscape. He and Amity stood on the tower of Sin Hanar, the great citadel that rose from the mountain. The fortress was the largest Korvin had ever seen. Clusters of towers rose in a ring around the mountain, connected with thick stone walls. Within this shell rose a second layer of walls, thrice as high, topped with parapets and massive towers whose height challenged even the Cured Temple far north across the sea. This citadel was old; its bricks were craggy, and many weeds grew between them, and men spoke of ghosts that haunted the halls. Two thousand years ago, the last survivors of the Goshar had built this fortress to protect their flickering civilization, yet their fortress had become their tomb. Today the Horde, this great army of many nations, ruled here.

Korvin turned his gaze to look down the mountains. Buried deep within them lay the arena where they had fought Behemoth. Korvin hoped to never enter that place again. The rocky, barren slopes stretched thousands of feet downward. The mountain range spread across the land like a raised scar, separating the northern desert and the southern arable lands where rivers flowed. In a mountain pass, Korvin could still see remnants of Ancient Goshar: a few chipped walls and the capitals of columns rising from the dust, hints of the civilization that had once ruled the path from desert to grasslands.

Across the southern grasslands now spread the tent city of Gosh Ha'ar, sister to the northern bastion of Hakar Teer on the coast. A towering sandstone archway led into the city, soaring as high as a palace, its crest gilded and topped with statues of warriors and dragons. Beyond spread countless tents and dirt roads. Hundreds of thousands lived here: warriors from many nations in iron and bronze armor, griffins with silver helms and leather saddles, and salvanae with long beards and chinking scales. Many women and children lived here too, for in the Horde, there was no distinction between the military and civilian life. All here served the Horde. All here were warriors, from the gruff swordsmen to the women whose wombs bore future fighters.

As Korvin watched children play below, he thought of his daughters. Fidelity and Domi were both adults now, but to Korvin they would always be some mixture of babies, children, youths--simply his daughters, always his children, no matter how old they all grew. He missed them. He had not stopped thinking of them since flying here.

Do you know that I'm alive, Fidelity? Korvin thought, staring down at the tents. *Do you miss me as I miss you? Do you still fly as a firedrake, Domi? Do you think of me too? Do you still love me, pray we meet again?*

As much as he mourned the loss of Requiem, Korvin ached with loneliness, with longing to see Fidelity and Domi again. Since Beatrix had murdered his wife, his daughters had been the reason he stayed alive, all he had in this world.

I'm still alive, daughters, and I'm thinking of you, and I love you, always. Always.

"This army will follow us, Korvin," Amity said, interrupting his thoughts. The red dragon pointed her claws down to the camp, and her eyes shone. "Imagine it! A host of a hundred thousand warriors, screaming and thirsty for the blood of the Commonwealth, storming the beaches, burning all in their path, heading toward the Cured Temple." She sneered. "I will cut off Beatrix's head myself."

Korvin grunted, smoke puffing out of his nostrils. "Will we be replacing the Commonwealth with the Horde? Where in all this does Requiem rise?"

The red dragon spun her head toward him, baring her fangs. "Once Beatrix is dead, I will pull the Horde back, and Requiem will rise from the ruins."

"Wildfire is easy to ignite." Korvin stared down at the hosts below. "It might not be as easy to put out."

Amity snorted. "Platitudes. I'm strong. I'm fierce. And we're fighting for justice, Korvin." Flames flickered out from her mouth. "Justice always prevails. Light always banishes the darkness."

"Does it?" Korvin sighed. "Beatrix thought herself a warrior of justice and light. She too was sure of her path, full of rage and righteous certainty." He shook his head sadly. "Blind righteousness is like a fortress of paper, likely to burn in the flame and collapse. Doubt is the path to wisdom. The winding, uncertain path through a dark forest leads to victory, not the brash warrior cutting down every tree along the way."

Amity beat her wings and took flight. "You'll have time for grim philosophy later. Come now. The coronation is about to begin."

Korvin watched her fly for a moment, chest tight. Amity was all fire and passion, sure of her path, her eyes bright and fierce. He had seen such fierce passion before. The last time he had gazed into eyes so lustful for glory and victory, he had been holding Beatrix in his arms.

He tightened his jaw. *I will not let Amity take that path to madness. I will not let her inner light burn her soul.* He beat his wings, taking flight. *Amity will be queen of the Horde, but I . . . I must guide her path, and I must keep her fire from consuming us all.*

The two dragons glided down across the mountainside, heading toward the sprawling tent city below. Amity dived near to the ground, leveled off, and flew through the White Arch. Korvin followed; the arch was large enough to dwarf even a dragon. A field of packed earth spread ahead, and a dais of giltwood rose here, a throne atop it. A hundred soldiers in bronze breastplates, bearing spears and round shields, surrounded the dais, and ten clerics stood at the base of a stairway, kneeling as the dragons approached. A crowd of the Horde--women, children, elders, and warriors--stood in the field. They cried out as the two dragons dived down and landed on the dais.

As soon as Amity's claws hit the dais, she tossed back her head and blew a shrieking pillar of dragonfire. The inferno rose into the sky, a beacon for all to see, and Amity roared out her cry. "Come see me, Horde! Come see your new queen crowned!"

The cry shook the stage, deafening. As the crowd cried out in response, waving swords and axes, Amity released her magic. She shrunk in size, returning to human form: a woman with short blond hair that fell across her brow and ears, brown breeches and a tan vest, and a crooked smile on her face. A sword hung at her side, and an axe was strapped across her back. She wore no gown, no jewels; she was a warrior of the Horde, and the Horde cared for steel, blood, and sweat more than silk or gems.

Korvin released his magic too and stood a foot behind Amity, hand on the hilt of his own sword. Amity waved to the crowd, crying out wordlessly, basking in the glory, but Korvin found himself scanning the perimeters of that chanting crowd. Not all, he saw, were pleased at this display. Many men slunk at the back, eyes dark, hands clutching their weapons, lips downturned.

Amity slew the old king, but our work here is not yet done, Korvin thought.

Amity stepped toward a chest, opened it, and pulled out the withered head of the fallen Abina Kahan. She raised the ghastly trophy high, displaying it for the crowd.

"Here is the rotting head of your old king!" Amity shouted. "I slew him, and I take his place as your leader. Under Kahan's rule, you rotted like his head rots now. You lingered here in the south, living in the dirt, in mere tents, polishing spears with no enemy to slay." She spat. "I promise you war and glory! Under my rule, we will swarm north, crush the Commonwealth, and send the Cured Temple crashing to the ground!"

The crowd cheered and Amity panted, teeth bared in a savage grin, chest rising and falling. When Korvin looked at her, his belly soured.

He closed his eyes, and the memories resurfaced: himself as a young man, only twenty years old, holding the woman he loved. He lay in her bed in the Cured Temple, a mere soldier, a humble man she had taken into her life. She stood before him, naked in the dawn pouring through the windows, a young priestess with rising power, beautiful and strong and noble, heiress to the world.

"When I'm High Priestess, the Horde will pay." Beatrix had clenched her fist, grinning savagely, a grin that twisted her face into a blazing mask. "All those who oppose me will burn in my fire. They will beg for mercy before I crush them. I will slay all the enemies of the Spirit. I will slay every last beast of the Horde, every last weredragon, every last heretic who resists me."

He had fought the Horde for her. As she preached in the light of the Temple, he fought on the beaches, in the mud, cutting down enemies, washing his hands and soul with blood, learning of the madness of war, the madness of the woman he loved . . . the woman he had to spurn.

Korvin opened his eyes and looked at Amity again, and that same fear clutched his old warrior's heart.

Clerics began climbing the stairs toward the dais, interrupting his thoughts. They wore crimson robes fringed with gemstones, and they held staffs carved from ancient reptile bones dug from underground. Bronze masks hid their faces, shaped as horned demons. Around their necks hung amulets shaped as hands with four fingers, the index finger nearly twice the length of the others--sigil of Adon, the Sky God. Each cleric had cut off a finger from his own hand, an attempt to grow closer to his god.

As the Adonite clerics stepped onto the dais, Amity knelt before them. For a moment, Korvin stood stiffly; he worshipped no god but the Draco constellation, the stars of Requiem.

Amity turned her head and glared at him. She gestured with her eyes: *Kneel!*

With a grumble, Korvin bent the knee, though he thought only of his stars, bringing their light into his mind as the clerics approached.

One of the clerics stepped toward Amity. He wore a crimson mask shaped like a lurid face, eyes large, jaw unhinged, tongue dangling. The mask's horns curled, and the symbol of Adon, a four fingered hand, was painted onto the brow. The cleric's own hands, their little fingers removed, held a crown molded of finger bones worked together with golden wires. The cleric came to stand behind Amity, holding the crown above her head.

"Hear me, Amity of Leonis!" he called out. "Five thousand years ago, the wise Adon, Warrior of the Sky, rode his flaming chariot into a desert, a land of rock and thirst and pain. When he pressed his holy hand against the mountains, rivers gushed forth, and the grasslands grew, and trees gave forth fruit. With his holy hand, he shaped the wet dirt, and he formed men and women to toil in the fields. Adon himself blessed the first king and queen with his holy hand. Now a new queen rises! Now a crown of cleric finger bones will bless you as Adon blessed our forebears." He began to lower the crown. "I bless you, Amity of Leonis, and by the glory of Adon, I name you Queen of--"

"Queen of Filth!" rose a shout from the crowd. "Queen of Whores! Queen of Reptiles!"

The cleric hissed and stepped back. Amity growled. Korvin stared into the crowd, and his throat tightened, and he grabbed the hilt of his sword and drew a foot of steel.

A man came walking through the crowd toward the stage. People stepped back before him, forming a path, bowing their heads. He was easily the largest man Korvin had ever seen. The brute towered over the rest of the crowd, over seven feet tall. His muscles bulged and rippled. He wore nothing but a loincloth, and he carried a mace and a round shield. A scar crawled up his cheek, through one empty eye socket, and across his bald head, the groove a deep canyon.

Korvin was a large man, but looking at this beast, he felt as small and frail as a stooped elder. Still he forced himself to step forward, and he shouted down from the stage, "Who are you to challenge your queen?"

The brute below laughed. Several griffins walked behind the giant, wings folded against their flanks, and on their backs rode warriors with shaved heads, bare chests, and round shields. All the men's shields, Korvin noticed, sported a red fist.

Amity cursed under her breath. "Shafel," she muttered, then raised her voice to a shout. "Shafel, leave this place! Your master is dead. Serve me or die too."

Korvin sneered. Shafel. He had heard that name before. Back in the war years ago, legends had spoken of a giant among the troops, a beast who snapped spines in his great hands, who cracked skulls and feasted on the innards, who stood twice the height of most men, whose skin was thick as armor. They had said that Shafel was only a boy yet stronger than any grown man in the Horde.

The boy had grown even larger.

"I will not serve the spawn of reptiles!" Shafel spat into the dirt. "As you slew our old king, I slay you now. I will rule the Horde!"

With a battle cry, Shafel leaped into the air. With what seemed like inhuman strength, he soared onto the stage and swung his mace toward Amity.

Korvin roared, leaped forth, and shifted in midair. His wings beat and his claws swiped.

Pain exploded as Korvin blocked the mace's blow. The iron head slammed into his paw, shattering two scales. Korvin yowled and would have blasted Shafel with dragonfire, had he not stood so close to Amity and the clerics.

"Careful, little man." A charcoal dragon, Korvin snarled down at Shafel. "You're big but not big enough."

With shrieks, the dozen griffins flew toward the stage, Shafel's warriors on their backs. Amity screamed, shifted, and soared as a red dragon. Korvin sneered and blasted fire skyward, trying to hold off the griffins, but the beasts mobbed him, flying in rings. Shafel leaped onto one griffin, brandished his studded mace, and charged toward Amity.

"Stop this madness!" shouted the head cleric. The man slammed his staff down, and thunder boomed. A blast of lighting rose from the staff, piercing the sky, sending griffins and dragons tumbling backward. "In the name of Adon, you will not shed blood in the holy city of Gosh Ha'ar!"

Korvin beat his wings, hovering in midair. Amity flew beside him. A dozen griffins flew all around. The cleric stood below, staff held before him.

"I will burn my enemies!" Amity sneered.

The cleric stared up from below, eyes burning behind his demonic mask. "Even a queen may not shed blood upon holy ground. Here in Gosh Ha'ar, Adon himself touched the mountains and spilled forth water. If you shed the blood of the Horde here, the crown will never be yours." The cleric stared up at Shafel next. "Stand down, Shafel! If you shed blood here, Adon will curse you too, and this crown will never sit upon your head."

The dragons and griffins landed on the stage beneath the mountains.

Shafel wheeled his griffin toward the crowd, and he raised his mace high.

"Hear me, Horde!" the giant shouted. "I am Shafel, son of Sha'ar, slayer of Ka'elor the Sand Asp. I slew thousands of Templers in the last war. I shatter boulders with my fists, and even dragons fear and dare not strike me. I am your new king! Kneel before me!"

Across the crowd, thousands knelt.

Amity stared in disbelief, then turned toward the cleric. "Crown me! Now!"

Yet Shafel stepped forth, knocking her aside, and snatched the crown from the old priest. When the giant tried to place it upon his head, Amity leaped out and grabbed it. The two stood facing each other, holding the crown between them.

The crowd stared.

Amity glared up at Shafel. He loomed above her, thrice her size.

"Choose a place," Amity hissed, eyes blazing. "Choose a place for me to slay you."

The giant snorted. "Wherever you walk, girl, I will hunt you. Wherever you step off holy ground, I will be there to crush you under my heel."

He yanked the crown backward. Amity tugged the other way. With a crack, the crown shattered, scattering finger bones.

Korvin stared, heart sinking.

We wanted to find an army. Now our army, like this crown, shatters.

FIDELITY

The dragons flew over the dark city of Nova Vita, a hundred firedrakes flying in pursuit.

Fidelity's heart pounded, and pain drove across her body. A crossbow's quarrel dug through her back, wind whistled through a hole in her wing, and several of her scales had fallen in the battle, revealing bleeding flesh. The city streamed beneath her, the firedrakes screeched behind, and her lifeblood dripped away, but Fidelity laughed.

Cade was free.

Her sister flew with her once again.

"Domi, can you keep flying?" Fidelity cried, tears in her eyes.

Her sister flew beside her. Her scales of many colors shone in the firelight, red and orange and yellow, though many were cracked or torn off, and she bled from the wounds. Yet the fiery dragon stared at Fidelity fiercely, and she nodded.

"Save your breath and fly!" Domi said. She narrowed her eyes and beat her wings with more fervor.

They flew onward, Fidelity leading the way across the city. When she glanced over her shoulder, she saw the hundred firedrakes pursuing, and more kept rising from the bowels of the Cured Temple, which now shone several miles away. At the rear,

Julian and Roen twisted backward, blasted out twin pillars of fire, then turned forward and flew onward. A hundred jets of flame blasted in answer, most too weak to reach them, but a few shrieked between the fleeing dragons. Cade screamed as fire licked his tail, and Fidelity grimaced as sparks landed on her wings. They kept flying.

"Requiem rises!" Fidelity cried as she flew. "Hear me, people of Nova Vita. I am a free dragon! Requiem is reborn!"

Though wounded and bleeding, Cade grinned as he flew beside her, and he cried out to the night. "Rise against the Temple! Remember Requiem! Remember Requiem!"

The time for subtlety was over. The time for smuggling books in shadows had ended. Now they roared their cry together, five dragons in the open sky.

"Remember Requiem! Remember Requiem!"

As they flew, hope began to rise in Fidelity. The firedrakes would not catch them. Cade was free from his prison, and Domi was free from the gilded cage she had surrendered herself to, no less a prison than one of bars and chains. Julian and Roen flew with her again--the wisest man she knew and the man she loved. And the most secret, forbidden of words now rang across the city--a cry of hope, of rededication, of memory.

"Remember Requiem!"

Before her rose the city walls, and beyond them the open night--darkness, wilderness, hope for escape, for life.

Fidelity was only seconds away from the walls when new fire blazed.

Her hope crashed.

Twenty firedrakes rose from the walls, blasting flame her way. She reared in the sky. The hundred firedrakes behind her shrieked with new vigor and stormed forth, trapping the dragons between them and the new foes.

"Soar!" Fidelity cried, beating her wings and shooting up toward the stars.

The other dragons curved their flight upward. Jets of flame blasted beneath them. One pillar of fire crashed into Roen, and the green dragon roared but kept ascending, his scales charred and cracking with the heat. Another fiery pillar rose by Fidelity, and she veered, knocking into Cade.

"Break past them!" she cried. "To the wilderness, fly!"

She could see nothing but fire, their flashing claws, their biting teeth. Beyond them lay the open night; the dragons could vanish there into shadow. Yet the firedrakes flew everywhere, forming a noose, shrieking, blasting flames. Paladins rode on their backs, and arrows flew. One arrow tore through Fidelity's wing, and she bellowed in pain. Another arrow slammed into her horn and lodged there.

"Break through!" She sneered and charged. "Requiem, with me!"

Fidelity screamed as she slammed into one firedrake. She lashed her claws. She bit at its scales. She swiped her tail, driving its spikes against the creature. The firedrake bucked in the sky, screeching, and she bit out its throat. It tumbled down, but an instant later three more beasts slammed into Fidelity. Their claws tore at her scales. Their riders' arrows slammed into Fidelity, most shattering against her scaly hide, but one drove through and cut deep.

Fidelity lost her magic.

She tumbled through the sky toward the city, a human again.

"Fidelity!" Cade cried.

As she fell, she saw her comrades fighting above, only four dragons, countless firedrakes surrounding them. The city roofs rushed up to meet her.

Remember Requiem.

She clenched her jaw, summoned every last bit of strength inside her, and shifted back into a dragon. She soared again.

Firedrakes swooped and slammed into her. More rose from the roofs around her. She blasted out flame.

"Fly into darkness, Requiem!" she cried. "Break through! With me! Rally with me!"

They swooped, blowing out flames in a ring, to join her flight. Fidelity roared her flames.

"Drive your fire forward!" she shouted. "Join your flames and break through!"

She blasted more fire. Their pillars joined with hers. The five fiery streams wove together, forming a gushing river of heat and sound and light. Firedrakes fled before it. The raging inferno carved open a path in the night. Ahead Fidelity saw the shadows, the open landscape, a chance to live. She flew there. The others flew with her.

They shot across the walls and over the fields.

We made it, Fidelity thought, tears in her eyes . . . and then the great beast swooped.

Mercy Deus had hovered above the battle, surveying it from the cold heights. Now the paladin swooped upon her great firedrakes, and her flames rained down. Ten other firedrakes flew with her, forming a wall of scales and fire.

"Slay them all!" the paladin cried. "Slay the weredragons!"

The firedrakes all blew fire, their jets weaving together in a gushing river, a raging inferno greater than Vir Requis fire, brighter than the sun, a flame to burn the world.

Fidelity reared in the sky, blinded by the light, screaming in pain.

A shadow flew forth.

"Fly, lassie!" the shadow cried, charging into the light. "Lead them on. Fly!"

"Julian!" she shouted.

The old silver dragon charged forth . . . into the woven jets of firedrake flames.

The dragon screamed as he burned.

Plowing onward, Julian beat his burning wings, laughed and screamed, and scattered the flames back onto the firedrakes. The old dragon blasted forth his own fire, a great fountain, and the firedrakes screamed and their riders burned.

"Father!" Roen cried.

"Julian!" Tears filled Fidelity's eyes. She couldn't even see the silver dragon anymore, only a burning phoenix, a beast of flame, laughing, holding back the enemy.

"Fly!" his voice echoed . . . and was gone.

Tears in her eyes, Fidelity flew.

"Follow me!" she shouted. "Domi, Cade! Fly! Roen!"

They flew past the burning firedrakes and into the open night. They streamed across the fields. When Fidelity looked over her shoulder, she saw the great blaze of firedrakes . . . and she saw a small, burning man plummet through the sky like a comet. Before Julian could hit the city rooftops, three firedrakes caught him, bit deep, and tore him apart. Limbs scattered. Fidelity's eyes watered and she looked away.

"Father!" Roen cried, voice torn in agony.

Fidelity forced herself to fly near the green dragon, to glare at him, to swipe him with her tail. "Silence! Fly silently, Roen. No fire. No sound. Fly!"

Roen's eyes were red and damp, but he obeyed. They all swallowed their flames. They soared higher and glided on the wind. Behind them, the firedrakes pursued, blasting out flame, seeking them in the night.

Five dragons had fought over the city. Four flew into the darkness, burnt, grieving. They had cried out, bled, killed for Requiem. As they flew in shadows, they left a light of Requiem behind, forever gone.

ROEN

My father is gone.

They flew through the night, four dragons where five had once flown. They flew through despair, bleeding, burnt, grieving. Roen could barely breathe, barely keep his wings flapping. The pain of his wounds blazed across him, and the pain inside him twisted his belly, clutched his heart, burned his throat and eyes. The sky itself seemed to shatter.

My father is gone.

If not for the firedrakes that still scanned the sky, he would have roared in agony. If not for Fidelity, whom he had to protect, he would have turned in the sky, charged back toward the enemy, and blasted his fire, burning them and dying, joining his father in the afterlife.

Father . . . Oh stars, Father.

The others flew beside him in the darkness: Fidelity, a slim blue dragon; Cade, a young golden dragon, his scales cracked and burnt; and Domi, just as battered and charred, her scales a mosaic of red, orange, and yellow in every shade.

And one dragon was missing. An old, silver dragon, his eyes bright, his smile ready.

Julian. My father.

The sky would always be empty.

As they glided in silence over the hills, Roen turned his head and looked back north. The city was distant now. The Cured Temple was only a spark of light on the horizon like a star fallen onto the earth. Yet other lights filled the sky, a hundred or more. Firedrakes. Their jets of fire rose and vanished every few seconds. Their shrieks tore across the sky. They flew everywhere, spreading out, seeking them.

Fidelity flew up beside Roen. She gazed at him with soft, damp eyes.

"Roen . . . I'm sorry." She let her wing brush against him.

He gritted his jaw, eyes stinging, not wanting to shed tears in front of her. He whispered, "Hush. Follow. We'll hide in Old Hollow."

She nodded, eyes gleaming, and kept flying close to him. Cade and Domi flew behind, silent on the wind. The firedrakes' flames now blazed miles away, and the grasslands gave way to the forests. As they glided lower, the pain grew stronger, an iciness spreading through Roen's belly.

I return home . . . without him.

The moon was a sliver but the stars were bright, and while Fidelity squinted in the darkness, unable to see, Roen's dragon eyes were sharp. He saw the crest of Old Hollow rising ahead from the forest, the tallest tree for miles, the only home Roen had ever known. He kept tapping Fidelity with his wing, guiding her onward, as they glided down. Domi and Cade followed, and Roen directed them to a small clearing where he had cut down several trees, creating a smooth surface to land on. The four dragons alighted onto the grass and shifted into human forms.

Crickets chirped, the forest surrounded them in black walls, and the stars shone. Directly above glowed Issari's Star, the eye of the Draco constellation. Roen stood still, watching the sky as if waiting for Julian to come gliding down, to tell them he's still alive, to laugh and embrace him. But no new dragon appeared, and Roen lowered his head.

The others stared at him silently. Fidelity was the only one who dared approach. She held his hand and touched his cheek.

"Roen, I'm so sorry."

He turned away. "Come, we go. We can't stand under open sky. The firedrakes are still searching for us."

As if to confirm his words, the cries of the beasts rose in the distance, and Roen spotted a shadow across the stars. The four Vir Requis, all in human forms, left the clearing and walked through the dark forest.

"I can't see anything," Fidelity whispered.

Roen held her hand. "Let me guide you."

He could barely see a thing either. Hardly any moonlight made it past the canopy, not with the moon so thin. He walked with his free hand held before him, making sure they didn't slam into any trees. If he hadn't known this forest so well, hadn't walked this path so many times, he wouldn't have found his way. But soon he found himself walking down a slope toward a towering shadow: Old Hollow.

Dragons Reborn

The ancient oak rose in the night, stretching its canopy toward the stars. It was the largest tree in the forest, perhaps in all the Commonwealth, rising from the ancient crater. As the Vir Requis walked toward the tree, their feet crunched fallen leaves.

"You'll find rest here," Roen said, voice hard, hoarse. "Food and drink and bandages. Follow me. It'll be crowded inside but we'll all fit."

The others stared at him, and he saw the pity in their eyes. Roen could not bear it. The lump swelled in his throat. He turned away and climbed the oak, moving from branch to branch, until he reached the hidden passageway that led into the hollow trunk. He slid down into his home. He stared at the place: walls of polished wood, a small table, only three stools, clay bowls, a pot of the stew his father would make . . . his father who would never cook this stew again, never fill this home with his laughter and life.

Fidelity slid down first from the branches, and Domi and Cade followed. All were silent, and Fidelity's eyes shone with tears. Roen could not bear to look at them.

I should never have left this place. Oh stars, I should never have fought in this war. I did this for you, Fidelity, and now he's gone, now he's gone.

He squared his jaw. There would be time for grief later. Shelves covered the walls, piled high with items, and Roen rummaged around until he found the bottle of spirits and the bundle of bandages. They spent a while bandaging their wounds and burn marks. Arrows had pierced their dragon forms. On their human bodies, the wounds were raw and ugly like the bites of wasps. Welts from the firedrake fire covered them; some were large and swollen and would leave scars.

As Roen bandaged a wound on Domi's leg, the memory would not leave him: Julian charging into the fire, falling as a burning man, and the firedrakes tearing him apart. Roen's fingers trembled. He hurriedly finished his work, binding the gash on Domi's leg, then turned away.

"You'll find food and drink on the shelves." His throat still felt so damn tight. "Eat. Rest."

With that Roen climbed out of the trunk. It was too crowded in there, yet too empty without his father. He could not bear it. He climbed down into the forest, walked across the fallen leaves, and stood facing the dark maples and birches. Finally he let his tears flow down his cheeks.

"This wasn't a war I wanted," he whispered into the shadows. "Oh, Father, I didn't want this fight. And now you're gone forever."

Footfalls sounded behind him, and Fidelity's soft voice rose in the darkness. "He gave his life for us. So Requiem can live. So--"

He spun around toward her, and now rage blazed inside him. "I don't care about Requiem!" He clenched his fists. "I did this for you, Fidelity! For you! Because you needed our help. I never cared about Requiem, and now . . ."

His hands loosened, and he fell to his knees before her. Fidelity knelt and embraced him.

"You're right," she whispered, holding him close. "I have no words of comfort. I cannot heal this pain. Just know that I'm sorry, that I'm here for you, that I love you."

He held her close, almost crushing her in his arms.

"I love you too," he whispered.

And as he held her, all his anger melted away, and he knew that he'd always fight for Fidelity, that he'd fly through fire and blood, that he'd give his own life for her. She fought for Requiem, and he would always fight for her. She was as precious to him as lost kingdoms, as dreams of rising again, as the stars and all they shone upon.

He looked up toward those stars, seeking the Draco constellation, but he saw fire.

"Firedrakes." He grabbed the axe that still lay on the forest floor. "A lot of them."

Fidelity grimaced and stepped back from him, staring up at the sky. Roen's heart sank. Several of the firedrakes swooped above, shrieking. Their claws shone in the firelight that escaped their maws. Above their cries rose a familiar voice--the voice of Mercy Deus.

"They're here somewhere! Burn down the forest! Burn down every tree!"

With blazing heat and shrieking wind, dragonfire roared down toward the forest, crashing through the trees like comets. One stream slammed down only a dozen feet away, engulfing an aspen. Red light flooded the forest.

Roen grabbed Fidelity and pulled her back. They raced toward Old Hollow.

"Bloody griffin bollocks!" Cade blurted out. The boy jumped down from the tree's branches.

Domi followed him, her red hair covering her face, and hissed like a wild beast. "That's Mercy above."

Cade grabbed her arm and began to run, dragging Domi along. "You don't say. Now run!"

They had taken only several steps before fire rained down, slamming into Old Hollow.

Flames cascaded over the ancient oak. Its canopy blazed. Its trunk creaked, the fire cloaking it. For two thousand years, this oak had stood here, a sentinel of the forest. Roen stood before it, the heat blasting him and stinging his eyes, watching this ancient tree, the only home he'd ever known, consumed with flame.

Fidelity grabbed his arm and tugged him. "Run!" she screamed.

The four Vir Requis ran together, keeping to their human forms. Another blazing jet slammed down before them, and another tree burst into flame. They swerved, dodging the inferno, and ran between maples, leaping over roots and fallen logs. Light bathed the forest.

"I see one!" cried a voice above. "Burn them!"

Roen cursed as fire crashed down before him, splashing up against his chest. His fur cloak ignited, and he tossed it off. He kept running, holding Fidelity's hand.

"Split up!" he shouted to Cade and Domi.

A burning tree slammed down before him. Roen and Fidelity paused, spun around, and raced around it. Cade and Domi leaped between the trees a dozen yards away. A firedrake swooped, grabbed a tree in its claws, and uprooted it. The roots rained soil, and the firedrake's rider fired an arrow. Roen ducked and the missile shot over his head.

"Cade, meet me at the tavern where we danced!" Fidelity shouted. "We have to split up!"

The boy nodded. As another flaming jet slammed down, Cade and Domi raced away, vanishing into the forest.

Roen turned and, holding Fidelity's hand, ran in the opposite direction. The firedrakes kept streaming above, roaring and blowing down their flames. Another one of the beasts swooped, and its claws tore up a birch. Roen and Fidelity swerved and raced down a hill between burning trees.

"We have to fly," Roen said.

Fidelity shook her head, braid swaying. "They'd see us in the sky. Keep running!"

They reached a stream and splashed through the shallow water. Trees blazed alongside, and the beasts kept flying above. As Roen ran, he slipped on a mossy rock hidden underwater, pitched forward, and banged his elbows. They bled. Fidelity pulled him up, and they ran onward.

She pointed. "There!"

A copse of maples rose along a hillside ahead, not yet aflame. Shadows still lurked between them. Roen and Fidelity ran out of the water and up the slope, moving between the trees.

When Roen glanced up, he couldn't see the stars; red smoke hid the sky. The firedrakes kept streaming back and forth. They must have lost track of their quarry.

"We need more distance between us and them," Roen said, then coughed madly. It was a moment before he could speak again. "Once we're far enough, we'll rise and fly."

He coughed again and almost fell, but he forced himself to keep running. Fire seemed to fill his lungs. He had breathed too much smoke; it felt as if embers blazed inside his chest.

I have to keep going. For the living. For Fidelity.

He kept running, holding Fidelity's hand. She too was coughing, and ash covered her face. One of her spectacles' lenses had smashed in the flight, and burn marks rose along her arms.

Along with the pain, rage filled Roen. Rage for the firedrakes who had killed his father, who had destroyed his home. Rage for them hurting Fidelity.

These monsters are who Fidelity has been fighting all these years, he thought as he ran. *I didn't want this war, but now . . . now I will burn them all.*

They kept running, leaping over logs and rocks, as the forest burned. Cade and Domi had vanished into the distance. The firedrakes kept blazing overhead, sending down death. Roen and Fidelity ran on, two souls alone in the inferno.

CADE

They flew between the smoke and stars, two dragons, one gold and one all the colors of fire.

"The damn paladins did us a favor," Cade muttered as they glided. "The smoke hides us."

That smoke blanketed the forest canopy below, crimson and white and black. The two dragons flew so high the air thinned out, and Cade could barely breathe. As he gazed down at the flaming forest, his eyes stung, and it wasn't only from the smoke.

Cade had never known such turmoil, such pain, such fear. The entire world seemed to burn, not just the forest below but all his life.

My home was destroyed. My parents were murdered. My sister is still captive. I'm a refugee, escaped from prison, and the Temple is burning the world to find me.

Cade did not know how to process such destruction, such a collapse of his life. He was only a baker! The only problem he had ever faced was a collapsing loaf of bread, not a collapsing world. He was used to fire crackling inside his oven, not spreading across sky and forest.

So many dead or missing. His eyes burned. *My sister. My parents. Korvin. Amity. Fidelity and Roen.*

His breath shuddered, and his chest felt so tight it almost crushed his lungs. He turned his head and looked at Domi, seeking some comfort.

She looked back at him, her eyes large and green. The firelight from below gleamed against her scales. She seemed like a flame herself, airborne, living fire. As he had so many times since his home had burned--in the darkness, in chains, in desolation--he thought about the time she had embraced him, whispered "Requiem" in his ear. Domi had first borne Mercy into his life, had tossed that life into a maelstrom, yet now, looking at Domi, Cade felt his anxiety fade. Domi had sparked this flame, yet now she soothed him. Now he saw goodness to her, the light of a fallen kingdom in her eyes. The Draco constellation shone above her, and as they flew, it seemed to Cade that the two dragons--the living Domi and the celestial dragon woven of starlight--were but echoes of each other. She was starlight woven into flame. She was Requiem risen in the darkness.

When Cade looked behind him, he saw the firedrakes in the distance, still dipping down to burn more trees. Ahead stretched the southern darkness. The two dragons kept flying until the smoke cleared below, until they left the fire behind. They glided down to fly lower in the sky, then finally landed in a field of grass.

Here they shifted into human forms. The fire was only an orange glow on the northern horizon, and the song of crickets and rustling grass filled the night.

"Domi," Cade said, turning to look at her. She stood before him, the grass rising to her knees. "Oh, Domi, I don't know how this all happened. But thank you. Thank you."

She only stared at him silently, then bit her lip and looked down at her feet. "Don't thank me. I served the Temple. I served our enemy."

He took her hands in his. "And you fought against them. You saved me from the dungeon."

A tear streamed down Domi's cheek. "But I couldn't save your baby sister; Eliana is still a captive in the Temple. I couldn't stop Mercy from burning your village, killing your parents."

Cade felt a lump in his throat. He wanted to tell Domi what he had learned in the Temple, that Beatrix was his mother, that Mercy was his true sister. He wanted to tell her about Korvin falling, Amity burning. He wanted to tell her about all the pain of the past few months, but he could bring none of it to his lips. So he just stared into those large green eyes, and then he embraced her.

She laid her head against his shoulder and wrapped her arms around him. They stood for a long time together in the night, holding each other, and she was warm and slender and eased his fear.

"Requiem," he whispered into her ear.

She nodded. "Requiem."

The world was burning, all its pillars crashing to the ground, but he had Domi again. They lay down to sleep in the grass, and she curled up against him. Cade held her close, never wanting to let go, and slept with her soft breath against his neck.

GEMINI

He pounded against the prison cell bars.

"Let me out, damn it! Domi! Mercy! Guards!" His chains rattled as he slammed against the bars again and again. "I am Gemini Deus, paladin of the Commonwealth! I demand that you release me!"

Nobody but the other prisoners answered, cackling, screaming, whispering, mocking, the voices of broken souls, their bodies and minds shattered. He could see no guards, no priests. Gemini slumped to the floor, chains rattling.

"Domi . . .," he whispered, tears in his eyes. "Why?"

He couldn't help it. The damn tears flowed down his cheeks. How had it come to this? He loved her! He protected her! He had freed her from this dungeon!

He balled his hands into fists. They trembled.

"The whore." He growled and rose to his feet. The chains around his ankles rattled. "You damn whore! I'm going to find you, Domi, and I'm going to gouge out your eyes, and rip out your entrails, and feed your head to the pigs!"

He fell back to his knees, weeping now. Blood dripped from his hands where his fingernails had cut his palms.

"Why?" he whispered. "Why, Domi? I love you. I love you."

He didn't understand. Why had Domi done this to him? Why had she punched him, knocked him out, chained him, locked him here?

"It wasn't me who imprisoned you here," he whispered. "It was Mercy. Only Mercy."

He stared between the bars. One cell was open, its prisoner released. The burnt corpses of guards lay strewn across the corridor--guards burnt with dragonfire, Domi's dragonfire. He had to think. He had to understand this.

She must have blamed me for her imprisonment, he thought. *She must think I knew, that I approved it.*

He took a shuddering breath. He had to get out of here. He had to find Domi, to explain that he had come to save her, that he hated his mother and sister. Domi had to understand that he loved her, that he'd always loved her, that he wasn't her enemy.

"Guards!" he shouted, banging against the bars again. "Guards, damn you!"

Nobody answered. He slumped back to the floor, curled up, and imagined that he held Domi in his arms.

He wasn't sure how long it was before he fell asleep, and it was a tortured sleep, something half between wakefulness and nightmares. In his dreams, he was making love to Domi, their naked bodies entwined, only to find that she was a dragon, that she was Pyre again, that in her lovemaking she dug her claws into him, bit him with her fangs, tore the flesh off his bones, ripped him apart, not even realizing she was a dragon, not even realizing that he screamed with pain and not with pleasure. He woke up drenched in sweat, curled up in the corner of his prison cell.

He waited. He slept again. His throat dried up and his lips cracked. He shouted himself hoarse. And still no guards approached, and still the corpses rotted in the corridor. Had Domi burned down the entire Cured Temple? Did Gemini now languish buried underground, the marble and gold palace toppled above him?

"I would have toppled this Temple myself for you, Domi," he whispered. "Why did you betray me?"

He closed his eyes, imagining that she was here with him, that he could hold her body, kiss her pale skin, stroke her red hair, gaze into her green eyes, protect her from the evil of the world, cherish her like a treasure.

He was drifting back into sleep when he heard the footfalls.

He bolted up, slammed himself against the bars, and stared out into the corridor.

Oh bloody Spirit spit.

His knees trembled. His heart sank. Walking daintily across the ashy floor, holding up the hems of her robes, came High Priestess Beatrix. His mother.

She came to stand before the bars and stared at him, face stoic.

"Hello, my son."

He pressed himself against the bars. "Get me out of here!" His voice was hoarse. Every word tore at his throat, yet still he shouted. "Get me out!"

The thinnest of smiles stretched her white lips. She took a step back. "You must learn to calm yourself, son. Hysteria does not become a son of Deus."

He blinked tears away, letting rage consume him. "The weredragon imprisoned me here. She escaped. Let me out! I will hunt her."

Beatrix sighed. "Both weredragons escaped, son . . . both your whore and your brother."

"My brother?" He laughed, spraying spit. "Has Mercy finally grown a pair? Mother, you've gone mad!" He grabbed the bars and shook them. "Get the keys! Open this door. I have to find Domi, I have to--"

"You will not utter that name here!" Beatrix frowned. "You brought that sniveling little reptile into my home. You brought a weredragon into the holiness of the Cured Temple."

"I didn't know that she--"

"You lie!" Beatrix sneered. "What kind of paladin are you? I raised you to slay weredragons, not to bed them, not to bring them into my home. She flashed her teats at you, and your brain turned to fog." She barked a laugh. "Perhaps now you learned of their treachery. Your weredragon whore imprisoned you here, the reptile you love. You wanted a weredragon? Enjoy her gift to you."

The High Priestess turned to walk away.

"Mother!" Gemini shouted, tears coursing down his cheeks. "Mother, damn you! Come back here! You're the whore, Mother!

You are! You cannot leave me here. Release me!" He pounded against the bars. "I am your son! Your son!"

She paused in the corridor, turned around, and stared back at him. "I have another son now. A son I will recapture. A son who will join you here."

"You can't leave me here!" Gemini cried.

Beatrix raised an eyebrow. She stepped back toward him, reached past the bars, and caressed his cheek. "Oh sweet child . . . sweet, innocent child. Don't you remember?"

He wept. "Remember what?"

She stroked his hair. "When you were very small, I told you that if you misbehaved, you will end up in this dungeon. You've been a very bad child. You have misbehaved. Enjoy the rest of your life, Gemini. A life of darkness."

She walked away, and she would not turn back even as Gemini screamed.

CADE

He woke up to a dawn of ash, of fading hope, and of a woman he loved sleeping against him.

Crimson smoke veiled the sun, and only soft red light fell upon the land. On the distant horizon, fire still blazed, and the smell of burnt wood wafted across the grasslands where they lay. Cade turned his eyes toward Domi and watched her sleep. Her hair was like a flame itself, wild and red and orange and shining yellow. Her body was slender, pale, dotted with freckles like the stars. The woman who had whispered "Requiem" into his ear. The woman he had dreamed of in darkness. The woman who had tied him, had borne Mercy upon her back, had ruined his life and then given him hope--here she lay in his arms.

She woke slowly, her eyes opening to slits.

"Cade," she whispered.

He pulled strands of her hair off her eyes and tucked them behind her ears. "Hello, Domi."

She nestled closer to him, her leg lying across him, and touched his cheek. "You're real. You're really here. Everything that happened--the burning city, the forest, the flight through the smoke--I thought it was a nightmare. But I can feel you, Cade. You're real."

He nodded, a lump in his throat. "I wish it were all a dream. Everything. From the first day when you arrived in my village, a wild firedrake, Mercy on your back."

She looked down. He saw the pain that caused her. When she looked back up, her eyes shone damply. "I'm sorry, Cade," she whispered. "I'm so sorry for that day. For who I was. For the things Mercy did while I watched and didn't stop her. I'm so sorry for your parents, for your village."

He nodded, looking away, not sure how he felt. Did he hate Domi? Did he love her? Was she his ally or his enemy, a great warrior for Requiem or one who fought against that fallen kingdom?

"You told me about Requiem," he whispered. "I never forgot how you whispered that word into my ear, how much I could feel it meant to you, to everyone. How much it came to mean to me."

She crawled up to straddle him, looked down at his face, and touched his cheeks. "And I never forgot you, Cade. Another Vir Requis, the first one I had met in years. I never forgot how, in a world of cruel paladins and the searing light of the Temple, you seemed good to me. Innocent. Almost childlike but . . . but strong." She lowered her eyes. "I often thought of you too. In the darkness of my lair, as I curled up, hurt, the lashes Gemini had given me blazing on my back, I thought of you. I pretended sometimes, when I lay in darkness, alone and afraid and cold, that you lay there with me, that I could hug you, kiss you, and--" She bit her lip and blushed furiously. "I've said too much."

Cade lay on his back, never wanting to move, never wanting her to leave. She seemed almost weightless upon him, her pale knees pressed against him, her feet folded underneath her, her head lowered, her hair brushing his face. He reached up to touch that hair, to tuck it back under her ears, and found himself stroking it again and again, then caressing her face, drowning in her eyes. She leaned down, and her lips brushed his, and he kissed her.

It was a hesitant kiss at first, a few pecks of the lips, but it morphed into a deep, passionate thing, a kiss he could drown into. Cade pushed himself onto his elbows, and Domi sat in his lap, her legs spread around him, and he kept kissing her, intoxicated by her, sure this too was a dream. This could not be real. It felt too good, too sad, too hazy, like thoughts after too much wine. And yet she felt real, her body soft and warm in his hands.

"Cade," she whispered into his ear, kissing him. "Requiem."

She straightened, still sitting in his lap, and pulled off her tunic and tossed it aside. She remained naked above him. Her body was white as milk, strewn with countless freckles, her waist slender, her breasts small, and he kissed every part of her. He did not know what he was doing. He had never made love to a woman before, but he had made love to Domi countless times in his dreams. Perhaps this too was but another dream. If so, it was one he never wanted to wake from.

They made love in the grass, slowly, gently, then wildly, desperately, and Domi bit her lip so hard he thought she would bleed, and she wrapped her limbs around him so tightly it almost hurt. Finally he cried out, and she gasped, and they lay together for a long time on the grass, spent, too weak to rise, too uncertain of what they had done, of the reality or dreams of this landscape and their lovemaking.

"Requiem," he whispered into her ear. "Domi."

He held her close against him, and he loved her--loved her more than Requiem, maybe more than he had ever loved anyone.

Finally they rose to their feet and got dressed again. They dared not fly as dragons; the firedrakes would be patrolling the skies. They walked through the grasslands, hand in hand, silent, afraid to speak, as if words could wake them up from this dream. The smoke spread above, and the sun did not emerge.

AMITY

She stood on the mountaintop, watching as her army drained away like sand between her fingers.

"They're going with him," she whispered to Korvin. "Oh bloody stars, they're going with the beast."

Below in the valley, she saw Shafel upon his griffin. A hundred other griffins flew around him, riders on their backs. Below them, thousands of men, women, and children were heading south, carrying their belongings in wagons or upon their backs. Gosh Ha'ar, the great settlement beneath the mountains, was falling apart.

"Follow, Horde!" Shafel's voice rose on the wind, distant but just loud enough for Amity to hear. "Follow your king!"

Korvin stood at her side, the wind whipping his long grizzled hair. "Let him leave." The old soldier grunted. "For years, many warriors in the Horde spoke of conquests in the south, of uniting the wild tribes who live beyond the rivers." Korvin scratched his stubbly cheeks. "Let Shafel go conquer. Let him get out of our hair. Enough have stayed loyal to you, Amity."

She spun toward Korvin, clenching her fists. "He's taking too many! The griffins. Thousands of warriors. Warriors we need to conquer the Commonwealth."

She spun back south. Only a few thousand remained camped before the marble archway in the shadow of the mountains. A few dozen salvanae--long coiling dragons with no wings or limbs--hovered between them. But the griffins were flying south. Tens of thousands of warriors were walking south with them.

"Enough have stayed loyal?" Amity whispered. "Korvin, he's taking two thirds of my army."

Korvin placed a hand on her shoulder. "So what will you do? Challenge him to battle? Risk dying? We came here to find an army. We have an army." He pointed below at the forces that remained. "And more soldiers of the Horde await us along the northern coast. Amity, let us take those of Gosh Ha'ar who remained loyal, and let us travel north back to Hakan Teer on the coast. Many there, seeing us approach with the salvanae and thousands of warriors, will swear allegiance to you. It will be enough."

"No." She trembled with rage. "No, I will not. I will not allow this! I will not allow the Horde to split in two, to rule in the north while Shafel lurks in the south, growing his forces. We'd be trapped between the southern Horde and the northern Commonwealth." She glared at Korvin. "The Horde must stand united. You don't understand. You're not one of us."

She saw the pain that caused him. His eyes hardened, and his cheeks flushed beneath his white stubble. He pulled his hand off her shoulder. "No. I'm not. I'm not one of the Horde. You're right, Amity. I'm a man of Requiem. The kingdom of dragons is all I care about. I thought you did too. Ask yourself, Amity, where your true loyalties lie."

She raised her chin. "I'm a daughter of Requiem. All my life, Korvin, I fought against the Cured Temple that rules it. The Temple that murdered my parents. The Temple that crushed Requiem, that raised the Commonwealth from its ashes. You want Requiem back? That will take a united Horde under one rule. Mine!"

With that, Amity spun around, raced across the mountaintop, and leaped into the air. Before she could fall and slam down against the mountainside, she shifted into a dragon, beat her wings, and flew. She blasted out a stream of fire, and she roared.

"Hear me, Horde!" She soared across the crowds below, crying out for all to hear. Her voice rang across the mountains and valleys beyond. "I am Amity, your queen! I will lead you to conquest across the sea. Turn aside from Shafel the False. Join me in the north! Join your queen!"

Yet Shafel kept flying away on his griffin, moving across the southern grasslands, heading toward the distant lands of wild tribes. The other griffins and the people below kept following. The warriors traveled along the rims of the camp, many riding horses, holding spears and swords and shields. Women, children, and elders walked in the center, leading donkeys and sheep, carrying their belongings across their backs or in wagons.

"Hear me, Horde! Turn back now!" Amity blasted fire across the sky. "Turn back and serve your queen. I will lead you to conquest!"

Ahead of her flew the griffins; there must have been over a hundred. Their riders turned toward her, and Shafel laughed--a deep, ringing laughter.

They cannot kill me here, Amity knew, baring her teeth. *We still fly over holy ground.*

But a few more miles, and they would swarm toward her.

Wings beat, scales clattered, and a charcoal dragon came to fly beside her. Korvin glared at her, eyes narrowed, smoke rising from his nostrils. "Amity, come back. Let them leave. The salvanae have remained loyal, and they're as fierce as griffins. Many warriors too remain, and we'll find more in the north."

Amity turned her head and gazed back toward the mountains. The salvanae still hovered over the foothills, the legendary true dragons of the west. Their bodies were a hundred feet long, slim and scaled and gleaming, and beards grew from their chins. From this distance they seemed like serpents floating on water. They were mighty warriors, Amity knew, able to cast lightning from their maws. Beneath them, thousands of men remained, armed with swords and spears, loyal to her, the slayer of their old king.

Is Korvin right? she thought. *When combined with the forces waiting in Hakan Teel in the north, will it be enough to crush the Commonwealth?*

"Do not let your pride lead you to insanity," Korvin said as they glided over those troops who had abandoned her. "I have seen what obsession can do, Amity. Do not risk your life."

She whipped her head toward him, glared, and spat smoke his way. "I am not Beatrix. I am not a madwoman. I do what I do for Requiem. I would fight for her. I would die for her." She snarled. "I will swarm onto the shores of Old Requiem with all the might of the south--of *all* the south--and my roar will send the Temple crashing down."

She beat her wings and flew faster, leaving him behind.

"Shafel!" she shouted. "Shafel, come face me, coward! We're no longer above holy ground." She blasted fire his way, and sparks rained down onto the hosts below. "I challenge you!"

The griffins were flying over the grasslands ahead. At the sound of her challenge, they turned as one, a hundred beasts, and all came flying toward her.

"Damn it, Amity!" Korvin said. He turned his head northward. "Salvanae, fly! Salvanae, to us--"

Amity slapped him with her tail. "No. I need no aid." She narrowed her eyes, growling, staring at the approaching griffins. "I'll slay them all myself."

With a roar, she charged forth and blasted out her fire.

The griffins scattered, rose higher, then swooped toward her. Their talons reached out, and their riders fired arrows.

Amity howled and blasted her dragonfire every which way. Arrows caught fire and burned. She soared and crashed into the griffins.

Talons slammed against her, scraping across her red scales. A beak drove down into her shoulder, drawing blood. Amity ignored the pain. She roared, blasting out flame, and the inferno cascaded around her, an exploding star in the sky. She whipped her tail, lashed her claws, snapped her jaws, and cried out as arrows slammed into her.

The griffins surrounded her, a ring of fur and feathers. Their beaks slammed into her. Their talons cut her. She roared, burning them. Fur ignited and feathers burned. A rider screamed, bathed in fire. Amity rose higher, closed her jaws around another rider, and cut the man in half. She tugged her head back, the rider's upper torso in her mouth, and spat it out. She swung her tail, slamming its spikes into a griffin, digging deep into its hide.

"Face me alone, Shafel!" Amity shouted, blood and organs in her mouth. "Are you a coward? Face me without your brutes!"

She rose higher, crashing between griffins and their riders, and saw him ahead. He flew on the largest griffin, a massive beast almost twice a dragon's size. Black armor covered the creature, and its yellow eyes blazed through holes in its helmet. On its back, Shafel wore a bronze breastplate, and he held a shield and a lance longer than two men.

"Move aside, warriors!" Shafel shouted. "Make way."

The other griffins swerved, and Shafel swooped toward Amity, lance gleaming.

Amity soared, shaking off blood, and blew her fire.

The jet blasted forth, screaming like a storm, blue in its center, exploding out with white and red.

The griffin before her screeched and reared in the sky. The fire crashed against its jeweled breastplate and blazed out in every direction, raining back down against Amity. She kept rising, crying out, jaws opened wide and claws outstretched.

Shafel stood in his saddle and thrust his lance.

Amity swerved.

The blade--long as a human arm--sliced along her flank, tearing out scales, digging a gash across her from shoulder to hip. Scales and blood rained, and Amity screamed.

The griffin flew past her, then spun around and prepared to charge again. A ring of other griffins closed all around Amity, above and below, hiding the world. Their eyes blazed, and their riders leered.

As Amity spun to face Shafel and his griffin again, fear flooded her.

Was Korvin right?

Pain blazed across her, and her blood kept dripping. Shafel readied his spear, and his griffin charged again.

Amity sneered.

No fear.

She charged forward.

Fire and blood.

She roared, soared higher, and blew her fire. The inferno rained down onto the griffin's back.

Shafel raised his shield, screaming as the fire cascaded across the metal disk. Amity kept spewing down her flame. The fire reached around the griffin's armor and ignited its wings.

Feathers blazed. Amity let her fire die, grabbed Shafel's shield, and tugged it free, exposing the man beneath. She lashed down her jaws, prepared to rip him apart.

His griffin swooped, then soared again. Shafel's lance drove into Amity's wing.

She cried out in pain, in fear, in rage. She swiped her claws and shattered the spear's shaft, but its top half still pierced her. She tried to beat her wings. She could barely fly.

Shafel's griffin burned, wings ablaze, but would not fall. The beast rose higher and slammed into Amity.

She yowled and tumbled through the sky, spinning madly. The hundred other griffins spun around her, a sea of endless wings and beaks and talons. They grabbed at her. They scratched her. They bit her. Their riders laughed and fired their arrows, and Amity knew she was going to die.

Fire blazed.

Gray scales flashed.

With a roar like thunder, Korvin soared into the sky, leading a host of salvanae.

The true dragons bugled, a cry like stones falling into subterranean pools, like silver trumpets, like ancient songs. Their crystal eyes shone, large as human heads and topped with long lashes. Their beards streamed like banners, and their scales glimmered, bright as polished coins. Lightning bolts blasted out from their jaws to slam into the griffins attacking Amity.

Korvin flew at their lead, blowing fire. His flames slammed into Shafel and his griffin.

"He's mine!" Amity roared. She was bleeding, hurt, maybe dying, but still she swooped. "Back off, Korvin!"

His dragonfire kept blazing across Shafel and the griffin. Amity dived right through the flames, reached out her claws, and plucked Shafel out from the inferno.

She soared, crashing through griffins and salvanae, clutching the burnt Shafel in her jaws. She rose higher and higher, emerging from the smoke and flame, then flew over the battle until she glided above the army below.

She spat out Shafel and caught him in her claws. He was still alive, his face melted away, his molten armor dripping over his red flesh. He was nothing but a chunk of metal molded with skin and muscle and burning blood, his ruin of a mouth gasping, his charred fingers twitching.

Amity tossed back her head and roared.

"See me, Horde!" she cried out. The lance still pierced her wing, and her flank still bled, but still she cried out to the people below, to the griffins who still flew behind her. "Hear me! I am Amity, Queen of the Horde! I hold the dying ruin of Shafel who defied me. So shall be the fate of any who challenge the Queen of the Horde!"

With that, she tossed Shafel into the air and blew out dragonfire. The jet slammed into Shafel, melting what remained of his armor, burning what remained of his flesh, extinguishing what remained of his life. The burning corpse fell like a comet. People rushed aside below, and the charred ruin slammed into the ground.

"Kneel before me!" Amity shouted, scattering flame all around. "Worship me!"

Below her, the deserters knelt. A chant rose among them.

"Queen Amity! Queen Amity!"

Smoke rising from her jaws and nostrils, she spun in the sky toward the surviving griffins and salvanae. The flying beasts stared at her, many burnt and bleeding.

"Lead the people back to the mountains," Amity said, blasting out sparks of fire. "We travel north. Across the desert. To the coast, then across the sea." She sneered. "To the Commonwealth."

She spun around, the lance still in her wing, and flew until she reached the mountains again. She landed on the mountaintop, a dragon wreathed in fire and light, and resumed human form.

She collapsed onto the stone, shivering, bleeding.

I did it, she thought, trembling, her blood staining the stone. *They're mine. The Horde is mine.*

The sun set around her, its light gilding the army below. Her army.

Wings beat and Korvin landed beside her. Healers leaped off his back, three women clad in the red robes of their order. They rushed toward Amity with bandages and ointment and prayer beads.

As they tended to her wounds, Korvin knelt beside her. At first his eyes were hard, but then they softened and he touched her hair.

"That was foolish, Amity. But I'm glad you're alive. Stars, don't do anything so foolish again."

"You shouldn't have helped me," she whispered, then grimaced as the healers rubbed ointment onto her wounds. She managed a grin. "I'd have looked stronger defeating him myself."

"You'd have been a corpse for Shafel to parade to his troops." He held her hand. "You must learn wisdom."

She cried out in pain as the healers splashed ointments into a wound, then managed another shaky smile and wink. "I'll leave wisdom to you, old man. I'll take the guts and glory."

As they wrapped bandages around her, the sun vanished and darkness cloaked the mountain. Holding Korvin's hand against her breast, Amity slept.

ROEN

He held Fidelity close as the world burned around them.

Ash rained from the sky, and trees burned on the horizons. Smoke churned above like clouds, and the smell of the fallen forest filled their nostrils. As Roen held Fidelity against him, he lowered his head, consumed with his love for her, with his grief for his father, with his grief for the forest.

Old Hollow, the most ancient oak in the woods, had burned. All the trees around it, millions of souls, had fallen in the fire. The maples he had tended to since they were saplings. The pine he had nursed back to health after a lightning strike. The coiling network of mossy roots, fallen logs, boulders rising from piles of fallen leaves--all living things to him, beings as wise as men. The animals of the forest--the swift hawks and falcons, the deer, the scurrying mice, the dragonflies and fireflies, all dearer to him than humans. All fallen to the fire. All gone. The forest that had been his home had been a nation to him, a nation as real as Requiem.

That nation is gone.

"I will no longer hear the birds," he whispered, voice hoarse. "I will never more watch dapples of sunlight dance upon fallen leaves. I will never more hear the rustle of branches, never more see the beauty of mist floating through autumn foliage, never more smell the fresh green spring, never more feel the crumbly soil beneath my fingers and the smooth trunk of Old Hollow." He rested his chin on Fidelity's head, squeezing her against him. "But I have you, Fidelity, and I promise to always protect you. To defend you like I could not defend the forest."

She placed her hand against his cheek. She stared at him through her battered spectacles; one of the lenses had smashed in the mad flight. Her golden braid hung across her shoulder, its tip seared. Burn marks spread across her clothes.

"I'm so sorry, Roen. I'm so sorry." She held him close and whispered into his ear. "You never wanted to fight this war. You wanted to remain in Old Hollow. With your forest. With your father. I came into your life, and now . . . now both are lost, and I cannot tell you how sorry I am, how much I grieve." She looked up at him again. "How much I love you."

He held her hands and squeezed them. "For a long time, I didn't understand. I didn't know why you cared so much for Requiem, for a fallen kingdom. But I know now. I understand. Requiem to you is like the forest, a memory of something precious, something lost. Something that meant the world, that meant countless lives all woven together into something beautiful. And you lost Requiem as I lost the forest. But we'll keep fighting, Fidelity. Always. To remember them. To keep the memory alive of both Requiem and its woods."

"And we'll plant saplings," she said. "In the ashes of the burnt forest. And we'll plant the seeds of Requiem and her memory across the Commonwealth. We'll regrow, rebuild, remember. I promise you. Together."

Her leg was cut and bandaged, and Roen lifted her in his arms. He carried her through the charred remains of the land as ash rained. She was a precious, broken doll to him, bandaged, burnt, her spectacles smashed, her eyes pained, her heart shattered. He could no longer save his father, could no longer save his forest, but he could save Fidelity. He could cherish her, heal her, keep fighting with her.

Roen carried her until they reached rolling grasslands and the fire was but a light on the horizon, a smell of smoke on the wind. The sun set but smoke still hid the moon and constellations. He could see only Issari's Star between the smoky strands, the eye of the dragon, named after an ancient priestess of Requiem. He lay Fidelity down by a stream in the darkness.

Their clothes were charred, torn, caked with ash and soaked with smoke. They undressed, wincing as the fabric brushed against their wounds, and stepped naked into the stream. It was only a foot deep, and they lay down together, letting the water stream across them. Their hands clasped together, and Roen closed his eyes as he lay in the water, smooth stones against his back, the cold stream flowing across him. He tried to let the stream clear away all his pain, all his grief, all his anger, to let all thoughts and memories flow away with the water. Fidelity squeezed his hand, lying naked beside him, almost invisible in the darkness.

Let this be a healing river, he thought. *If you can hear my prayers, Issari's Star, let us find healing.*

Fidelity turned toward him in the water and kissed his cheek, and they climbed out onto the grass and lay in the night, naked in the darkness.

To me, you are soothing and healing like water, Roen thought, closing his eyes, holding Fidelity close, trying to lose the pain as he embraced her.

He kissed her cheek, and then in the darkness, he found himself kissing her lips. She kissed him back, and he stroked her hair, and she wrapped her arms around his back, and he did not mean to, did not expect to, but he found himself making love to her, flowing inside her, moving atop her as she gasped, wrapped her legs around him, buried her hands in his hair. He made love to her in the darkness with the same urgency and passion as their first time. He lay with her for his love, for his grief, for a world that collapsed around him. Perhaps Fidelity was all that remained of his world, all that mattered to him, the sum of all goodness and comfort and light.

"I love you, Fidelity," he whispered, kissing her neck.

"I love you, Roen." He felt her tears on his cheek. "Even as worlds crumble, I will always love you."

They held each other, entwined together, and slept through darkness and dawn.

DOMI

She walked with Cade down the dark cobbled streets of Lynport, seeking the Old Wheel, the tavern where she had spent a summer in her youth, the tavern where she would now find hope or crushing grief.

Did you survive the flight, Fidelity? Domi thought as she walked along the shadowy streets. *Do you wait for me here?*

This was an old neighborhood, and this was an old city, an ancient port on the edge of the Commonwealth. Some of the houses here predated the Commonwealth itself. They were built of wattle and daub, the timbers dark and chipped, and their roofs were triangular and tiled, not the clay domes of those houses the Temple had built across the realm. Lantern poles rose at every street corner, and flames flickered within the glass panels of their lamps. Domi could not yet see the ocean ahead, but she heard its whispers calling to her, and she smelled the salt on the air, a smell that triggered so many memories that she shivered.

"They'll be here, Domi," Cade said softly. He patted her hand. "Fidelity and Roen are swift dragons, faster and stronger than any drake."

She nodded silently. Cade could not understand her, she knew. He had no memories of the lamplight against the wet cobblestones, the sound of waves, the smell of salt, but to her Lynport was a place of an older life. In her mind, she was a child again, visiting here with her father and sister. They walked along the boardwalk, bought fresh oysters from a stall, and shucked them on the beach. Domi and Fidelity had gagged and squealed at the taste, and Korvin had ended up eating them all. Again, Domi and Fidelity were playing beneath the cliffs of Ralora along the beach, pretending to be old heroines of Requiem like the legendary Queen Lyana, the warrior Agnus Dei, and the famous Tilla Roper who had lived in this very city hundreds of years ago. In her mind, Domi sat again in the Old Wheel tavern, tasting ale for the first time, and eating the best fried fish she had ever tasted.

It was a summer of family, of innocence, she thought, remembering her time here. *A last holiday of joy before I fled our home, before I chose the life of a firedrake, before war burned us and took my family away from me.*

She turned to look at Cade.

Are we all that remains, Cade? Are we the last whispers of Requiem?

They kept walking and stepped onto the boardwalk. Only several lanterns cast their light here; the boardwalk stretched long and dark across the coast, the sea whispering to the south, a row of buildings rising in the north. The place was barren. A few stray cats scampered along the beach, the only sign of life. The moon was a faded glow behind the clouds, and the waves whispered.

Finally Domi saw it ahead, a three-story building of wood and clay rising along the boardwalk. The Old Wheel tavern. *Meet me at the old tavern!* Fidelity had cried, and here it stood, and here Domi's fear swelled.

Be here, Fidelity.

Domi reached out and clutched Cade's hand, seeking some comfort from his presence. He held her hand tightly, and they approached the tavern together. The boardwalk was dark and barren, but Domi found the tavern door unlocked. She and Cade stepped inside.

The common room was large enough for six or seven tables, most of them in shadow. A hearth lay cold and dark at the back, and casks of ale rose along one wall, looming over a bar. A wagon wheel hung from the ceiling, candles burning upon it, their light the only illumination. Two figures, shadowed and hooded, sat at the back of the room, the only people here.

Domi stood still, anxious, the sea wind at her back. Suddenly she feared that it was Mercy and Gemini in the shadows, ambushing her, ready to drag her back to the dungeon. The figures leaped to their feet and ran toward her, and Domi hissed and prepared to shift into a dragon and blow her fire.

"Domi!" cried one of the shadowy figures. "Cade!" The candlelight entered the figure's hood, shining on spectacles with only one lens. The second figure stepped forward too, and the light revealed Roen's beard and warm brown eyes.

"Fidelity!" Domi cried, and tears budded in her eyes.

Her sister leaped onto her, embraced her tightly, then laughed and turned toward Cade, and soon they were all swapping hugs and laughter.

The innkeeper emerged from the kitchen, and soon the companions sat at the table together, and Domi tasted that ale again, and a bargirl placed the same old fried fish before her, and her sister sat beside her again, and once more Domi felt safe, felt loved, and it was too much. And it scared her. And her father was not there. And though she did not eat the fish, she felt as if a bone were lodged in her throat. The room spun around her. Her eyes burned. Her fingers shook and she could not breathe. She rose from the table and fled the tavern, leaving her companions behind.

She raced across the boardwalk, legs weak, and leaped onto the moonlit beach. She walked along the sand until she reached the sea and stood with her bare feet in the water, and she closed her damp eyes.

It hurts too much. The memories are too real. The joy is too painful.

She stood for a long time, breathing deeply, listening to the waves. Finally she heard soft footsteps behind her, and she felt a hand on her shoulder.

"Domi?"

She turned to see her older sister. Fidelity stared at her with soft eyes.

"Are you all right, Domi?" she asked.

Domi shook her head, and her tears fell. "No. I'm so sorry, sister. I'm so sorry."

Fidelity held her hand. "For what?"

"For . . . for doing this to our family." Domi looked down at her toes. "For running away. For becoming a firedrake, a traitor. For bearing Mercy on my back and serving Gemini, as both a firedrake and a woman to mount." She trembled. "I ran from our family. From father. From you. And I miss those old days, and I'm so scared. Where is our father? Oh, Fidelity . . . where is he?"

Now Fidelity's eyes watered, and she pulled Domi into an embrace. "I wanted to tell you at Old Hollow. I was going to. But the firedrakes arrived too quickly, and . . . oh Domi. He fell." She squeezed Domi so closely it almost hurt. "It was over the sea. He fought the firedrakes, and Mercy stabbed him, and I tried to save him, but I couldn't. I saw him fall into the water, and Cade and I had to flee. I don't know if he lived or died, but he's lost, Domi."

Domi trembled.

Father. Lost.

"It's my fault," Domi whispered. "Oh, stars, it's my fault. I bore Mercy on my back to Sanctus. I took her right to the library, and now . . ."

Domi could speak no more. She couldn't even stay standing. She fell to her knees, trembling. Fidelity knelt and embraced her.

"You helped us flee the library," Fidelity whispered. "Without you, I would be dead. You saved me."

The waves rose ahead, wetting their knees. Fidelity hugged her close, and Domi could only lie on the sand, a lump in her throat, grief and guilt in her heart.

I'm sorry, Father. I'm so sorry. I miss you so much.

"I just wish he were here again," Domi finally whispered. "That I could tell him that I'm sorry. That I could tell him that I love him." She tightened her lips. "He's still alive somewhere. I know it. Korvin is a tough old bastard, the toughest man I know." She sat up, fists clenched in the sand. "I'm going to believe that he's still out there, still fighting, that I'll see him again." She turned to look at Fidelity. "We're going to find him. And until then, we're going to keep fighting for him. For Requiem."

Fidelity nodded, unable to speak, only to embrace her sister. They sat together, watching the waves. The clouds parted, revealing the head of the Draco constellation. Issari's Star shone down upon them, the dragon's eye, forever guiding their path.

CADE

When the sisters returned into the Old Wheel tavern, they all sat together at the back table, cloaked and shadowed.

"We burn them." Cade pounded the tabletop. "We sneak into the city again. We rise at night." He rose to his feet as if to demonstrate. "We burn down the whole damn Temple!"

"Hush!" Fidelity glanced around the common room, then glared at Cade. "Keep your voice low and don't pound the table."

Cade glanced around him too. Candles burned atop the wagon wheel chandelier, casting flickering light across the common room. Casks of ale rose along one wall, and before them stood the old innkeeper, polishing the bar. Several round tables stood scattered across the scarred oak floor. A fire crackled at the hearth. A collection of fisherman and tradesmen raised their eyes to stare at Cade, then shook their heads or grunted and returned to their drinks.

Cade sat down. "I'll be quiet now. But when we burn the Temple, I'll be roaring."

He looked at his companions one by one. Fidelity sat beside him, wrapped in a burlap cloak. Her spectacles were still smashed, and her golden braid was cut to half its previous length; the bottom half had burned in the battle. Across from Cade sat two other hooded figures. Roen hunched over, elbows on the table, looking as uncomfortable as a bear trapped in a barn. Cade saw little more than the woodsman's beard and darting eyes. Beside him sat Domi, barely half Roen's size, her cloak wrapped around her. She was busy sipping from her ale and watching everyone, silent, her face blank.

"The wisest course of action," said Fidelity, "is to continue our work. To keep printing our books. To--"

"Fidelity!" Cade rolled his eyes. "They burned down the whole damn forest. That includes our printing press. They were waiting for us at the paper mill, and you better believe they've got more men in every paper mill in the Commonwealth. By now they've probably seized every book we've printed and burned it." As she glared at him, Cade forced himself to lower his voice. "Books won't be enough anymore. We need to attack."

Fidelity tugged at her braid so mightily Cade thought she might rip off what remained of it. "Attack? You saw what happened last time we attacked." She lowered her eyes.

Cade glanced at Roen, then at his drink. "I know." His voice was soft, barely a whisper. "I didn't know Julian well, but he was kind to me. I can't imagine the pain his loss brings to those who loved him." He looked up and gazed at the three others. "We must continue the fight. We can't let Julian's death be in vain. We have to stop this cursed Temple, and we have to save my sister." His eyes stung. "Eliana is still there in the Temple, just a baby. We have to save her."

For the first time since they'd entered the tavern, Domi spoke, her voice soft. "Eliana is safe. I saw her in the Temple, Cade. I know you want to save her, and I promise you: I will do what I can to help. But know that she's safe, that she's being treated well."

"Being raised to become a paladin," Cade said. "Like Beatrix wanted for me."

Domi frowned and leaned forward. "She wanted you to become a paladin?"

Cade lowered his eyes again and clasped his hands beneath the tabletop. "She . . . when I was there, in the Cured Temple, she . . . the High Priestess that is . . . she told me that I'm her son." He looked up at the others, seeing them through a haze. "That Mercy and Gemini are my siblings. That she wanted me to consume tillvine, give up my magic, and become a paladin." He barked a mirthless laugh that sounded almost like a sob. "Mind games."

Domi and Fidelity both gasped.

"Impossible," said Fidelity.

"Lies," said Domi.

Roen, meanwhile, only grunted and hunched down further. "The High Priestess spoke truth."

Cade frowned. He stared at the hulking forester. What did Roen know of such things? Cade felt anger rise within him. He had never liked Roen, not since the first moment, not since he had seen Fidelity and the brute exchanging secret glances. Did Roen blame him for Julian's death, and was this some kind of feeble attempt at revenge?

"What do you mean?" Cade demanded. "How can it be true?"

Roen sighed and, for the first time since entering the tavern, raised his mug of ale. He drank slowly, emptying the mug in a single, long gulp.

"It was years ago." The forester wiped suds off his beard. "I was only a boy, about the age you are now, Cade. It was the day your father came to Old Hollow, seeking aid. The day he came there with you."

Everyone was staring at him. Cade wanted to vanish underground.

"My . . . father," he whispered.

Roen nodded. "Aye, don't remember him much, to be honest. Couldn't tell you what he looked like. But he was wounded--badly. I remember that much. Burnt and cut and feverish. And he carried you in his arms, a little babe wrapped in swaddling clothes. Our two fathers knew each other; they spoke like old friends." Roen stared into his empty mug as if wishing it were full again. "For the first time, I learned about High Priestess Beatrix. My father had only told me that the world outside the forest was dangerous, that bad people would hunt us for our magic. Your father spoke of Beatrix . . . of his wife. Of your mother." Roen pulled his hood lower over his face and lowered his voice. "He spoke of his other children being purified, of Mercy and Gemini. He spoke of wanting to save his third child . . . to save the babe's magic. To save your magic, Cade. To raise you in Old Hollow, hidden in the forest."

"What . . . what happened?" Cade whispered. "Why didn't he stay?"

Roen's eyes darkened. "I'm sorry, Cade. His wounds were too grievous. He died that very night. And you, Cade, well . . . we couldn't care for you. We had no mother's milk. You'd have died too. My father flew off with you in the darkness, said he'd find you a home, a new family. Said he knew a pair of old friends, bakers in a distant town called Favilla, who'd raise you as a son."

"Derin and Tisha," Cade whispered. "Oh stars. It's all true." His eyes stung. He looked to his side. "Fidelity . . ."

Her eyes softened, and she pushed her chair up next to his, and she wrapped her arms around him. Domi leaped from her seat, rushed forth, and joined the embrace.

"It's all right, Cade," Fidelity whispered. "It doesn't matter even if it's true."

Domi nodded. "You're still a child of Requiem. That's all that matters." She touched his cheek and turned his head toward her. "Do you remember how I first told you about Requiem?"

Cade nodded. "I remember," he whispered.

Domi's eyes shone with tears. "It was a dark day. A day of death and mourning. You grieved for Derin and Tisha, those who raised you. They were your real family." She leaned forward and kissed his forehead. "And we're your family now. My sister and I. And Roen too. All Vir Requis are family."

With the two sisters holding him, Cade shut his eyes. It was true. He had always known it was true, deep down. He had known it since Beatrix had told him, since he had stared at Mercy's face and seen his own face reflected.

"I need another drink," he whispered.

"Me too," Roen grumbled. "More than one."

The tall, bearded woodsman rose to his feet and flagged down a serving girl. Soon four new mugs of ale stood on the table. For a long time, the companions drank in silence.

Finally it was Domi, still seated beside Cade, who spoke. She reached under the table to clasp Cade's hand, and her voice was low.

"Cade was right. The time for books is over. The time to burn is here. But not burn the Temple. We don't have the strength for that."

"So burn what?" Cade asked.

Domi smiled thinly, green eyes gleaming. "The very source of the Temple's power. The weapon that lets them steal the magic of Requiem. And I know where to find it."

"Find what, Domi?" Cade asked.

She squeezed his hand. "Beatrix's fields of tillvine."

GEMINI

For a long time, he simply waited.

In his prison cell, he did not know day from night, minute from hour. There was nothing but darkness here, screams, the smell of blood, his chains chafing his ankles. Sometimes a guard brought him a meal, a bowl of gruel thick with lumps and, more often than not, hairs or bugs or other surprises.

"Mother!" he called weakly sometimes, slumped against the bars. "Mother! Sister!"

Yet they never returned. The guards came and went. They had dragged out the burnt corpses of their friends long ago. Now only the other prisoners remained for company; he could barely see them from his cell, but he could hear their screams. He could imagine their broken, shattered bodies. Sometimes he saw the torturers walking down the corridor, carrying the tools of their trade: pliers, pinchers, whips, hammers, hooks, blades. Then the screams rose loudest. Then Gemini huddled at the back of his cell, covering his ears, trembling, his childhood nightmares come true.

"Let this be a dream," he prayed, huddled up in the corner. "Please, Spirit, let this just be another nightmare. Let me wake up back in bed, back in Domi's arms."

Yet he never woke. And the screams never died. And Domi never came to him.

Domi had placed him here.

Domi had placed these chains around his ankles, shoved him into this cell, left him to rot.

"You did this to me!" He leaped to his feet, raising his arms as far as the chains would allow. "You did this, you filthy weredragon! I'm going to find you, Domi, and I'm going to break every bone in your body, and I'm going to toss your torso to the dogs! I--" Tears coursed down his face. "I'm sorry." He fell to his knees and curled up. "I'm sorry, Domi. I'm sorry. I love you. Please come back. Please free me."

Yet she, like his mother and sister, never returned.

He languished on.

He lay for a long time, waiting to die. He realized that his mother had been serious; she would leave him here, not just for hours, not just for days, but for the rest of his life.

Next time a guard arrives with a meal, Gemini thought, *I won't eat. I'd rather die. In shadows. Alone. Without anyone. That's always been my life, a life alone. So let me die alone.*

He closed his eyes and thought of Domi, pretending that he held her in his arms, until he heard the heavy footsteps. He opened his eyes to slits, saw a guard's boots, and closed his eyes again.

"I'm not hungry!" Gemini shouted. "I don't want the slop you serve. Get rid of it."

Keys jangled, and Gemini squinted to see the barred door creak open. He grimaced. The guards had always shoved his meals between the bars, not opened the door.

"Go away!" he shouted, shielding his eyes against the torchlight. "Get lost. I don't want to eat that filth."

But the guard's boots thumped across the cell, and metal pieces jangled. Gemini blinked, his eyes adjusting to the light, and screamed.

The guard was not bringing him food--but a toolbox of torture.

"No!" Gemini cried, tears leaping into his eyes. "Spirit, no!"

The burly, balding man lifted a pliers in one hand, a hammer in the other. He wore a leather apron splotched with old blood, and more dried blood encrusted his fingernails and clung to his hairy arms. He spat on Gemini. "High Priestess's orders. She said to treat you like any other prisoner." The man snorted. "I bet you'll scream louder than the others, though. Most don't scream till I get started, and you're screaming already."

The torturer leaned down to grab Gemini's wrist.

"Wait. Wait!" Gemini tried to tug back his hand. "Stop. Please."

The guard ignored him, placed his pliers around Gemini's fingernail, and tugged.

Gemini screamed.

He screamed louder than he'd ever screamed.

Across the dungeon, the other prisoners cackled and howled.

"Please!" Gemini cried, weeping, shaking.

The guard snorted. "You think I haven't heard men beg before?"

"Not me! You haven't heard *me*." Gemini scampered back, chains rattling. "You haven't heard the son of a High Priestess. I can help you. I can . . . I can give you wealth! Riches! Women! Ask for it and it's yours."

The torturer paused. He stared down at Gemini, eyes narrowed. "You're powerless. Your mother rules the Temple. Your sister will rule after you." He spat again and backhanded Gemini, knocking him to the ground. "You're nothing but flesh to break."

Gemini stared up, tasting blood in his mouth. "I'm second in line to the throne. Free me . . . and I will kill Mercy Deus, and I will kill High Priestess Beatrix . . . and once the Temple is mine, you'll have more wealth than you, your kids, and grandkids would know how to spend." He reached up a shaky, bloody hand. "Do we have a deal?"

The torturer grabbed his hand and squeezed so hard Gemini screamed again.

DOMI

She flew through the night, a dragon with three riders on her back, feeling like Pyre again, like a beast trained for war.

Only this time, Domi flew against her old masters.

The fortress of Castellum Luna rose ahead in the night, still distant, torches flickering on its walls. Here was one of Requiem's most ancient fortifications, built in the days before the great war with Tiranor over a thousand years ago. In the old books of Requiem, this had been a mere outpost rising from the forest. Today a town sprawled around the ancient fortress, a few scattered lanterns gleaming among its clay huts. Farms spread around the town, dark squares in the night: fields of barley, rye, wheat . . . and the cursed plant Domi would burn.

"Tillvine," she whispered. She looked over her shoulder at the others. "Ready?"

They sat on her back: Cade, Fidelity, Roen, all clad in their burlap cloaks and hoods. Four dragons would be too visible over the plains, even in the darkness. Domi was the smallest among them, and with only her flying, no firedrakes had noticed them yet. Black paint covered her scales; she vanished into the darkness.

Her companions nodded. One by one, they leaped off her back, silently shifted into dragons, and fanned out.

As practiced, Cade and Domi flew close together, gliding down in the sky. She looked at Cade, and he met her eyes and nodded.

It will be our fire that blazes down.

Meanwhile, Roen and Fidelity flew farther out, flanking them. Both bared their fangs and stretched out their claws, prepared for battle.

And they will slay any enemy that rises to stop us.

Domi stared ahead and bared her fangs. She saw the enemy there.

"Firedrakes," she grumbled.

Several of the beasts stood around the field, hulking black lumps in the night. They could have passed for great bales of hay if not for the fire in their jaws, flickering lights that reflected against their scales. Several human soldiers stood here too, patrolling the field, armed with longbows. Domi had flown here enough times as Pyre to know the defenses.

The four dragons kept gliding downward, jaws shut, fire hidden, scales painted black, mere shadows in the starless night. The field grew close, and the fortress loomed ahead, a great shadow topped with fire. Domi could smell the tillvine already--an acrid, burning smell.

Domi glanced at Fidelity, who flew to her right, and at Roen, who flew far to her left. She blew a single spark from her maw, a mere flicker . . . then swooped.

The others swooped at her sides.

Air shrieked around her, and the firedrakes below reared and their eyes blazed.

"Remember Requiem!" Domi cried, and the other dragons answered her cry. "Remember Requiem!"

She shot down toward the field. As the firedrakes burst into flight, screeching madly, Domi blew her flames.

The jet crashed down toward the field, and an instant later, Cade sent down his own shrieking pillar.

A row of tillvine caught fire.

Arrows flew from below.

The firedrakes rose and prepared to blow their flames.

Instants before the great reptiles could attack, two shadows swooped. Fidelity landed upon one of the drakes, lashed her claws, and ripped out its throat. Roen shot toward the other drake, spewing flame. The two dragons, blue and green, rose higher, then plunged down and showered dragonfire against the soldiers below.

Rows of tillvine blazed in the field, but most of the plants still grew, and more firedrakes came flying from the fortress above.

"Again!" Domi shouted to Cade, then looked toward her sister. "More drakes from the fort!"

Domi beat her wings, rose higher, and spun in the air. She dived and spewed more fire, igniting another row of tillvine plants. Cade glided at her side, his fire raining, and more tillvine burned.

"Agai--" she began to shout when two firedrakes slammed against her.

Domi cried out in pain. Their claws tore at her scales. One's jaws closed around her shoulder, biting deep. Paladins rode on their backs, thrusting lances. Domi screamed, blasting fire every which way, and dipped in the sky.

A roar rolled down.

A blue dragon swooped and crashed into the firedrakes, a mad beast, jaws snapping, claws digging into firedrake flesh. Fire blazed as Fidelity fought, ripping the drakes off Domi.

"Fly, sister!" the blue beast shouted.

Domi gasped, bleeding and burnt, but managed to soar and dive. She blew more fire onto the field. Another row of tillvine burned.

"Slay them!" a voice sounded in the town. "Archers, fire!"

Domi looked up and her heart sank. Archers were racing out from the town. They tugged back bowstrings, and flaming arrows flew through the night.

"Roen, Fidelity!" Domi shouted and soared.

She was too slow.

An arrow slammed into her tail, and another shot through her wing. Domi yowled. These were longbows, their arrows thick and deadly, capable of punching through breastplates and dragon scales.

Domi gritted her teeth and dived to burn another row of tillvine.

She rained down her fire, then bellowed as an arrow scraped across her back. Another glanced off her horn.

"Fidelity!" she shouted.

The blue dragon streamed overhead, and Roen followed. Their fire blasted forth, hitting the archers. Cade swooped at Domi's side, scattering flames, burning more tillvine. The fire was spreading below now, engulfing the field.

When Domi looked over her shoulder, she saw a dozen more firedrakes rising from the town, riders on their backs. Their cries shook the world.

"We're done, let's get out of here!" Cade shouted.

Domi nodded and beat her wings. Two arrows were still embedded into her. When she tried to fly higher, a firedrake flew her way, and she roared out her flames; they washed over its rider, and the man screamed, burning. Domi flew higher.

"Come on!" she shouted. "Roen! Fidelity!"

More arrows flew. More firedrakes cried out, and the beasts' flames shot across the night. The fields blazed below. The four dragons joined together and rose higher.

"Remember Requiem!" Cade shouted and laughed. "Requiem is reborn!"

The clouds spread above them, thick and charcoal. The dragons flew into their cover.

"On my back!" Domi said.

One by one, her companions flew above her, released their magic, and landed on her back as humans. The firedrakes still screeched behind, but only one small dragon, her scales painted black, Domi vanished into the clouds.

"Find them!" rose a cry behind. "Find the weredragons!"

Columns of fire rose through the clouds. Domi banked, dodging them, swerving left and right. The flaming columns rose everywhere, a burning cathedral.

One of the drakes rose ahead of Domi, its black teeth ringing a maw of fire, and its eyes smoldered like molten metal. Domi hissed and dived, flying beneath it, then soared through the clouds. More fire blasted ahead; she glimpsed another firedrake flickering through the clouds, only flashes of its scales showing and vanishing. She soared higher, rising above it, and flew onward.

Arrows whistled through the clouds, but the paladins firing them were blind in here. The firedrakes kept blowing their fire, revealing their locations. Streaks of orange and glowing red splotches spread everywhere. Domi flew like she had never flown, silent, barely letting her wings churn the clouds, dodging the flames, avoiding the light.

It seemed hours before the sounds and lights of pursuit finally faded.

Domi dipped in the sky, emerged from under the clouds, and beheld wild grasslands leading to distant mountains. No more firedrakes. No more flame.

A weight lifted off her back. The other Vir Requis fell through the sky, then shifted and rose to fly around her.

Even as she bled and hurt, Domi allowed herself a tight grin.

For the first time in a hundred years of the Cured Temple's reign, the dragons of Requiem were fighting back.

She spoke through the fire in her mouth. "Requiem is reborn."

MERCY

She stood in the Chamber of Birth, staring at the bursts of light appearing and fading on the map, at all those diseased souls flickering into a broken world.

Her mother stood beside her on the balcony, staring down with her at the craggy landscape carved of white stone. "They are diseased." Beatrix's face was blank, her hands tucked into her long sleeves, but her rage showed in the slight downward curve of her lips, the stiffness of her back. "They are born diseased, and the beasts burned the only medicine to cure them. What do we do, Mercy?" The High Priestess turned toward her daughter, piercing Mercy with those cold blue eyes. "How do we deal with a poison when the anecdote has been stolen?"

Mercy stared down from the balcony again. Whenever she stood here, Mercy felt like a goddess staring down from the clouds at the world. The chamber was massive, as large as an emperor's throne room, and a great map of the Commonwealth covered the entire floor. Hills and valleys, carved of white stone, rolled hundreds of feet across. Great mountain ranges, tall as a person, rose like the spines of dead dragons. Towns, cities, villages, farmlands--all rose on the map, their little buildings carved of clay. Directly in the center rose a crystal sculpture of the Cured Temple, a beacon of light.

And other lights glowed here. Every moment, a light flickered to life somewhere on the map, glowed bright, then faded. Whenever such a glow appeared, scribes in other balconies--a dozen balconies rose around the chamber--scribbled into scrolls. Each flicker of light was a flicker of life, a child born in the Commonwealth--babes here in Nova Vita, babes in distant farmlands, even babes born in the wilderness.

Babes diseased with dragon magic, Mercy thought, staring at the new life appearing in her empire. *Babes we must cure with tillvine.*

"Well?" Beatrix said. "Solve me this riddle, Mercy. The dragons which you let flee, which you failed to kill, have burned five tillvine farms so far. Our stocks run short. How do we burn out the dragon curse?"

"We dip into our stores." Mercy watched a light flicker in Lynport, an ancient city in the south. "We have plenty of tillvine in the cellars from last harvest, and--"

Beatrix interrupted her. "That tillvine is meant to last until next harvest. That next harvest was coming up this month. It will be another year before the fields yield new crops. Our stores will not last until next autumn." She narrowed her eyes, staring at Mercy. "So I ask you again, daughter. Without enough tillvine this year, how do we deal with diseased babes?"

Mercy stared into her mother's eyes, and she saw the answer there.

"Spirit," Mercy whispered and took a step back.

Beatrix smiled thinly. "So you understand."

Mercy shook her head. "They are children of the Spirit, people of the Commonwealth. I will not do such a thing."

The High Priestess's smile stretched a little tighter. "You will, my child. I have no tolerance for disobedient children. Ask Gemini how I treat a child who defies me. I will not tolerate the disease in my empire. Leave. Now. Seek them out. And . . . *cure* them." Beatrix turned to leave, then paused and looked back. "And Mercy? That babe you adopted, the precious little thing you call Eliana? If you fail at this task, it will be Eliana who pays the price. Get rid of these diseased babes . . . or I'll get rid of yours."

With that, Beatrix left the balcony, robes swishing.

Mercy stood for a moment longer, staring down at the map. Her jaw tightened and her fingernails drove into her palms. For that moment, all she could do was stand stiffly, barely able to breathe.

Finally she shouted, "Give me the lists!"

Within an hour, three hundred firedrakes took flight from Nova Vita, paladins on their backs, and flew to all directions of the wind.

"To purification," Mercy whispered and leaned forward in the saddle. Below her, Felesar grunted and snorted out sparks of flames. The firedrake's wings creaked, and his scales clattered. He was an aging beast but the largest in the capital, scarred and sturdy and ruthless in a fight.

As they flew beneath a shimmering sun, Mercy reached across the saddle to stroke Felesar's copper scales. They were hot and smooth, and Mercy thought back to her years riding Pyre. She had chosen Pyre because of her scales; she had been the only firedrake of multiple colors, each of her scales a different shade of fire, ranging from deep red to bright yellow. What Pyre had lacked in size and strength, she had made up for in speed, stealth, and beauty.

Mercy closed her eyes, trembling, disgusted, betrayed, shocked.

For years I rode you, Pyre . . . and you were a weredragon. The weredragon Domi. The weredragon my brother bedded.

Mercy wanted to gag.

So many truths were collapsing around her. About Pyre. About her missing brother--Cade, a weredragon she had hunted, a weredragon who had fled her again. About her mother and the depths of her cruelty, a mother who'd send her out to slay innocent babes.

"But I must protect you, Eliana," Mercy whispered, tears in her eyes.

For the past few months, Eliana had become like a true daughter to her. Mercy had found wet nurses to feed the babe, servants to change her swaddling clothes, and priests to pray over her. But every evening, Mercy would enter the babe's chamber, lift her, hold her close, vow to protect her.

Mercy shivered.

"And now you would kill her, Mother? Kill her unless I slay a thousand babes?" She grimaced, eyes stinging. "How you know our weaknesses. How you use them against us, High Priestess. How you know how to terrify your children."

A mile outside the city, Mercy spotted the farmhouse. Two other drakes flew with her, paladins upon them. They descended, their wings beating back the stalks of wheat, their cries ringing across the land.

"Purification!" Mercy shouted, as she had shouted on so many missions. "Bring out your babe to be purified!"

The three firedrakes landed, their claws tearing through a vegetable patch, and Felesar blasted flame skyward.

"Bring out the babe!" Mercy shouted again.

The farmhouse door opened, and a husband and wife emerged, clad in burlap, holding their newborn. They knelt before Mercy, and the mother held out her child. The baby screamed, face red.

"Here, my lady!" said the mother. "Her name is Sania. Purify her, my lady, and may the Spirit bless you."

Mercy took the babe in her arms and gazed upon her. The child still cried, tears flowing, but as Mercy held her, the babe slowly calmed. Her crying stopped, and she gazed up at Mercy with inquisitive blue eyes. Her tiny hand reached toward Mercy's hair.

She looks so much like Eliana, Mercy thought, heart twisting.

Her two fellow paladins placed down the wooden altar, and Mercy laid the babe upon it. She had performed the purification so many times. She had performed it on Eliana herself. She had done so with pride, with commitment to the Spirit, with a prayer to bring about the Falling. Today Mercy moved stiffly, throat tight, like a woman tying a noose.

She had always brought two herbs to every purification ceremony: ilbane to test for the curse, tillvine to cure it.

Today she had only one of the two.

She produced the ilbane from her pouch, the plant that burned the skin of weredragons. As she raised the leaves above the babe, she prayed silently.

Please, spirit, let this babe be one of the few. Let her be the one in a hundred who are born without the curse. Let her be like Gemini, pureborn, raised to breed pureborn children. Please, Spirit. Her eyes stung. *Don't let her be cursed.*

Her fist shook around the ilbane--the only herb she had here this day. She winced, not even daring to breathe, as she lowered the plant.

Please, Spirit, let the leaves not burn this child. Please.

She touched the ilbane to the baby's arm.

The skin sizzled red, and the baby screamed.

Mercy lowered her head.

"She is cursed," she whispered.

Oh stars, she is cured.

The babe's parents looked at each other, relieved.

"She's not pureborn," whispered the father. "She won't be forced to breed." He wiped a tear from his eye. "Thank the Spirit. She will be purified and returned to us."

Mercy's eyes clouded, and when she stared down at the weeping babe, she couldn't tell her apart from Eliana, couldn't tell herself apart from her mother.

She had no tillvine today. But she had a dagger.

The blade rose.

The blade plunged down.

The weeping died.

The parents screamed.

Mercy rose onto her firedrake, and as she took flight, her tears streamed down her cheeks, and the hot blood stained her armor. Below, she could still hear the parents scream.

She flew onward. She flew to the village in the valley. She landed and cried out: "Bring out your babe!"

Her knife drove down again.

Another babe's scream died.

She flew again, blood on her armor.

She flew from village to town, from farm to city, and her dagger drank the blood of the curse. She was Mercy Deus, a paladin, a purifier, a killer of infants, a savior of her daughter, a holy warrior for the Spirit, a holy warrior for her mother. Her knife rose and fell again and again, taking lives upon a hundred altars, a purification of the Commonwealth, a sacrifice of blood.

"For you, Eliana," she whispered as she purified. "For you, my mother. For you, my god."

She flew on. She killed on. She eradicated the disease with her steel and the ice in her heart.

As the sun set, casting red light across the sky, Mercy turned to fly home. As she flew over farmlands and villages, she heard the screams below. The lands of the Commonwealth wailed with their sacrifice. All across the empire, hundreds of other firedrakes had purified the land with steel.

"You did this, weredragons," Mercy whispered, fists trembling. "You brought this death, Cade the weredragon. You burned our tillvine. This blood is upon you."

She reached the walls of Nova Vita and flew above them. A dozen firedrakes were still streaming across the city, rising and landing, and screams rose from homes. The blood of innocents flowed down the cobbled streets of the capital. Rising from the center of the city like a rotting jewel, the Cured Temple reflected the setting sun, blazing out with white and red light, blinding Mercy, blinding the world, a heart of burnished metal and crystal, the heart of an empire, the heart of a vengeful god.

A twin to my own heart.

She entered the Cured Temple and walked down its halls. Priests and servants knelt before her, and she ignored them, marching forward, eyes staring straight ahead, blood staining her priceless white armor, blood staining her soul. She walked until she entered the chamber and closed the door behind her, and then she closed her eyes, and she fell to her knees, and she had to clench her fists and hold her breath to stop her tears.

A soft, gurgling sound rose through her pain.

She opened her eyes, rose to her feet, and walked toward the crib. Baby Eliana lay within, staring up at her, smiling.

Mercy lifted the babe and held her in her arms. She examined the child--the wide hazel eyes, the soft brown hair.

"The moment Cade fled me, Eliana, I vowed to protect you," Mercy whispered. "When I burned his village down, I had to save you, and I still fight for you. I will drive this blade into the hearts of ten thousand infants, and I will watch forests and cities burn, before I see you come to harm. You are mine now, Eliana. You are my daughter now." She squeezed the baby tightly, desperately, and tears coursed down Mercy's cheeks. "You are mine. You are mine. You are always mine. Always. I swear. I swear."

The baby screamed, crushed in the embrace. Mercy held her daughter close, her tears falling, wanting to never let go.

GEMINI

At midnight, he stumbled out of his cell, bearded, shivering, clad in bloody rags, and free.

He left his chains behind.

The torturer stood in the dark corridor, staring with hard eyes.

"When will I get my treasure?" the man asked, crossing his hairy arms. His toolbox lay at his feet, including the pliers which had ripped off Gemini's fingernail. Gemini shivered to see it.

"Once the Temple is mine," Gemini whispered, lips cracked, tongue dry like a strip of leather. "Once my mother and sister are dead."

He sucked in breath, imagining it. How wonderful it would be! He would plunge the blade into their backs himself, hear the breath gush out of their mouths, feel the hot blood splash him. This was no work for an assassin; he would do the work himself. Perhaps he would kill Domi too. Perhaps he would make love to her one last time, then kill her. Or maybe the other way around. Yes. That would please him.

All women are cruel, he thought, fists trembling. *All women are backstabbers.* His mother had tormented him since his birth. His sister had always looked down at him as if he were a maggot. And

Domi . . . Domi was the worst of them all, the whore who had slipped into his bed for his money, for his power, then left him to rot in this dungeon. She would pay. They all would pay. They--

"Waiting for another guard to show up?" the torturer said and smirked. "Go kill the daughters of dogs. I want my treasure."

"Oh, you'll have your treasure," Gemini said. "Maybe I'll give you a weredragon. Domi would make a good prize for you."

The guard sneered and raised a hammer. "You said money."

"Money you shall have too." Gemini began to walk, taking shaky steps across the corridor. "Make your own way out of the city. Wait for me in Oldnale at the windmill. Once Beatrix and Mercy are dead and my reign is secure, I will come to you."

The torturer grabbed Gemini's shoulder and squeezed, forcing him back. "Slay them now! Tonight!"

Gemini stared at the brute and shuddered. The man was twice his size, and the blood of countless victims stained his apron. "I can't slay them tonight! Are you mad? Do you have any idea how many soldiers guard them? You think Beatrix and Mercy would let me just show up with a dagger in my hand? I must first gather my allies, regain my strength, muster my resources, arrange my forces for attack, and--"

The torturer's hand squeezed tighter. Gemini grimaced; he thought the man would shatter his shoulder. "Tonight. Kill them." The brute drew a knife from his belt and handed it to Gemini. "Use this blade. I did not free you to run and hide like a dog. I will not wait. I demand my treasure. Tonight!"

Gemini stared at the dagger. He gulped. "But . . . the guards . . ."

"You are their paladin! They will obey you." The torturer shoved the dagger's hilt into Gemini's hand. "Kill the High Priestess tonight. If you cannot, I will return you to your cell, and I will make you scream." The guard's lips peeled back in a hideous smile, revealing yellow teeth. "I will start by crushing your manhood with my pincers, then move to shattering the segments of your spine, one by one. Perhaps I will cut off your fingers next."

Gemini held the dagger with a shaky hand. Sweat dripped into his eyes, stinging. His knees knocked. "I . . ." He gulped. "I . . ."

How could he do this . . . tonight? He had planned to escape first, perhaps with a few of the loyal firedrakes. To find allies in other cities, to raise an army, to fly back as a general, to seize the city with great force and might. How could he get past a hundred guards tonight, alone, clad in rags, a haggard prisoner with a mere knife for a weapon?

"Go." The torturer sneered and raised his pliers. "Go now. Do it. Kill them. If you cannot, I will drag you back into your cell, and we'll get to work. How would you like to lose more fingernails? How about losing your entire fingers? Your nose? Your entrails? Your skin? I can take them all from you and keep you alive. Kill them! Now! I demand my prize."

Gemini was shaking wildly. He almost dropped his dagger. Stars, he had to do it tonight. He had to! He would have to attack all the guards, even if he died assaulting his mother's chambers. And surely he would die. Yet death was better than torture, wasn't it? But . . . he needed his revenge. He needed--

"You will not go?" The torturer reached out to grab Gemini's shoulder. "Very well. Your pain continues. Your--"

Gemini screamed, a howl that tore through his throat, that echoed through the dungeon, that brought blood to his lips, and as he screamed he thrust his dagger.

The blade slammed into the torturer's cheek, scraped across the bone, and drove through the eyeball and into the skull.

Gemini tugged the dagger back with a spray of blood.

The torturer stood for a second longer, then crashed down.

Gemini spat on him.

"More meanness than brains to you." He stared at bits of brain on the blade. "Definitely not much brains anymore."

His voice cracked and he stumbled back, shaking violently. Sweat washed him, and he had to lean over and breathe deeply, struggling not to pass out. It was the first time he had killed.

"But I will kill many more times," he whispered. "I will kill you all. All those who hurt me."

The prisoners in the other cells were laughing. Laughing at him. Gemini straightened and ran, wobbling, through the dungeon. He ran out the door, up the stairs, into the palace hall, out the back door into the night. He stumbled down the stairs into the city, and he laughed, and his head spun, and he stretched out his arms. He breathed the fresh cold air. He was free. He was powerful. He was Gemini Deus, future High Priest of the Cured Temple.

"Firedrake," he whispered, still laughing, still crying. "I need a firedrake."

He would fly for now. He would flee for now. And he would return with the might of a god.

CADE

He stood on the hill, the wind whipping his burlap tunic, and lowered his head. His fists clenched at his sides, and his eyes stung.

They're dead. So many dead. Because of me.

The village nestled in the valley miles away, its lanterns glowing in the sunset. Even from this distance, Cade heard the mournful wails. All across the Commonwealth they cried out in agony. Angels of death had flown across the realm, and now parents--grieving, crying out--buried the innocents, buried the slain, buried a generation.

"We wanted you to grow into Vir Requis," Cade whispered, staring at the land. "We wanted you to grow with your magic, to become dragons of Requiem." He closed his eyes. "Now your light will never shine."

The wind gusted, and Cade did not hear anyone approach, but he felt a hand on his shoulder. He turned to see Domi standing on the hill, her hair billowing in the wind like a torch's flame. The setting sun reflected in her eyes.

"It's our fault," Cade whispered to her. "All those dead babes . . . if the Temple still had tillvine, they'd purify them. They would lose their magic, but they'd live." His fists shook. "Now they're dead, all of them, and still dying every day, every moment. Because of us." His throat tightened, squeezing his voice into a hoarse whisper. "Because of us."

Domi pried open his fingers and held his hands. She stood staring into his eyes. "We could not have known. We did what we thought was right."

Cade laughed mirthlessly. "Those who meant well have kindled some of history's greatest wildfires. Good intentions have spilled as much blood as devious plans." Tears burned in his eyes. "Oh, Domi . . . what have we done?"

He expected her to embrace him, to stroke his hair, to whisper into his ear. But instead Domi snarled and her eyes flashed.

"We did nothing!" She pulled her hands back and glared at him. "Do not place this blame on me, on yourself, on any of us. We did not sink our knives into the hearts of babes. Mercy did that. Mercy and her fellow paladins. The only blame is on them, and I will not allow you, Cade, to feel guilt, and I will not allow you to spread your guilt among us. Blame the Cured Temple. Fight the Cured Temple. Keep fighting. I will."

"Fighting for Requiem," Cade said, and the words tasted bitter in his mouth. "Domi, I never wanted this fight. I just . . . I just wanted to be a baker. I never wanted any of this." He held his head. "Not to lose Derin and Tisha and my sister. Not to run, hide, get captured, learn that Beatrix is my mother. Fight for

Requiem? I never knew what Requiem was until a few months ago."

Domi dug her fingernails into his hands. "Well, you know what Requiem is now. And you can't go back to being a baker. So you have a choice now, Cade. You can either let guilt, grief, and regret overpower you, or you can keep fighting. Do you think I wanted this?" She barked out a laugh. "I never wanted this war. All I wanted was to live as a dragon, a firedrake in disguise, to fly free. Do you think Roen wanted this? All he wanted was to live in a forest with his father. That father is dead now. The Temple forced this war on us. The Temple killed these infants. So now, yes, I will fight. Will you?"

Two shadows climbed the hill to join Domi and Cade. The sunset fell on Roen, bearded and dour, wrapped in his furs. He stared at Cade, eyes dark. Fidelity stood beside the forester, one of her spectacles' lenses still missing, clad in her old vest with the brass buttons. She too stared at Cade.

"Why do you all look at me?" Cade said. "What do you want me to say?"

Fidelity stepped closer and touched his shoulder. "Just one word: Requiem."

Domi nodded. "Requiem," she whispered.

Roen grumbled under his breath, and his fists clenched and unclenched, but then he raised his chin and spoke in a deep, clear voice. "Requiem."

Cade stared at them one by one. Fellow Vir Requis. His friends. The only people he had left, the only people who understood. Yes. He would fight with them.

"Requiem," he said. He closed his eyes, thinking of the first time he had heard that word: the feeling of holiness, of magic, of home. He could not abandon the dream of Requiem, not even as blood washed the world. He took a deep, shuddering breath and looked at his companions again. "I don't know how I can keep fighting. I don't know what to do. But I will not forget our kingdom, our magic. We will keep Requiem alive."

GEMINI

He burst out of the stables at dawn, riding his sister's firedrake.

"Fly, Felesar!" he cried, laughing. "Fly!"

The burly copper beast, among the oldest and largest of the firedrakes, beat his wings and soared over the city of Nova Vita. His scales clattered like a suit of armor, and his wings creaked. Fire flickered out of his great maw.

"Fly south! Fly, Felesar!" Gemini wore no spurs, but he pounded his heels into the animal's tenderspots.

With beating wings, they soared higher, flying across the city of Nova Vita. The temple shone behind them, and countless domed huts sprawled out below. Streets crawled across the city like spiderwebs. The rising sun glowed behind a veil of clouds, and a flock of pigeons flew below.

Gemini expected battle--hordes of firedrakes and archers on the roofs. He expected to fight his way out of the city with fire, blood, and screams. But no enemies emerged. The firedrakes who perched on the city walls merely glanced up at him, then back toward the horizons. Guards stared up, then returned to their patrols. All here could recognize Felesar, a fabled firedrake, the oversized copper mount of the Deus Family.

They don't know, Gemini realized. *The guards, the drakes . . . they don't know that it's me, or they don't even know that I was imprisoned.*

He laughed as he flew over the walls and across the fields. He tossed back his head and breathed deeply of the sweet, cold air, and he kept laughing.

"I'm free." His grin hurt his cheeks. "I'm free and I stole Mercy's favorite pet, and I'll never let them hurt me again." He ground his teeth, forcing himself to keep laughing; to stop laughing meant to weep. "I will be the one hurting them."

He still wore the same housecoat he had been imprisoned with. His face was stubbly, his hair a mess, and more stubble grew on the left side of his head--the side paladins normally shaved every morning. He would need to shave it. He would need armor. He would need weapons. He would need aid.

"We'll find allies, Felesar," he said to the beast as they flew over farmlands, leaving the city behind. "We'll find new armor, new weapons, new soldiers, new firedrakes. We'll return with an army."

As the sun rose, Gemini wrapped his robe more tightly around him and considered. Aid. Where could he find aid? From his friends, of course. He had plenty of friends left! He could summon . . .

He tapped his fingertips against his palm, wincing with pain as his injured finger, the one missing its nail, brushed against his skin. He had always been close to the priests who brought him women to breed with, but they still lived in the Cured Temple. He could track down some of those women, he supposed; they might have brothers, fathers, uncles, strong men who'd fight for him.

"Don't be a fool," Gemini told himself. He had no use for priests or peasants. He needed an *army*. Soldiers. More firedrakes. Horses and chariots.

There had to be some lord who'd agree to lend him his army. The lord of Castellum Luna, for example. He had an army! He had many firedrakes and soldiers, and . . .

Gemini frowned, trying to remember that lord's name. He could recall seeing a tall, beefy man with a wide mustache. The brute had been close to Mercy, would often talk to her about old battles.

Gemini groaned. "I can't enlist that fool." He spat across the saddle. "If he's friends with Mercy, he's an enemy of mine, and I will slay him too."

He tried to bring to mind all the other lords he knew across the realm, but he only remembered men in bright armor visiting his sister, drawing swords and drilling with her, riding firedrakes with her, fighting alongside her. Gemini had never had time for such nonsense. He was a pureborn; he had spent his days and nights bedding the women the priests sent him, doing his duty to the realm, not wasting time on wars like a common soldier.

Gemini's heart sank.

Could it be true? Had he squandered away his youth with lowborn women and wine while his sister built a network of allies? No. There had to be someone. Gemini sneered.

"I have friends. Powerful friends! There's Domi. She's a wild beast. She can become a great dragon named Pyre. She . . ." He sighed. "She bedded me for money, then tossed me into a dungeon."

With horror, Gemini realized that Domi--this very woman who had betrayed him--was his only friend.

His eyes stung.

"Are you still my friend, Domi?" His lips wobbled. "Oh stars, Domi, I'm sorry. I'm so sorry. I don't know what I did." His chest shook, and he stared at the cuts along his wrists, the cuts the shackles had left. "I need you, Domi. I need you to forgive me. I need your help. I need to hold you again, to protect you, to tell you everything will be all right." His damn tears flowed again. "I need you to love me."

I need to find you.

He stood up in the stirrups and stared down at the farmlands.

"Domi!" he shouted. "Domi, can you hear me?"

A few birds cawed below. A group of sheep scattered across a meadow. Gemini slumped back into his saddle.

It was a large empire. The search would take a while.

"Where do we look, Felesar?" Gemini said. "You knew Pyre. Sniff her out! Follow the scent."

The copper firedrake snorted. Gemini answered with a snort of his own. It was just a dumb reptile, not a bloodhound. Gemini clutched his head.

Think.

He tried to remember the stories Domi would tell him in bed, stories of her childhood. Of wandering from town to town, lost, a weredragon alone in a world that hunted her. Spirit, she had spoken of so many places! Of the library in Sanctus, but Mercy had already destroyed that place. Of time spent in the forest south of the city, but Mercy had already burned that forest. Spirit!

Gemini closed his eyes, trying to remember the other stories Domi would tell him. Mostly, as Domi would speak to him in bed, Gemini would busy himself with kissing her neck, passing his hands along her curves, and admiring her intoxicating eyes, not listening to her tales. He tried to imagine that he lay with her again, his one hand stroking her hair, the other exploring her body, as she prattled on.

"That tavern had the best ale," Domi said in his memories, eyes wistful, as he kissed her neck, moving down to her breasts, her belly, the sweet hills and valleys of her pale, freckled body. "We used to drink there sometimes, my sister and I, and even dance. There was an old harpist, and . . ."

Yet his memories morphed into him kissing her, making love to her, sleeping in her arms.

No. No! He ground his teeth, forcing himself to remember. What had she told him? What tavern?

"We used to watch the sea from the windows." Domi spoke in his memory. "Sometimes when Lynport was all silent, we'd walk along the beach, and--"

Gemini stood up in his stirrups. "Lynport!" he shouted and laughed. "She has a favorite tavern in Lynport! Her forest burned.

Her library fell. Where else would she go?" He pointed south. "Fly, Felesar! Fly to her. We're going to find her. And she's going to help us."

He sat back down in the saddle, and he found himself trembling. Spirit damn it. He had wanted to seek Domi with rage and hatred, to find her, burn her, make her pay. But by the Spirit . . . he missed her. He needed to kiss her again, to forgive her, to love her.

I need your help. I need you Domi.

They flew on, crossing the last farms. The burnt forest spread below them, smoldering, a pile of ash and charred wood. The whole world was burning, and he followed the memory of green eyes.

He flew all day, crossing the forests, until the sun fell. They landed by a farm in the evening, and Felesar blasted down his fire, roasting several sheep. The beast ate ten of them, and Gemini-- famished after his imprisonment and flight--ate what felt like an entire sheep himself. At only one point did the farmer emerge from his home, see the feasting firedrake and near-naked man, and quickly rush back inside and slam the door shut.

They slept in the fields and flew again at dawn.

For six days, they flew across the lands of the Commonwealth. They drank from streams. They ate what they stole from farms, feasting on sheep, chickens, squash and corn and turnips. Every dawn rose upon a free world, a wilderness of fields, mountains, grasslands, forests. Every night, the stars spread above, millions of them, bright and blessing him. Gemini wanted to fly here forever. This life--just him and a firedrake--filled him with vigor. The fuzz that had always covered his mind in the capital, brought on by endless wine and languor, began to lift. Without the stream of women, booze, smoking pipes, rich feasts and sweets, a new strength filled Gemini, a lust for life, for freedom.

Decadence chained me as surely as chains of iron, he thought as they flew. *I'm free now, a free man, a warrior. I left the capital a miserable wretch. I will return a conqueror.*

On his seventh day since leaving the capital, he soared over the vast plains south of the forests, the warm lands north of the Tiran Sea.

"Domi!" he shouted as he flew. "Domi, where are you?"

The sun had fallen, and clouds hid the moon, when he saw the coast ahead. He had reached the end of the Commonwealth; beyond lay the Tiran Sea which led to the continent of Terra where the Horde mustered. A cluster of lights glowed on the coast--the city of Lynport. The city Domi had spoken of in his bed.

Are you there, Domi?

"Fly on, Felesar," he said to his firedrake. "Let's find her."

They flew over dark farmlands until they glided over the city. Lynport was perhaps smaller than the capital, but with a hundred thousand souls, it was the largest city in the southern Commonwealth. Many huts rose here, and even older homes from the Lost Age before the Cured Temple had ruled the land--

houses built not of clay but of wood and stone. A boardwalk stretched along the coast, and several ships swayed in the water.

"How the Abyss am I supposed to find some piss-soaked tavern in a city this size?" Gemini grumbled from the saddle, flying in circles above Lynport. "She could be anywhere here, if she's even in this city at all." He leaned over the saddle and shouted at the top of his lungs. "Domi! Domi, where are you? Domi, come to me! I forgive you, Domi!"

He heard no reply from below. He kept flying, rising higher, spiraling over different neighborhoods.

"Domi!" he shouted, voice hoarse. "Domi, it's Gemini! If you're here, fly to me. Domi!"

He kept scanning the city, waiting for her to rise, a dragon of many colors, the old dragon he had called Pyre, the dragon he had loved. Yet she never emerged, and he kept flying. His firedrake glided above the boardwalk, and he kept scanning the buildings, waiting for her to rise, seeing only shadows, only emptiness.

"Domi!" His damn eyes kept spilling those damn tears. "Domi, please. Domi. Be here, Domi. Be here. I love you, Domi!" He lowered his head, and his voice dropped to a whisper. "I love you."

She's not here, he thought. *I'll never find her. I--*

Shadows rose in the night.

Felesar bucked in the sky, wings beating madly. Gemini gasped.

A dragon was soaring up toward him--then another joined it. A third. A fourth. The dragons streamed upward, barely visible in the darkness, no fire in their maws.

"Domi?" Gemini whispered.

An instant later one of the dragons slammed into Felesar's belly.

Gemini screamed as the firedrake tumbled.

A second dragon slammed into Felesar's flank. When Felesar opened his maw to blast out fire, a third dragon shot forward and grabbed the beast's snout, shoving the jaws shut.

Gemini rose in his stirrups, fear washing across him.

"Domi . . ."

A fourth dragon descended from the darkness above, silent and almost invisible, and talons wrapped around Gemini's body.

He cried out as the dragon yanked him from the saddle and held him in midair.

He screamed. The dragon lifted him higher. The claws tightened around Gemini, as hard and unyielding as the iron chains in the dungeon. Below him, he saw the three other dragons slamming into Felesar, biting and clawing, ripping out flesh. With a great snap of its jaws, one dragon--a burly green beast--tore out Felesar's throat. Blood rained in the night, and Felesar--greatest of the capital's firedrakes, an old beast of legend--tumbled from the sky and slammed down onto the beach below.

Then the dragon clutching Gemini flew even higher, and they vanished into the clouds. When he tried to scream again, the claws tightened around him, and he couldn't even breathe, and all he saw was clouds and wings and blazing dragon eyes.

DOMI

She flew through the clouds, holding Gemini in her claws, squeezing him until his screaming died. She narrowed her eyes, refusing to let any feelings she might have had surface.

He is my enemy. He is a son of the Temple. And I'm a warrior of Requiem.

Fidelity flew at her side, and Cade and Roen flew close behind. They glided lower in the sky, leaving the city behind, and flew along the coast. The waves whispered to their right, tipped with moonlight, while the dark cliffs of Ralora rose to their left, a wall of stone overlooking the southern sea. In the shadows of those cliffs, a mile out of the city, Domi glided down and tossed Gemini onto the beach. She landed before him, and her fellow dragons landed around her, claws sinking into the sand.

Domi had always known Gemini to be handsome, at least in a pale, slender sort of way, but the young paladin now looked like a drowned rat. He still wore the same housecoat Domi had last seen him in; it was now tattered and stained with blood. Brown stubble covered his face and the left side of his hair, and brown roots showed where his hair was long and bleached white. He coughed, struggled to rise in the sand, and began to run.

Still in dragon form, Domi pounced and knocked him facedown. She placed her paw against his back. She was careful not to nick his skin, but she placed enough weight to keep him pinned down.

"Release me!" Gemini shouted, thrashing. "I'm looking for Domi. Where are you, Domi?"

Domi sighed. Her scales were still painted black to conceal her during her night flights. He did not recognize Pyre, his dear old dragon. She turned her head toward her companions and nodded.

Standing in the sand, the three other dragons released their magic. They stepped forward, humans again, and untied the ropes that served as their belts.

"Let me go!" Gemini screamed. "Release me! I'm a paladin of the Cured Temple, and I order you to release me, weredragons!"

Domi kept him pinned down as Roen bound the paladin's wrists. Cade meanwhile held down Gemini's kicking legs while Fidelity tied his ankles together. Once Gemini was securely tied up, Domi finally removed her paw off his back and released her own magic.

She knelt beside her poor, bound paladin.

"Gemini," she said.

He blinked sand out of his eyes, spat sand out of his mouth, and looked at her. At first his eyes widened, then narrowed.

"Domi," he whispered. "Domi!" He began to thrash madly, floundering in the sand. "Release me! Domi, why? You whore! I'll kill you, you whore!" His cheeks reddened, and he began to weep. "Why . . . why, Domi? I love you. I love you. Why?" His words blended into unintelligible blubbering.

Cade knelt beside Domi and raised an eyebrow. "Bloody bollocks, Domi, is this the man you lived with? I've seen toddlers throw lesser tantrums."

She sighed and lowered her head. She reached out to stroke Gemini's cheek, then pulled her hand back when he tried to bite. "He's always been a broken man. A child, really. I think his mother stole his childhood, leaving him stuck somewhere between adulthood and--"

"Release me!" Gemini shouted, interrupting her. "Domi, who are these people? Who are you? Why do you bind me?" He lowered his voice to a frightened whisper. "Don't hurt me. Please, don't put me back into the dungeon. Please. Please! Don't put me back there. They hurt me. I only wanted to find you, to love you, to protect you. All I ever wanted was to love and protect you, Domi. That's all I ever wanted. You have to believe me."

Cade whistled appreciatively. "Blimey, Domi, you broke his heart good."

Domi reached out to stroke Gemini's hair, and this time he did not try to bite, merely curled up and sobbed and let her stroke him. She had pinned him down with disdain in her heart, but now pity filled her.

"Poor, broken child," she whispered.

She thought back to her times with him. She had served as his firedrake, the beast Pyre, whipped and kicked and hurt with his lash and spur, taking his pain for a chance to fly and breathe fire. She had lived with him later as a woman, seeking shelter, food, protection, and a chance to learn more about her enemy, to collect information about the Cured Temple and its hunt of her friends. Yet finally, at the end, had Domi learned to love him?

I could have stopped him from making love to me, she thought. *I willingly let him bed me, and . . . I enjoyed it.* She lowered her head. *I enjoyed the feeling of him inside me, and I enjoyed sleeping in his arms, and I enjoyed telling him old stories as his lips brushed across my body.* Even now she flushed to remember those days, his emphatic yet gentle lovemaking, the peace and luxury and splendor of her life with him. Yes, perhaps she had learned to love him at the end. Perhaps she had found pleasure with her enemy.

But those days were over. Now she was no longer Pyre the firedrake, no longer Domi the serving girl. She was a warrior of Requiem, and he was a paladin of weredragon hunters.

"We've captured Gemini Deus," Fidelity said, coming to stand beside her. "The second in line to the High Priesthood. The third most powerful person in the Commonwealth." Her lips tightened, and fire burned in her eyes. "He knows things. He knows how the paladins always find newborn babes. He knows how many firedrakes fly in the world. He knows if . . . if other Vir Requis exist."

Lying bound in the sand, Gemini turned to look at the librarian. He spat at her. "Go to the Abyss, weredragon! I'll never tell you a thing. Release me now or my mother will bring an army here to burn you all."

Roen approached. The bearded forester grabbed Gemini's neck and spoke for the first time. "Your mother can't save you now, boy. And you will talk. I will make sure of that."

Gemini's eyes dampened again, and once more he screamed.

ROEN

He stood atop the cliffs of Ralora, stared down at the miserable wretch, and felt an overwhelming urge to kick the bound paladin down to his death.

"Domi," the paladin whimpered, lying bound between Roen's feet and the cliff's edge. "Domi, where . . . where are you? I love you. Please."

Roen's eyes narrowed. He couldn't believe what those eyes saw, what his ears heard. This pathetic, sniveling creature, barely a man at all, was a paladin? Was the son of High Priestess Beatrix herself? Was one of the mightiest men in the Cured Temple, that Temple which had stamped out Requiem, hunted down the dragon magic to near extinction, and crushed the Commonwealth under its heel? This worm at his feet?

Look at him, Roen thought. *A begging boy trapped in a man's body. A coward stripped of his armor, lying before me weak and groveling. A paladin. A firedrake rider. One of the men who killed my father.*

Whatever pity Roen might have felt burned away. Rage overflowed him, and he balled his hand into a fist.

"Domi," Gemini whispered. Ropes still bound his ankles and wrists, chafing them raw. "Domi, where are you? Are you here, Domi?"

"Domi can't help you anymore," Roen said, voice gravelly. "It's only you and I here above the cliff. The others are gone. You won't see them again, not unless you answer all my questions."

Rage flooded Gemini's face. "I have nothing to say to you, weredragon! Let me go. Release me now. Do you have any idea how much I can hurt you? I-- No! Wait!" As Roen raised his fist, Gemini cowered, curling up into a ball. "No. Don't hurt me! Please. Oh, Spirit, please don't hurt me. I just came here to help you. Yes!" Gemini's face brightened, and a shaky smile stretched across his lips. "I came to help Domi, and you're her friend, so I'll help you too. I hate the Cured Temple. I hate it! I--No, wait!"

Roen's rage burned inside him, hotter than dragonfire. He grabbed a fistful of the paladin's hair and dragged him toward the edge of the cliff. He shoved Gemini forward until the paladin teetered over the drop. Three hundred feet below, boulders rose from the sand.

"Wait!" Gemini screamed, and liquid trickled down his leg as he lost control of his bladder.

"I've heard enough of your pathetic groveling," Roen said, trembling with rage now, twisting Gemini's hair. "How dare you shrug off your culpability? How dare you disavow your family? I was there that night. The night Domi and Cade escaped from your clutches. The night your firedrakes killed one of us." He shoved Gemini another inch forward, and Gemini screamed, nearly falling, his bound hands grasping at the rock. "The night you killed my father."

"I didn't kill any of you!" Gemini shouted. "I've only ever killed one man in my life, and he was my mother's soldier. A torturer. I killed him escaping the Temple's dungeon! I too was a prisoner. I too hate the Temple."

Roen snorted. "You are a paladin of that Temple."

"I was imprisoned! Ask Domi! She . . . she placed me in the dungeon. And my mother left me there to rot. I came here for your help fighting her." He blubbered. "Don't shove me down. I came here to help. To help Domi fight the Temple. To help all of you."

Roen trembled with grief and anger. This worm was trying to trick him. Roen knew it. It was like that in the world. People lied. Deceived. Betrayed. Stabbed one another in the back. He knew enough of the world to know of men's lies. His father had raised him in the forest to escape such cruelty, and as soon as they had emerged to help that world, the firedrakes had slain Julian. So why should Roen now pity a man of that world?

"You are a liar," Roen said. "I will get no information from you."

He shoved Gemini another inch.

Gemini screamed again. "Domi! Domi, please! Domi, tell him! Tell him I was imprisoned. Tell him I'm a good man. Please." He shook wildly. "Tell him I'm good . . ."

Roen's eyes narrowed.

By the stars.

Gemini was weeping like a child now. Could the man be speaking truth?

Roen grunted and tugged him back. "I told you, Domi won't help you now. Only I can grant you life or death. I want answers. How does the Cured Temple find newborns? How do the firedrakes know where to fly to?"

Gemini shook, glanced back toward the cliff, then gulped. Sweat dripped down his forehead. "A map. A magical map, yes. A huge map, large as ship, all with hills and valleys and towns carved of stone. It's old magic. The Spirit himself created the map, the priests say. Lights glow whenever a babe is born."

Roen grabbed Gemini's shoulders and dug his fingers, twisting the paladin's arms. "Where is this map? How many guard it? How many firedrakes lurk in the Temple?"

For a long time, Roen asked questions, and Gemini answered. The paladin wept, begged, shouted threats, called for Domi, and groveled, but he kept answering.

Dawn was rising when Roen had heard enough.

"Silence," he spat. Gemini was begging again to see Domi. "I'll let you live for now."

Roen shifted into a dragon, grabbed the bound paladin in his claws, and took flight. He glided to the beach below, tossed Gemini onto the sand, and shifted back into human form.

"Stay here," he said to Gemini and walked along the beach, heading toward the others.

Fidelity, Cade, and Domi stood together at the edge of the water. They turned toward Roen as he approached.

"He talked," Roen said.

"Did . . . did you hurt him?" Domi whispered.

Roen scrutinized the young woman. There was real pity in Domi's eyes. Perhaps Roen felt some pity within himself too.

He grunted. "He's hurt enough already. He claims to have been in the Temple dungeon, and he's got the scars to prove it, both on his body and his mind. Been tenderized already. Barely had to touch him before he started speaking."

Roen glanced back toward Gemini--the paladin still lay tied in the sand--then back toward his fellow Vir Requis. He spent a while conveying the information Gemini had given him, speaking of the map, of the positions of firedrakes in the city of Nova Vita, of the number of soldiers guarding the High Priestess, and of the Temple layout.

Fidelity sighed and tugged her braid in frustration. "The Cured Temple is too powerful. How can we defeat so many firedrakes, so many soldiers? Even should we slay the High Priestess, another ruler would rise in her stead. How can we crush the Cured Temple with force, only four dragons?"

Roen cleared his throat. "We might not have to crush the Temple. We might . . . be able to strike a deal."

The others all stared at him, eyes narrowing.

"A deal?" Fidelity whispered, eyes widening.

Roen grumbled. "I think you'd better hear it from the man himself. Come with me."

GEMINI

He lay on his back in the sand, head tilted sideways. He watched the waves in the dawn and thought of home.

As the morning sunlight fell upon the waves, Gemini tried to pretend that he lay back in his bed at home. He missed that bed, the bed where he had planted his seed into so many women, creating pureborn children; where he would lie drinking wine, then sleep until the afternoon; where he would hold Domi close, the first woman he had ever loved, stroking her hair, whispering his secrets to her.

Why do things have to change? Gemini thought. *Why does the world have to shatter?*

He had shed too many tears. No more would fill his eyes. He had screamed too much. No more cries rose in his throat. He just wanted to lie here, to watch the waves, to think of home. Perhaps the weredragons would leave him here. Perhaps they were already flying away, and he would linger here, bound in ropes, and die on the beach. Crab food. It wasn't a bad place to die.

It's beautiful here, he thought, watching beads of light on the waves. *The sand is soft and I'm at peace.*

He breathed deeply of the salty air and heard a shuffling sound. He looked aside to see small, pale feet walking toward him across the sand. He raised his gaze to see freckled legs, a burlap tunic, and . . .

"Domi." A lump filled his throat.

She stared at him with those large green eyes of hers, eyes he had been lost in so often. But she was different now. She was the real Domi here, not Pyre the firedrake, not the serving girl she had pretended to be. He had known, even in the Cured Temple, that she was a weredragon, but now he truly saw her as one--a child of fallen Requiem, a strong woman, free, not needing his protection. Now it was he who needed her. Now it was she who perhaps would protect him.

I'm the weak one now, he thought, and he hated the feeling. All he had ever wanted to do was protect her. And she had bound him in chains, and now in ropes.

The other weredragons walked behind Domi, still a few feet away. Domi stepped closer, leaving her companions behind, and sat down beside him.

Gemini returned his eyes to the sea.

"I know that you don't love me," he said softly. "I know that . . . that you lied when you pretended to. When you lay in my arms. When you kissed me. When we walked through the gardens, looking at flowers, and when we lay outside at night, gazing at the stars. When we told funny stories and laughed, or sang old songs, or just sat holding each other, watching the fireplace. I know it was an act, Domi. I know that now. I know that you wanted information--about the Cured Temple--so that you could fight us. But . . . it was real to me." He still could not bear to look at her. "I love you, Domi. I love you so much. I was so happy with you. Sometimes when we sat together in that big armchair back in my chambers, your legs slung across my lap, I'd look at you, and I'd think: I'm so happy, and I don't know what I did to deserve such a blessing, such a wonderful woman to love me." A lump filled Gemini's throat. "I was happier than I had ever been with you. And I understand now. I understand what I did to deserve you. I am my mother's son. That's all I've ever been. To Beatrix, I was a stud to plant my seed into women. To Mercy, I was nothing but a dolt. To you I was a tool, an enemy to seduce." He finally dared turn his head and look at Domi. "But still I love you. I can't stop."

She closed her eyes, and he saw a tear stream down her cheek. She lay down beside him in the sand, gazing into his eyes.

"Gemini," she whispered, "I know. I know." She touched his cheek. "My sweet Gemini. I do not deserve your love."

"You have it nonetheless."

Her fingers intertwined with his. "Gemini . . . Roen said that you wanted to help us. That you would tell me how you can help."

Gemini raised his eyes and saw that Roen, Cade, and Fidelity were listening from several feet away. He returned his eyes to Domi.

"I want to build you a kingdom, Domi. A safe place. I . . . I realize we can't be together again." Gemini's voice shook, and he clasped her hand, that soft, slender hand he had held so often, had dreamed of holding for so long in the darkness. "I know we can never go back. Never be together again in the Temple, walk through the gardens, laugh together, whisper together. I know that we can never return to Sanctus, never return to that fort where we first ate a meal together. Do you remember that fort over the sea, Domi? That life is over. I know this." He reached out to touch her cheek. "But I still want to protect you. I still want to give you a new life. If that can't be a life with me, let me give you a life of your own, a land of your own. For you. For your kind. Let me give you Requiem."

Domi narrowed her eyes. "What do you mean? The Cured Temple rises around our column upon the ruins of our fallen palace. The Commonwealth spreads across our land." Anger filled her eyes. "How will you give me Requiem?"

"I cannot give you a new palace, nor can I dismantle the Temple around King's Column. I cannot return to you all the lands of my family." The tide was rising, and the water flowed around Gemini's feet, stinging the wounds around his ankles. "But I will give you a stretch of land. Maybe here along this coast. A place to build a village. For you. For your friends. A small kingdom, a new Requiem, a buffer between my empire and the Horde in the south. A place where you can be free, Domi. Free to fly as Pyre again. Free to live with the others. The kingdom you dreamed of. It's what you wanted. Let me give you this gift."

Feet stomped across the sand, and Roen approached and knelt above Gemini, fist raised, teeth bared.

"You're in no position to give us anything!" The woodsman spat on the sand. "Your own mother imprisoned you. You're no longer a paladin. You're nobody. Nobody but our prisoner, disgraced."

Gemini turned his head to gaze into Roen's eyes. He spoke calmly. "I'm nobody now. I'm only a prisoner now, bound in your ropes. But I'm still the son of High Priestess Beatrix. I'm still of holy blood. I've come here to form an alliance with Domi. I ask you to join me, Roen, you and the others." Even with his arms bound, Gemini managed to push himself up. He stood on the beach, staring at them one by one. "Fly with me back to the capital. Storm the Cured Temple with me, four dragons roaring fire. We will kill the High Priestess. And we will kill Mercy. And then . . . then the Temple will be mine, and a kingdom will be yours."

FIDELITY

"We can't trust him," Roen said. "A man who'd kill his own mother and sister? Such a man is fully corrupt, and he won't hesitate to stab us in the back once it suits him."

They stood along the boardwalk of Lynport, the southernmost border of the Commonwealth. To one side stretched a row of buildings: seaside temples, libraries of holy books, a silo of grain, an ancient windmill, many domed huts of clay, and several old buildings from the days of Requiem, their wooden timbers hundreds of years old. On the boardwalk's other side stretched the port. Two breakwaters embraced the sea, forming a cove. Piers stretched into the sunlit water, and a hundred ships docked here, mostly the small boats of fishermen. Farther back, near the edge of the cove, several great brigantines had set their anchors, massive warships of many sails. More brigantines sailed in the open sea, patrolling the coast, their sails painted with tillvine blossoms.

Fidelity stood with her companions, the sea breeze caressing her face, the afternoon sun warming her. With one lens of her spectacles broken, she found the world flatter, less alive, less real; only her right eye now saw clearly. Spectacles were a treasure, a lens worth more than gold. It would perhaps be many years before she could afford a new lens. Fidelity sighed, hugged herself, and stared out at the port. She watched a merchant ship, a great carrack with tall masks, navigate into the cove and set down its anchor, and she wondered what treasures it brought from foreign lands, if it had perhaps even been to the Horde itself at the continent of Terra.

Roen was talking some more, and Cade and Domi nodded and added their own words, but the conversation faded in Fidelity's ears, seeming as blurred as the world in her left eye.

The Horde lies beyond that sea . . . where my father fell.

Her one eye might now be blurred, but Fidelity could still clearly see that old vision; she had been seeing it for months now whenever she gazed into the distance, whenever she closed her eyes, whenever she thought of him. Her father, the brave gray dragon Korvin, facing Mercy. The paladin's lance driving into his neck. The gray dragon losing his magic, falling as a man into the sea, and Amity burning, and Fidelity wanting to fly to them, and Cade dragging her away, and tears and so much pain and fire, and—

"What do you think, Fidelity?"

She blinked, realizing that Roen had stepped closer to her. His eyes softened as he looked at her, and he reached out to hold her hands. Fidelity breathed deeply, feeling some of her anxiety ebb away like the retreating tide. In a world of death and chaos, Roen was her anchor, no less grounding than the anchors of the merchant ship before her.

She wrapped her arms around him and leaned her head against his broad, warm chest, seeking shelter in his embrace. His beard tickled her forehead. The tall woodsman held her and kissed the top of her head.

"He offers us a kingdom," Fidelity whispered. "Yet he wants us, only four souls, to attack a temple full of an army."

She glanced aside, peering out from Roen's embrace. Gemini stood several feet away, talking to Domi in hushed tones. Both wore heavy burlap robes and cloaks, and both kept their heads lowered.

"Do you trust him?" Roen said.

Fidelity sighed, watching the paladin talk to her sister. A gull landed between the two, and Gemini tried to kick it away, incurring a curse and glare from Domi.

"No," Fidelity confessed. "I don't trust him. This could all be a ruse, a plan for Gemini to lure us back into a trap. He would profess to lead us on an assassination attempt, only for soldiers to leap onto us. Domi believes him. I don't even fully understand her relationship with him. I don't think she does either. She trusts him, but I don't." She raised her head and stared into Roen's eyes. "Yet if we cast Gemini aside, what other hope awaits us? There are only four Vir Requis left that we know of, that's all. We have no army to storm the Temple with, no other aid, no--"

"I'm telling you!" rose a voice along the boardwalk. "Two bloody weredragons in the south. They lead the bloody Horde, they do."

Fidelity frowned and spun toward the voice. Roen stared with her.

The merchant ship had docked along the boardwalk, and dockworkers were busy offloading its wares: wooden crates, burlap sacks, and bundles of canvas. A portly man in lavish, purple robes and a plumed hat stood on the boardwalk by the gangplank, speaking to a lanky priest.

"You been drinking Terran spirits again, Yaran?" said the priest, frowning.

"Aye, I have been," said the rotund merchant. "And you should drink your fill too before the fire reaches this town. Abina Kahan, old ruler of the Horde, is dead and burned. Weredragons killed him, and they're mustering, my friend. Mustering for war. The Red Queen rules there now, and she's thirsty for the blood of the Temple, they say."

Fidelity gasped. Leaving her companions, she rushed toward the merchant. Her knees shook, and her breath rattled in her lungs.

"Pardon me, sir," she said, struggling to keep her voice calm. "The . . . Red Queen?"

The merchant turned toward her, and his eyes softened. Fidelity supposed that she made rather a pitiful sight: a girl wrapped in a tattered burlap cloak, one lens missing from her spectacles, bruises and scrapes covering her skin. She probably looked like a dock rat, an urchin who lived on the boardwalk, scrounging for fallen morsels and whatever seaweed washed ashore.

"Get out of here, scum!" the tall priest said, glaring at her. His lip peeled back in disgust. "You're speaking to Ferin of Vale, a wealthy man. He has no time for dock rats."

"It's all right, Yaran!" said Ferin, raising a pudgy hand in a conciliatory gesture. "It's all right. The child has a right to good, juicy merchant gossip as much as any priest." He gave a jovial laugh, turned back toward Fidelity, and his eyes gleamed. "Aye, the Red Queen they call her. A weredragon woman. In the days, she's a tall proud warrior, a barbarian of the Horde. In the nights, she turns into a great red reptile, beating wings like sails and blowing fire."

Fidelity trembled.

Amity.

"You . . . you said there were two dragons?" she whispered.

"Were you eavesdropping?" demanded the gaunt priest.

"Yaran!" barked the merchant, turning toward his friend. "Let the girl ask! She's certainly a better audience than you. Go bless the crates and pull that stick out of your arse." As the priest stormed off, the merchant turned back toward Fidelity, and a grin split his face. "Oh, quite an audience! Very nice."

Fidelity glanced to her sides and saw that her companions had joined her. Roen stood to her left, while Domi, Cade, and even Gemini stood to her right. Others from along the boardwalk stepped up: fishermen and their wives, scrawny urchins, and a few boys busy chewing on apples and jangling dice in their hands.

As dockworkers continued to offload crates, the merchant raised his arms, voice booming out, the consummate performer with a captive audience. "Aye, they said the Red Queen slew a hundred griffins herself, tamed the great Behemoth, and wears the old abina's shrunken head around her neck as an amulet. She has a companion too, they say, a dark, hulking, brutish warrior." The merchant stamped his feet and leaned forward, his face twisting into a demonic mask. Children squealed and fled behind their mothers' skirts. "He's a weredragon too, you know. Aye. The brute can turn into a great gray beast with blue fire, and he follows the Red Queen wherever she flies, burning any who dares challenge her reign."

A gray dragon, Fidelity thought, trembling. *Korvin. My father.*

"Do you know their names, kind sir?" she asked, unable to hide the tremble in her voice. "Of the red and gray dragons?"

"Ah!" said the merchant, raising a finger. "They are known by many names. The Red Queen and the Brute. The Weredragons of Leonis. Queen Am--" The merchant slapped his mouth shut, and his eyes widened, staring over Fidelity's shoulder. "Oh Spirit."

Fidelity spun around, and her chest seemed to shatter into a thousand pieces.

Oh stars no.

A hundred firedrakes or more darkened the sky, paladins on their backs, flying over the city of Lynport.

"Surrender the weredragons!" shouted a familiar voice from the sky. "Surrender Gemini, the rogue paladin! Bring me the outlaws or this city will burn!"

* * * * *

Fidelity stared up and saw her there, flying on a pure white firedrake with ivory horns.

"Mercy," she hissed.

Footsteps thumped. Cade ran up to Fidelity and grabbed her arm. "Come on! We have to run!"

She shook her head. "No! Cover your face with your hood." She stared at the others. "Be calm. Follow me. Walk slowly."

She pulled her hood over her head, and she walked along the boardwalk. Her heart thudded and her fingers trembled, but she forced herself to walk calmly. Her fellow Vir Requis walked at her side, as did Gemini; the paladin was cursing and hissing, but Domi guided him onward, whispering soothingly.

"We seek four weredragons and an outlaw paladin!" Mercy shouted above. Her white firedrake dived. It glided so close above the boardwalk its belly nearly hit Fidelity's head. The blast of its wings ruffled her cloak, and Fidelity had to grab her hood to hold it down. "Surrender the criminals or your city will burn!"

Fidelity kept walking, leading the others. Many other people crowded the boardwalk, some staring at the firedrakes and pointing, others rushing back to their homes, and a few even knelt and prayed as if the beasts were deities.

A hundred thousand people live in this city, Fidelity told herself, taking a shuddering breath. *We'll vanish into the crowd. Mercy will never find us.*

The firedrakes screeched overhead, a hundred or more, diving and racing over the city roofs, streaming across the sea, blasting out fire. Their roars were deafening. Their beating wings blasted down storms of air. Debris scuttled across the boardwalk, and fiery streams crisscrossed the sky.

"Surrender yourself, vermin!" Mercy shouted from her firedrake. "Do you hear me, Gemini? Do you hear me, Domi, you harlot? I know you're here! You've been seen, maggots!"

Fidelity turned her head to stare at the others. They stared back from the shadows of their hoods. Fidelity's heart sank. The battle over the beach, kidnapping Gemini, killing his firedrake . . . somebody had seen them in the night, perhaps a fishermen, perhaps a pair of lovers walking along the shore.

"Keep moving," Fidelity whispered, tugging her hood as low as it would go. "We return to the tavern." She looked ahead and saw the Old Wheel only a few steps away. "She won't find us. She--"

Mercy's firedrake dived again, skimming along the boardwalk, and the paladin's voice pealed. "I will burn one house at a time until you emerge, Gemini!"

Her firedrake's wings beat, and the beast soared toward the sun, moving in a straight line. Thousands of feet above, it turned in the sky and swooped, roaring, Mercy clinging to the saddle. The firedrake opened its jaws wide, and dragonfire cascaded down to slam into the Old Wheel tavern.

Fidelity leaped back, the heat bathing her. The ancient tavern, a relic of Requiem, the place where Prince Relesar Aeternum himself had lived during Requiem's great civil war, burst into roaring flames. Sparks showered out, landing against Fidelity's robes. She hurried back, brushing off the sparks, and stared in horror at the inferno.

"Surrender yourselves, weredragons!" Mercy shouted as her firedrake soared again. "Surrender yourselves or the destruction of this city will be upon you."

Fidelity stared at the flames, the heat blasting against her, stinging her eyes, singeing her nostrils and throat. Screams rose inside the tavern. Children leaped out of the windows, burning. A man burst out of the doors and ran across the boardwalk, a living torch. Timbers cracked and shattered, and the screams fell silent.

More death. More killed. Because of us. Fidelity trembled. *Because of us.*

"Fidelity, we have to get out of here!" Cade grabbed her arm.

Roen held her other arm. "Come, Fidelity. Away from the fire."

She let them drag her away. People were screaming now and running all across the boardwalk and streets. A few leaped into the water and began to swim, only for firedrakes to blast down flames, burning them.

"None will flee this city!" Mercy cried. "None will live unless the weredragons surrender themselves!"

Mercy's firedrake turned in the sky, plunged down, and blasted fire. The flames crashed into a hut, baking the clay dome. The firedrake's claws slammed into the hot clay, tearing it open, and more beasts blew fire into the hole. The flames blasted out of the windows. People screamed inside. Firedrakes flew along the streets, torching hut after hut. Fire exploded across Lynport. Smoke raced along the streets like demons, and the firedrakes kept roaring, and Mercy kept screaming. Burning people ran, screaming. A firedrake skimmed along the boardwalk, claws outstretched, scooping up people and tossing them into the air.

"Gemini!" Mercy cried above, laughing. "Where are you, dear brother? Will you burn with them all?"

Mercy's firedrake dived across a street, roaring out fire. The street burned. People screamed and ran.

Fidelity ran with them. The fire crackled all around her, and cries of pain tore across the city. She clung to Roen with one hand, to Cade with the other. Domi and Gemini ran ahead. The narrow streets burned around her, and huts kept collapsing at her sides, firedrakes tearing into their roofs. Thousands of people clogged the roads, clawing over one another, desperate to flee the inferno.

We'll burn here with them all, Fidelity realized, heart sinking. *Mercy will kill every last soul in this city to slay us.*

Fidelity stopped running.

The huts crackled around her, and people ran back and forth, screaming. Yet Fidelity stood still, lips tight.

Cade tried to tug her forward, but she wouldn't budge.

"Fidelity, come on!" the boy shouted. "The whole damn street is burning!"

They'll burn the whole city, Fidelity thought. *They'll burn the whole world to find us.*

"We have to fly," she whispered.

The others stared at her, eyes wide.

"Are you mad?" Gemini shouted. "There are a hundred firedrakes up there!"

Fidelity nodded, eyes burning. "Enough to burn the whole city. Enough to kill us all. A hundred thousand people." She clenched her fists. "My father is alive. So is Amity. I know this. I know it! They're in the south across the sea. It's time to fly. And it's time to find them."

She stepped back, shouted wordlessly, and shifted into a dragon.

She beat her wings, blasting back the flames and smoke, and soared into the sky.

Around her, countless firedrakes screeched, spun toward her, and began flying her way.

Fidelity flew higher, spun in a circle, and blasted out a ring of fire.

"Remember Requiem!" she cried, flew higher, and charged toward the enemy.

She screamed as she slammed into them, as fire washed over her, as claws drove against her. She roared, blasting out fire, and snapped her jaws.

"Remember Requiem!" she cried, battling countless firedrakes, surrounded with scales and steel and dragonfire.

"Remember Requiem!" rose more cries below, and the other dragons soared around her.

A green dragon, Roen barreled into several firedrakes, and his fire washed across a paladin in his saddle. Cade shouted beside him, a golden dragon, and closed his jaws around a firedrake's neck and ripped out flesh. Domi rose too, the heat melting the black paint off her scales of many colors, and Gemini rode on her back.

"Slay them!" Mercy howled, and Fidelity raised her head to see the paladin flying her firedrake toward the battle. A hundred other firedrakes flew around the paladin, and their riders readied their lances.

This is a battle we cannot win, Fidelity thought. *Not yet. Not this day.*

"To the sea!" she cried. "Requiem, to the sea! Follow!"

Fidelity could barely make out the coast ahead, only flashes of blue amid the smoke, the fire, and the drakes. She beat her wings, screamed as a firedrake's claws tore at her blue scales, and blasted forth a great river of fire. Cade flew at her side, adding his flames to hers. Roen and Domi joined her, and the four streams wreathed together, forming a gushing torrent of heat. The inferno slammed into a firedrake, melting its scales, melting its rider. The four dragons flew forward, cutting a path through the enemy.

Arrows flew from behind, clattering across Fidelity's scales. Pain blazed across her haunches, and she yowled but kept blowing her fire. Gemini screamed on Domi's back, tearing off his burning cloak, but the paladin laughed and shouted at his sister.

"I'm free, Mercy!" Gemini cried, face sooty, chest shaking as he laughed. "I'm free and strong, and I'll be back, you dog's daughter! I'll be back with an army!"

More arrows flew, and fire washed across Fidelity's tail. She kept flying, kept blowing forth flames, melting all in her path, bathing the sky with the light and heat of a sun. A firedrake swooped from above, and she flipped over, lashed her claws, and tore its belly open. As its innards spilled, she righted herself and kept flying forward, and her companions flew with her, and they blasted back the last firedrakes and flew across the beach and over open water.

The firedrakes chased them, scores of the beasts. Mercy still howled curses behind, and arrows still flew. But the four dragons kept flying--singed, bleeding, but still crying out for Requiem, still beating their wings.

"Remember Requiem! Remember Requiem!"

Four dragons, one outcast paladin, and a host of firedrakes streamed across the sea, leaving a blazing city behind.

MERCY

Again she had killed.

Again she had slain innocents on her quest for purification. Purification of her empire. Purification of her soul. Purification from her mother's grip that reached Mercy even here, far above the southern sea, gripping and squeezing her heart like an iron vice, like chains that forever bound Mercy to the glittering Cured Temple that rose from her empire like a crystal shard from flesh. The fires blazed behind her, consuming the city of Lynport, consuming any last traces of pity Mercy might have felt for those under her domain.

The blood of infants coats my hands. There is no more compassion in my heart. There is no more cruelty I will shy away from. There is no more mercy for those who harbor the enemy.

Even if she had to burn down her entire empire, lay waste to cities and forests, dry the sea, topple the mountains, build new mountains of bones--Mercy would do these things to catch them. To end this curse. To bring about the Falling even if the world itself fell with it.

The city burned behind her, and the weredragons flew ahead, carrying her brother with them. All those she sought, all her enemies--all flew ahead of her, not even a mile away, yet

Mercy knew that she had lost them. She knew that they would cross the sea, escape her again. She led a hundred firedrakes, but strong as the beasts were, they would eventually tire and need to find land. The weredragons could take turns riding one another, alternating between human and dragon forms, able to fly for days on end. They had escaped her this way when traveling to Leonis in the east; they would escape her this way today, flying south to the continent of Terra.

"Turn around!" Mercy said. She tugged the reins, spinning her firedrake around in the sky. "We return north."

Jaw tight, she flew away from the weredragons, heading back to the burning city, to the Commonwealth, to the lands she would someday inherit.

She would need more than firedrakes. She would need a great army, an armada of a thousand ships.

This would not be merely a hunt, she knew.

This would turn into a war.

She flew over the burning city. She kept flying north.

She flew over the village where she had first found Cade, the village she had razed to the ground. She flew over the forest she had burned, the forest where the weredragons had hidden from her. She flew over towns and farmlands where mothers still cried to the heavens, weeping for their slain babes, babes Mercy had killed after the weredragons had burned her tillvine. As she flew, no pity filled her, only ice, only iron.

My babe died too, she thought. *My babe died and so I will kill everyone, I--*

Mercy gnashed her teeth so hard she almost chipped them.

No. No, she would not let that thought fill her. That life was gone. That life was false. That life was only a nightmare. She was Mercy the paladin, her soul, her steel, her womb dedicated to the Spirit. That was all she was, a sword for the Spirit to wield. Never more a priestess. Never more a mother. Never more one to heal, only one to kill.

They flew for days, crossing the bleeding lands of the Commonwealth, flying over ruin, over graves, until finally they reached the city of Nova Vita, capital of her empire.

The city still screamed.

No tillvine grew this year, and paladins marched across the streets, shattered doorways, grabbed babes and slit their throats. Screams of parents rose. White flags of mourning rose from clay huts across the city, as inside parents grieved.

Let them grieve. Mercy's fists trembled around the reins of her firedrake. *Let them grieve like a young priestess once grieved. Let the whole world feel this pain.*

Mercy left her firedrake in the courtyard and entered the Temple, walking alone. She passed through lavish halls and sought her mother in the Holy of Holies, but could not find her there. She searched the libraries, the chapels, the gardens, but the high priestess was nowhere to be found.

As she searched, a fear grew in Mercy, and she placed her hand atop her belly, feeling the pain there, the emptiness. She quickened her step, and soon she was running. She raced down marble corridors, priests and servants leaping aside. She ran until she reached her bedchamber, yanked the door open, and barged inside.

High Priestess Beatrix stood within, holding baby Eliana in her arms.

Mercy froze.

She reached for her sword.

"Put her down," Mercy hissed.

Beatrix stared at her, and a smile stretched across her face, though it did not touch her eyes. "Welcome home, daughter! I was just putting the babe to sleep. One cannot trust servants to do all child rearing. Eliana is like a granddaughter to me now."

Mercy would not release the hilt of her sword, ready to draw the blade. "Put her down. Never touch her again. I would burn the world for her."

The High Priestess sighed, rocking the sleeping babe. "It seems that you've already burned the world. The forests burn. The city of Lynport burns. And still . . . no weredragon corpses. No sign of your brother either. Fire and death and nothing but defeat." Beatrix tsked her tongue. "All your battles, all your flights, and still you fail me." She raised her eyes and stared at Mercy. "This babe has softened you."

Amity took another step closer. "Put. Her. Down."

Beatrix stared at her, eyes hard, burning cold, and her fingers tightened around the babe. One hand strayed toward Eliana's throat, a menacing caress. "This child is a privilege for you, Mercy. Not a right. I would not hesitate to steal this prize from you, just as you've stolen babes from mothers across this city."

"I did as you ordered me!" Mercy shouted, rage and pain blinding her. Eliana woke up and wailed. "I killed them for you! I killed them because you ordered me to kill! I killed them like he killed my son, like--"

Mercy froze, trembling wildly. She couldn't breathe. She couldn't speak. She couldn't weep. She could only stand, frozen in horror. No. No. No, that was only a dream, only another life, not real. Not her. Not her life. Not her past. And yet she had spoken of it, made it real. She fell to her knees.

"Please," she whispered. "I beg you, Mother. Please."

Beatrix glared at her just a second longer, eyes blazing, and then her face softened all at once, as quickly as if she had placed on a mask. She knelt, laid the wailing Eliana on the floor, and embraced Mercy.

"Of course, my child!" Beatrix patted Mercy's back. "Of course, my sweet daughter. Mother didn't scare you, did she? I would never hurt your adopted daughter. I know that you would do everything in your power to make this world safe for Eliana, to bring about the Falling."

Mercy lifted her daughter and held her close, rocking her until she calmed. She stared over the soothed baby at Beatrix. "Mother, the weredragons have fled to the Horde. Not just the island outposts but to Terra itself. Weredragons lead the Horde now. The Red Queen Amity rules both the mountains and coast, and they say a million souls flock to her. It must be war. Allow me to summon the armada. Give me a thousand firedrakes and a thousand ships. The time for war has come, a time for fire to engulf the world, for the light of the Spirit to crash through the heathens and shine upon even the southern continent."

Beatrix rose and stepped toward the window. She stared out into the night, and the soft breeze rustled her white robes. She spoke softly, and for the first time that Mercy could remember, perhaps the first time in her life, it seemed like some humanity filled Beatrix's voice, some emotion, not just calculating sweetness or cold cruelty but true doubt, true fear.

"For long years I've feared this day," Beatrix said, gazing out onto the city. "For long years, I stood at my windows, gazing into the darkness of the night, and I felt a chill not of the wind, not of winter nor early spring's frost, but a chill that comes from the great, hot land overseas, the deserts and stony mountains, the fire of a mob gathered from many nations, from all those heathens we failed to bring under our light. The Horde has been gathering for many years, throughout my reign, throughout the reign of my mother, forever a thorn in our sides. Yet now they're no longer a thorn." She turned toward her daughter. "Now they are a spear aimed at our heart. Now weredragons fly with them. Now weredragons lead them. Now they would seek to supplant us, to crush this Temple, to undo the Commonwealth and bring back the heathen kingdom of Requiem. We cannot sit in wait while our enemy rises. When an enemy rises to slay you, you must slay him first. History is full of fallen empires, of kings and queens lost to memory. Survivors strike first. Survivors cut down all who would rise to slay them. And so we will strike first. War is upon us. We will muster the fleet. We will summon the firedrakes from across the empire. And we will strike. And you will lead our forces south. You will return with your shield, or you will return upon it. You will return victorious, or you will not return at all. You will bring the lands of Terra under our dominion, or all light will go dim in this world."

Mercy nodded. "I will win."

That night Mercy did not place Eliana in her crib, but she took the babe into her bed, and she held the child in her arms, stroking her hair. She never wanted to let Eliana go. She never wanted to see the babe in danger again, to feel that loss again, that grief that tore out the soul.

She had spoken her secret.

She had brought that banished memory to her mind.

She had spoken of her true child.

In the darkness of her chamber, Mercy grimaced, clinging to the babe in her arms like a drowning woman to floating debris. Again she felt his fists pummeling her belly. Again she screamed, giving birth to her daughter, to a stillborn babe, to a life of memory and pain. Again she thrust her sword, driving the blade into her husband's heart, the first time she had killed, the first time she had known the joy of killing.

She had doffed the robes of the priesthood then, and she had donned armor. Armor of white steel. Armor to protect her from memory. To protect her from loss. To protect her from all emotion, from those things that hurt, that dug deep.

And she kept killing.

And she would forever keep killing. No longer just a huntress but a great general. She would kill thousands, millions. She would kill everyone else in the world until none were left but her and her new daughter, this precious child she had found.

"I vow this to you, Eliana," she whispered. "I will love you forever. Forever. Our love will burn the world."

AMITY

She had left Terra's northern coast dragged behind a horse, beaten and whipped and waiting to die. She returned from the mountains a red dragon, roaring out her pride, as her army marched below.

"The Horde musters!" Amity cried, voice rolling across the desert. "The Red Queen will lead you to victory!"

She grinned as she flew. Her wounds still ached--the wounds from her battle against the firedrakes in Leonis, from dragging across the desert behind Abina Kahan's horse, from fighting Behemoth, from slaying griffins and burning Shafel the false king. But every scar made her stronger, every bolt of pain pumped her with ambition.

I am stronger than giants, mightier than gods. I am Amity of the Horde, and I'm coming for you, Beatrix.

She stared around her at her forces. Five hundred griffins flew to her right, great lions with the heads and wings of eagles, each the size of a dragon. The sunlight shone upon their armor, and riders sat on their backs, holding bows and the banners of the Horde: five coiling serpents on a golden field. Their homeland, Leonis, had fallen to the Commonwealth. Now these griffins fought for the Horde, for a chance to reclaim their ancient isles.

When Amity looked to her left, she saw the salvanae, several hundred strong. Here flew the true dragons, creatures who had no human forms like Vir Requis, not even a human form burned away like firedrakes. Their bodies were a hundred feet long, thin and coiling, covered in gleaming scales. They had no limbs, no wings, but swam across the air like snakes on water. Their eyes were like crystal balls, topped with long white lashes, and their beards fluttered like banners. No men rode them, for they were ancient creatures, wiser than men and honorable and sad. Their homeland, the mythical realm of Salvandos, lay under the dominion of the Cured Temple, and firedrakes now flew over its mountains.

When Amity looked down, she saw her ground troops below: thousands of warriors on horses, clad in patches of armor forged from bronze, iron, and steel, and myriads of infantry soldiers, armed with axes, spears, sickles, hammers, or simple clubs, wearing armor from metal and leather. Their women and children moved with them, leading flocks of sheep, goats, and camels. Wagons held rolled-up tents, blankets, sacks of grain, boxes of fruit and vegetables, and treasures of gold and gems.

And among the soldiers, rising like a moving mountain, walked Behemoth.

The beast dwarfed the soldiers around him, as large as an anthill among ants. His six feet pounded the earth, tipped with claws the size of men. His tail dragged behind him. A great disk of bone crowned his head, large as a gatehouse, topped with horns like towers. On his back rode a dozen archers, and more men sat atop his horns in crow's nests like men atop the masts of ships.

A voice rose beside Amity. "The beast has not seen sunlight in thousands of years. It's already killed a dozen troops, feasting on their flesh, their bones, their armor and weapons. It's a danger to us all."

Amity turned her head to see Korvin gliding a few feet away. The burly dragon was larger than her, his scales thick and deep gray like plates of armor. His dark eyes stared down at Behemoth, and his jaw twisted. She grinned at him.

"Imagine the danger he'd be to Beatrix. The beast can smash through the Cured Temple like a drunkard through a tavern's door."

Smoke blasted out from Korvin's nostrils. "Assuming you can ship it to the north. We'll need a big ship . . . or you'd better hope it can swim."

Amity grinned. "He'll make it across the sea if you and I have to carry him." She gestured ahead with her chin. "And there is the sea before us."

The coast stretched ahead, and beyond it the blue waters of the Tiran Sea that led to the Commonwealth. Thousands of years ago, the ancient civilization of Eteer had spread across this coast, building the world's first ships and raising its first buildings of stone. Today only ruins remained of that lost culture: a few shells of walls, a few columns along the beach, and old stories.

The city of Hakan Teer sprawled ahead of her, the place where Amity had first faced the abina she had later slain in the southern mountains. Countless tents rose along the coast, and a great mass of people bustled among them. Griffins and salvanae flew above them. A hundred ships sailed in the water: brigantines and carracks captured from Commonwealth merchants, their old banners replaced with sigils of the Horde; locally constructed baghlah ships with elaborately carved hulls and elongated prows; and many small dhow boats of warriors, traders, and fishermen.

"We'll muster hundreds of other ships," Amity said, gliding toward Hakan Teer. "We'll muster countless more warriors. From all across the lands of Terra, we'll summon the vast multitudes of the Horde and cross the sea. The Cured Temple will shatter before us."

The army below, seeing Hakan Teer in the distance, cheered at the sight. They had marched for a long time across the desert, leaving the mountains of Gosh Ha'ar behind in the south, and here they would enjoy feasts around campfires, music and dancing, and the pleasures of camp followers from many lands. As they reached the tent city, the people of Gosh Ha'ar unburdened their mules, raised new tents, and kindled thousands of fires. Women beat timbrels and danced, men dueled with swords and spears, and children scampered about, firing arrows from homemade bows.

Among countless tents rose a single permanent dwelling: the villa where Amity had first confronted Abina Kahan. Stone walls surrounded the complex, holding within their embrace flowering gardens, a grove of pines, a columned bathhouse, and finally the adobe villa itself, the coastal home of the Horde's monarch. Amity and Korvin glided down, landed on a pebbly path between cypress trees. A dozen griffins landed with them, riders on their backs, their long platinum hair streaming like their banners. Guards stood outside the villa, clad in bronze breastplates.

Amity tossed back her head and blasted flame.

"Bow before Abini Amity, Queen of the Horde!"

She shifted back into human form, and they bowed before her. Surrounded by guards, Korvin at her side, she marched into the hall.

Here the abina doomed me to death, she thought. *From here I will launch an army to conquer the north.*

She gazed around at the main hall: a round chamber, the floor a mosaic of many Terran animals, the columns engraved with vines, the ceiling painted with murals. Trees grew from stone pots, sending forth flowers, and birds flitted between them. A throne of precious metals rose ahead, and columned windows afforded a view of the sea.

"Beats the old prison cell, doesn't it, big boy?" Amity patted Korvin's cheek.

The gruff warrior stared around. White stubble covered his leathery, tanned face, but his thick eyebrows were still black as coal, and his shaggy mane of hair was still more black than silver. With his craggy countenance, tattered clothes, and scars and bruises, he seemed as out of place here as . . . well, as she herself was, Amity supposed.

The old abina had been a vain man, filling his hall with several bronze mirrors, and Amity regarded her reflection in one. She saw a bruised, beaten woman, clad in rags. Her yellow hair was growing longer, almost long enough to reach her chin now, tangled and caked with dirt. Dust and grime covered her skin, but not enough to hide the cuts and burns that spread across her body. A tall woman. Strong. Powerful and lithe. A scarred warrior. A queen. A conqueror. A lost girl.

As the sea whispered outside the windows, as guards moved about the hall, as the beating of timbrels and the song of men and birds rose outside, Amity stared into the mirror, and she saw a young girl, frightened, fleeing, her parents gone. A girl swimming across the midnight waters. A girl shivering in the dark, weeping, so afraid. Always so afraid. She saw weakness. She saw pain. And it seemed to Amity that woman and girl were one, that weakness fueled pain, that forever the scared girl and the proud warrior would fight within her.

She tightened her lips and spun away from the mirror. She faced Korvin.

"I need to get out of these clothes," she said. "And so do you."

He frowned. "Now is hardly the time."

She groaned. "Was that a joke, big boy? You know what I mean. Now come, there's a bathhouse somewhere in this place. I saw it from above. Let's go find it."

They left the villa and walked outside until they found the bathhouse, a stone pool surrounded by columns, and here Amity peeled off her clothes. Guards stood around her, and Korvin stood at her side, but they did not shy away from her nakedness, for the Horde regarded the human body as no more shameful than a suit of armor. She stepped into the water and called to Korvin to join her. He undressed slowly, grumbling and wincing as his tattered clothes brushed against his wounds. His body too was covered with wounds: cuts, burn marks, the stripes of whips. He stepped into the water; it rose to his shoulders.

"Look at us," Amity said. "Two beaten up chunks of meat."

"Living chunks of meat," Korvin replied, "which is more than I expected."

"Ruling chunks of meat." She clasped his hands. "Together." Suddenly her eyes stung, and tears streamed down her cheeks.

"Amity?" Korvin's eyes softened. "Why do you shed tears?"

She blinked furiously and rubbed them away. "It . . . it always happens in water."

I have to swim! I have to flee! The little girl again, scared, orphaned, alone, swam across the midnight ocean, so afraid, so weak, forever inside her.

Her vision cleared, and she touched Korvin's cheek. "Can we truly do this?" she whispered. "Can we truly rule this mass of armies, people, creatures, truly take them overseas? Can we win?" She closed her eyes. "I'm scared, Korvin. I'm so scared."

He waded closer in the water, and his arms--large, wide arms, strong and scarred--wrapped around her. He held her close and stroked her wet hair.

"I don't know," he said, voice a low grumble, soothing as rolling thunder in a dying storm. "But whatever happens, I'm with you. Whatever enemies we face, I will fight them with you. Always."

She caressed his prickly cheek and kissed his lips. "I love you, big boy." Those damn tears flowed again. "You know that, don't you?"

That night they held a great feast in the villa. Trestle tables were laid out in the main hall, and cooks brought out the bounty of the Horde: steaming pies of all kind, full of fish, fowl, and fruit; roasted peacocks on silver platters, their garish tail feathers reattached; skewers of lamb and camel meat on beds of rice; golden bowls full of grapes, persimmons, figs, and a hundred other fruits; and honeyed clusters of nuts and dried berries. Hundreds of men and women filled the hall, the generals of her army, feasting, drinking wine and spirits, and singing old songs. Musicians moved between the tables, playing lyres and drums, and dancers performed in silks that revealed more than they hid.

Amity sat at the head of the table, singing hoarsely, drinking deeply whenever servants filled her cup, pounding on the table and laughing whenever a jester stumbled. She wore iron armor and a resplendent red cloak, and Korvin stood at her side, ever her guardian, wearing a dark gray breastplate and a charcoal cape. As silent as he was, Amity was loud--clapping, singing, laughing, drinking, belching, shouting, for her cries drowned the pain, and the wine drowned the memories, and she drank more and more and cried out more and more, all to hide that old fear, to bury that scared little girl beneath endless laughter, endless wine.

The feast lasted into dawn. When the last warriors stumbled out of her hall, they left a disaster: shattered tables, piles of bones and apple cores and apricot seeds, spilled wine, toppled jugs. Amity rose to her feet and swayed. She was tired. Bone tired. So tired the memories of that little girl were almost drowned, too muzzy to claim her.

"Let's find a damn bed in this hovel." She spat. "Korvin, help me walk."

He held her hand, and they walked together through the villa, her swaying, him a solid pillar. They explored several hallways until they found a staircase, climbed it, and discovered a bedchamber. The room was massive, almost the size of the hall downstairs. It had no fourth wall, only a portico of columns affording a view of the sea. The floor was tiled, the walls painted with murals of birds, and a great canopy bed stood in its center.

"Perfect," Amity said, tugging Korvin toward the bed. "Now, undress again."

He frowned at her. "We've already bathed."

She snorted. "Do I have to rip your damn clothes off? Undress!"

She tugged at the straps of her armor, and the iron plates clanged to the floor. She all but tore her clothes off, and when she grabbed at Korvin's clothes, she did tear them, ripping through the cotton, tearing through the lacings, tearing at his skin with her fingernails.

"Make love to me now," she said.

His eyes narrowed. "You're in no condition to--"

She growled and shoved him onto the bed. He lay on his back, and she stared at his naked body, the many scars and bruises, the contours of his muscles, the peace he brought to her, the strength he gave to her life, the anchor of her soul. She climbed onto the bed, and she straddled him, and Amity rode him, head tossed back, fingernails digging into his chest, and she cried out again--shouting as she had in the feast, shouting as she did in battle, shouting as she had in her childhood, fleeing across the sea. The bed rattled. The sheets tore. His skin tore beneath her fingernails, and still she rode him like a woman riding a dragon, and still she cried out, not caring if the entire camp heard.

She did not even remember falling asleep. She knew only dreams--dreams of drinking in an endless feast, endless masks floating around her, and dreams of riding a dragon across the sea. The dragon kept calling to her, opening his mouth to roar, but only a knocking sound left his jaws, knock after knock.

Her eyes opened.

The knocking continued.

Amity was lying sprawled out in the bed, still naked, the sheets damp with her sweat. Korvin lay beside her, still sleeping. Afternoon light fell into the bedchamber.

Knock. Knock. Knock.

Amity growled and rose to her feet.

"Enter!" she barked.

The door opened and a serving girl entered the chamber, clad in a white tunic. The girl lowered her head, looking away from Amity's nakedness.

"My abini." She knelt.

"What is it?" Amity glowered. "Why do you disturb me?"

The servant gulped, and her eyes flicked up, full of fear. "Dragons, my queen. Four dragons flew in from the sea . . . and they're looking for you."

FIDELITY

As Fidelity stood on the southern coast of Terra and beheld the great, sprawling camp of the Horde, more fear than she had ever felt flooded her. Countless humans and beasts mustered here, preparing for war--griffins, salvanae, and warriors from many lands--but Fidelity cared for only one man.

"What if he's not here?" she whispered. "What if the merchant's story was false, if . . . if we don't find him?"

Standing at her side, Domi reached out and clasped Fidelity's hand. Fidelity turned to look at her little sister, seeking comfort in Domi's presence.

"He's here." Domi's red hair fluttered like a torch's flame in the wind. "I know it."

Fidelity looked to her other side. Roen stood there, and he reached out to hold Fidelity's other hand. The tall, bearded forester had never liked crowds, and it was hard to imagine a more crowded place than this camp, but he seemed to Fidelity a pillar of calmness, one she could tether her anxiety to. Behind him stood Cade and Gemini, both wrapped in cloaks, both looking as out of place as pups who'd wandered into a wolf's den.

Fidelity took a deep breath and looked around her. Two massive statues rose at her sides, hundreds of feet tall. They were shaped as rearing stallions, carved of sandstone, and their kicking hooves were gilded. Here were the fabled Eras and Elamar, Guardians of Terra. Beyond this gateway spread the camp of the Horde. Fidelity's left lens was still missing, but through her right lens, she beheld a massive camp that spread toward the horizon. Tens of thousands of tents rose here, bustling with activity. Soldiers were drilling with swords, and griffins flew above in formations, their riders tossing up clay targets and shooting them with arrows. In the sea, a hundred ships or more were hoisting banners, and rowboats kept moving back and forth, bringing soldiers from the land onto the warships' decks.

The Horde prepares for war, Fidelity thought. *Do you truly lead them, Amity? Are you truly here with her, Father?*

Roars sounded above.

Wings beat, blasting sand and dust across the camp.

Fidelity coughed and rubbed her eyes, and then she saw them flying above.

A red dragon blasting out fire. A charcoal dragon, scales like iron plates, burly and creaky.

Fidelity's chest shook, and she couldn't breathe, but she could cry out, and she cried with all the strength in her lungs: "Father! Father!"

Tears flowed down her cheeks, and she ran through the camp, reaching up to him. Domi ran with her, and the dark gray dragon dived down, hit the dirt between the tents, and shifted into a man.

Fidelity's eyes watered as she ran.

It's him. Oh stars, it's him, he's alive.

There he stood--her father, the old soldier. Korvin was gaunter than she remembered, and his skin was tanned deep bronze, sharply contrasting with his white stubble. His eyebrows were as bushy and black as ever, and his hair was still a great, grizzled mane that flowed halfway down his back, the black streaked with more silver than before. He wore fine steel armor now, and a sword hung at his side--a soldier again. Yet despite the changes in him, it was still her dear father, the man who would bounce her on his knee years ago, who had lived with her in the library, who had fought with her for Requiem, who brought tears to her eyes and made her chest shake.

"Father!"

He held out his arms, and Fidelity leaped onto him, crying against him, holding him close. Her body shook with sobs, and she laughed through her tears.

"Fidelity." Korvin held her close, and she was surprised to see his eyes dampen. She had never seen her father shed tears before, and she knew she would never forget this moment. "My daughter . . ."

He could say no more, only hold her close, nearly crushing her slender frame against his armor.

A soft voice rose behind them. "Father?"

Fidelity turned around, still wrapped in her father's arms, to see Domi standing on the dirt path between the tents. Her orange hair once more fell down to hide her face, and her green eyes peered between the strands, hesitant. She dared not step closer.

Gently, Korvin released Fidelity from his embrace, and the two stepped toward Domi.

"My daughter," Korvin said, reaching out to embrace Domi.

Domi took a step back. She seemed like a wounded animal, torn between fleeing and fighting. She began to tremble, and then tears flooded her eyes, and she leaped forward and wrapped her limbs around Korvin, squeezing him.

"I'm sorry, Father," she whispered. "I'm so sorry for running away, for being Pyre, for everything I've done. I'm so sorry. I love you, Papa. I love you."

As around them bustled an army of soldiers, chariots, and flying beasts, they stood together--father and daughters, holding one another close, united in the shadow of looming war.

GEMINI

"It seems like it's the time for family reunions," Gemini said, watching Domi and her sister hug the grizzled old warrior. He turned to look at Cade. "Should we finally have our own proper reunion? They tell me you're my brother."

They stood in the tent city, two young men in the center of chaos. The Horde bustled around them. Burly, bare-chested warriors rode horses back and forth, both men and beasts clad in ring mail. A leathery old man walked by, leading a chained griffin, a massive beast with the body of a lion and the head of an eagle, even larger than most dragons. Tall, noble women and men walked all around, clad in pale steel armor, their platinum hair streaming like banners, their eyes blue like the sea--Tirans of the desert, a proud and ancient race, their sabers filigreed and their skin deep gold. Even a salvanae streamed by, its scales chinking, a serpent of the air, seeming to Gemini almost like a great sculpture of jewels. The creature blinked its crystal eyes at him--each as large as Gemini's head--fanning him with its eyelashes, and its beard streamed along the ground as its body hovered. And all around, past warriors and creatures, spread the tents of Hakan Teer--some lavish and embroidered, others simple dwellings made of animal hides stretched over cedar poles.

Gemini was used to the order and cleanliness of the Commonwealth. Back home, every soldier wore the same exact armor--paladins in white steel plates, commoners in chain mail so meticulous that each soldier wore the same number of rings in his armor. Every home in every city was the same, a clay hut with a domed roof, built to perfect specifications, identical to its neighbors. Each city street, each warship, each saddle on a firedrake, all were created with precision, part of a flawless whole.

The south, however, was a motley mess. No two tents were alike, and most seemed homemade. No two suits of armor matched. Warriors simply cobbled together whatever makeshift armor they could, strapping on hunks of iron, bronze, and copper, scraps of ring mail, sometimes simply boiled leather studded with bolts. Some men wore beards while others were clean shaven. Some women wore long gowns while others walked around bare chested, not a scrap of modesty to them, and Gemini would have thought them harlots if not for the swords at their hips. He didn't even see commanders, no units of troops, no order, only a great mass. The smells were just as plentiful and confusing and intoxicating: sweat, oil, perfumes, horse dung, cooking fires, fruits and roasting meats, a sickening and sweetly aroma.

This was, Gemini decided, not an army but a mob.

He looked back at Cade.

Perhaps, he thought, *this boy is the only thing I have left in this land of barbarians.*

He stepped closer. "Well, Cade? Aren't you going to say anything?"

The boy stared at him, eyes hard. He was shorter than Gemini, younger, his hair brown, not bleached like the hair of a paladin, his eyes hazel, not blue like Gemini's. But Gemini saw the resemblance; Cade had a face remarkably like his own.

It's true. We are brothers.

Finally Cade spoke. "I had a true family once. A kind father. A loving mother. A sister." The boy clenched his fists. "Your family slew my parents and stole my sister. You are no brother to me."

Gemini raised an eyebrow. "It sounds like I'm the only family you have left."

Cade growled and grabbed Gemini's collar. "Be silent! Don't think that I trust you." He twisted the collar in his fist. "I know that you hurt Domi. I know of all those that your family hurt. I am not one of you." His cheeks flushed and his eyes reddened. "Do you hear me? I'm not part of your sick, twisted family."

Gemini sighed and pried Cade's hand off his collar. "Sick, twisted family." The words tasted flat. "Yes. We are that. My mother. My sister. They're . . . not the most pleasant of people. I know of their sins--the people they killed, tortured, imprisoned, deformed." He shuddered, the nightmares of the dungeon never far from consuming him. "But that's them. They're the ones in power. I've never been like them, Cade. They hurt me too." Gemini winced, closed his eyes, and took a shaky breath. "You can't imagine what it was like--growing up with Beatrix as your mother, with Mercy as your sister." He barked a laugh, opened his eyes, and looked at Cade again. "Can you?"

Cade's fists loosened. "No."

Gemini placed his hand on Cade's shoulder. "Listen to me, brother. I'm here now. Helping you. Fighting with you. You are my brother, and I swear to you . . . we will fight back against our family." He sneered. "We will kill Mercy and Beatrix, and then we--the Deus brothers--will rule the land."

"I want nothing to do with your land." Cade glowered. "I fight only for Requiem."

Gemini nodded. "Requiem is what you'll get if you fight with me. Against my mother and sister. *Our* mother and sister." His eyes stung. "Spirit, Cade, their cruelty, their bloodlust . . . Such horrors, brother. Such horrors. And I've always felt very alone. I sought love with women. With wine. With Domi. With firedrakes. Seeking some relief, somebody to understand." He was surprised to find tears stinging his eyes. "But I found you. A brother. A real brother. Somebody to fight with me."

Surprising himself again, Gemini hugged Cade. The boy stood stiffly at first, then relaxed.

"My brother," Gemini whispered. "My little brother. I promise that I'll never hurt you like Mercy hurt me. I promise to always fight with you."

Cade pulled himself free. He stared at Gemini with a mix of confusion, contempt, and wonder, then turned and walked several steps away. The boy stood with his back to Gemini, staring toward the water.

I don't know if we can ever be friends, Gemini thought, gazing at the boy. *I've never had a brother, never had a friend, never had anyone love me, never loved anyone but Domi who betrayed me.* His damn eyes stung again. *Please, Spirit, let this boy, this brother, be a friend to me. Let him fight with me against the world, against all those who hurt us.*

"Gemini!" The voice rose behind him. "Cade, you too! We're going to find something to eat. Gemini, come on!"

Gemini turned around to see Fidelity gesturing to them. He raised his chin, dried his eyes, and nodded. He walked toward the others, the weredragons, those who had captured him, who perhaps would fight with him, who perhaps would be the only people in the world to love him.

MERCY

Her firedrake perched upon the tower, the tallest point in Altus Mare, and from the saddle Mercy watched her armada muster.

"Altus Mare," she whispered into the wind. "The great Eastern Light of the Commonwealth. From here our greatest beam of righteousness will shine forth."

Below her spread the second largest city in her empire, the greatest port of the Commonwealth, larger than three Lynports. Altus Mare was an ancient city, harkening back to the days of the Osannan civilization which had first built a port here three thousand years ago. The eastern sea pushed into the continent here, a cove of calm warm water, and the city spread along the coast, embracing the bay. Hundreds of monasteries rose here, their steeples white and soaring, and great tillvine blossoms shone in their stained glass mirrors. Between the temples, thousands of cobbled streets rolled along hills toward the water, and countless houses rose alongside them. The homes were all built of the same white clay, their windows round, their roofs domed. Among them rose libraries, silos, workshops, and fortresses.

Altus Mare--fabled for its beauty, for its white spires like crystal shards, for its crystal blue waters, for its wisdom, its music, its history and holiness. Altus Mare, the Jewel of the East.

Today it was home to an army.

Hundreds of warships filled the cove: towering brigantines with many sails, their decks lined with cannons; carracks topped with archers and soldiers ready for war; longships lined with oars and shields; portly cogs laden with barrels of gunpowder and siege engines; and a hundred wooden hulks bearing firedrakes upon their decks. Ships had come here from across the coasts of the Commonwealth, forming the greatest armada the empire had ever seen. On the horizon, Mercy saw many more masts rising, drawing closer, more ships come to join the greatest invasion of the age.

Thousands of troops gathered here too. They stood along every boardwalk, mustered in every square. They wore white robes painted with tillvine blossoms over chain mail, and they held shields and swords. A thousand paladins commanded them, clad in white plate armor, bearing great lances and banners. As Mercy watched from the tower, hundreds of rowboats were busy moving back and forth, ferrying troops from the boardwalks and onto the warships.   Dozens of firedrakes flew overhead, gliding down to land on decks. Hundreds more would fly above the armada as it sailed, swapping places with the beasts on the decks every few hours, forever forming a cloud of scale and fire above the fleet.

Lynport lay far southwest from here, and Sanctus far north. Altus Mare was not only the largest of the Commonwealth's port cities but also the closest to her destination: the great tent city of Hakan Teer in the continent of Terra . . . the great army of the Horde.

"We will face them in battle, Talis," Mercy said, leaning across the saddle to stroke her firedrake's white scales. "We will burn them all."

Talis was a young firedrake, not yet fully trained, jittery but fast and mean and strong. He was smaller than Felesar, her old mount which Gemini had stolen, but quicker, crueler. Scales as pure and pale as snow flowed across his muscular form, and his jaws kept snapping, and his claws kept digging into the steeple of the monastery he perched on. He gurgled and cackled as she stroked them, then spread his wings wide, tossed back his head, and blasted upward a great fountain of fire, an inferno that shrieked and roared, blue in its center, spreading out to white and blazing red.

"Yes, Talis," Mercy said. "Soon you'll blast this fire onto the weredragons. Soon they will cower before you and die in your flame."

Suddenly pain drove through Mercy, and she closed her eyes. Again she felt the agony in her belly, her husband's fists killing the child who had slept within. She shivered, biting her lip so hard she bled, and her eyes snapped open. She stared at the fleet below.

"I do this for you, Eliana," she whispered. "I will lead the Temple to its greatest battle, and I will purify the world so that you never know pain. So that you never know war. I will bring about the Falling and raise you in a world of light . . . even if my life is one of shadow and flame."

She dug her spurs into Talis's tenderspots, and the beast took flight. His wings beat madly, and he cried out, a bugling cry, eager for the fight. They dived over the city streets, over thousands of domes, thousands of soldiers. They soared, scattering flame, rising high above the cove, and they circled above the hundreds of ships that spread for miles. Mercy's banner rose high, thudding in the wind, displaying a golden tillvine blossom upon a white field. The sun beat down, shining on Talis's white scales and her white armor.

"Hear me!" Mercy cried to the army below, to the multitudes, to the wrath of the Temple. "I am Mercy Deus, and I will lead you to victory! We are the light of the Spirit! We are the blade of the Cured! Sail forth, armada! Sail forth, holy warriors!"

Across hundreds of decks, men blew into silvery horns. The cries rose from below, growing and multiplying, a thousand clarion calls, calls for holiness, for war, for triumph. The last rowboats reached the warships, and the last soldiers climbed onto the decks, and with the roar of drums and horns and chanting men, the armada began to sail.

Talis turned toward the east and flew, leading the way out of the port, blasting fire and screeching, his cry rolling across the cove and city. A thousand other firedrakes took flight, blowing fire, their cries shaking the sky. Below them, the ships raised their anchors and began to sail: brigantines, carracks, hulks, hundreds of vessels bearing a hundred thousand soldiers. Cannons blasted out in triumph. Priests led chants, and countless voices rose in song upon the decks. All along the cove, men and women cheered, waved flags, and blew horns. Sunbeams fell upon the water, and Mercy felt as if the Spirit himself watched from above, blessing her with light.

It was an army the Horde could not stop. It was a light the weredragons could not extinguish. It was the great battle of Mercy's life--for her mother, for her daughter, for her god.

And for the fear inside me, she thought. *For the emptiness that I cannot fill.*

The great army of the Cured Temple sailed out of the cove into open water. Ahead, across the horizon, they waited: the continent of Terra, the weredragons, her brothers, and her triumph or her death in fire.

KORVIN

A gray dragon, he perched atop Elamar, one of the great horse statues that guarded the coast of Terra. The colossus rose three hundred feet tall, almost as tall as the Cured Temple in the north. Clutching one of the horse's raised, gilded hoofs, Korvin felt as small as an eagle on an oak's branch.

Amity sat perched on the horse's second kicking hoof. The red dragon spat out fire, and smoke rose from her nostrils. She turned her scaly head toward Korvin and grinned, showing all her teeth.

"We're almost ready," she said.

Korvin grunted, puffed out smoke, and stared at the coast below. Behind him sprawled the tent city of Hakar Teer, the great northern garrison of the Horde. Before him in the water, the ships of this empire spread across the sea. Many were old ships captured years ago from the Commonwealth in battle: brigantines, carracks, and caravels, the tillvine blossoms scratched off their hulls, their banners now displaying the serpents of the Horde, and cannons lined their decks. Among them sailed hundreds of vessels built here in Terra: dhow ships with lateen sails, some small with only one mast and a dozen men, others sporting three masts and a crew of a hundred; massive baghlah ships, long and curved, their hulls masterworks of engravings and precious metals; hulks and cogs, massive ships the size of forts; longships like great centipedes lined with oars; and countless smaller vessels, some oared and some raising single sails, like bustling flies around the larger warships.

On the fleet's decks, the warriors of the Horde roared for battle and brandished their weapons. Osannans, the descendants of outcasts from their lands in the north, wore scraps of iron, leather, and wool, and they wielded axes, hammers, spears, and longswords. For the first time in hundreds of years, they would sail back to their ancestral home in the northeast, the home the Temple now ruled. Among them roared warriors of the Terran tribes, survivors of the fallen civilizations of Eteer, Goshar, and the other city-states that now lay buried under the sand. They were shorter and darker, their skin olive toned, their hair black, their eyes green, and they wore bronze breastplates, suits of scales, and ring mail, and they brandished scimitars and khopeshes and spears tipped with iron. Thousands of Tirans sailed here too, tall and noble people with golden skin, piercing blue eyes, and long platinum hair, warriors hailing from the deserts of the west, come to join the great Horde in its conquest.

Not only men and women topped the ships but beasts too. A thousand horses stood within the hulls of lumbering cogs, and several ships even held elephants in their bowels. Griffins stood atop massive wooden hulks. Salvanae lay curled up on other decks like serpents, scales bright in the sun.

Finally, on the beach, loomed Behemoth itself. No ship was large enough to ferry the beast; he was large as the largest carrack. Crow's nests had been attached to his many horns, and archers stood within. More men stood on the beast's back in a great wooden howdah. As Korvin watched, riders shouted commands and lashed crops, guiding Behemoth into the sea. The creature walked through the water, moving between the ships. He would swim the ocean as he had in eras long ago, before the ancient lords of the Horde had imprisoned him in the mountain.

"This host has the might to sweep across the Commonwealth," Korvin said. "Lynport burned to the ground. We will land there in the ruins, facing little resistance, and make our way north--north across charred forests, north to the capital, to the Temple, and we will send that Temple crashing down." He looked at Amity. "And I don't know what land we will find when the Horde has done its work."

"We will find Requiem," Amity said.

Smoke seeped out of Korvin's nostrils. "The Horde might not be as willing as you think to retreat."

Amity snarled, and fire flickered between her fangs. "I will slay anyone who resists me. I will grant the Horde the lands of Osanna in the east, from Lanburg Fields to Altus Mare. I will grant them the forests of Salvandos in the west, the mountains of Fidelium in the north, the swamps of Gilnor in the south, all those lands annexed to the empire that was once our kingdom. Those will be the prizes of the Horde for their war--more than half the Commonwealth. For us, Korvin, I will keep our ancient kingdom, the classical realm of Requiem as it was in the days of King Benedictus."

Korvin twisted his jaw. "The old borders of Requiem leave us a small kingdom, fragile. It was the kingdom that fell so many times to invaders. If we carve but a small land for Requiem, we'll still have to face the Horde--a vast Horde, stronger than ever before, ruling not only the southern continent of Terra but wrapped around Requiem in the north too, a noose that will ever crave to tighten."

Amity grinned. "Big boy, I intend to rule both the neck of Requiem and the noose of the Horde, forever keeping one away from the other. I will be queen of both." She spread her wings and took flight. "Now fly with me! It's time to sail." She blasted forth a jet of flame. "The invasion of the north begins!" She roared, a cry that rolled across the land and sea. "Sail north, Horde! Sail beneath the Red Queen! To blood! To fire! To war! To war!"

The Horde roared beneath her. A hundred thousand warriors raised their weapons--men, women, youths, elders, all wearing patches of armor of metal and leather, brandishing swords and spears, hammers and axes. A great mass, a mob, a seething pot of anger about to overflow. They bellowed. They sang for her. Their voices rose together, shaking the sky.

"To war! To war!"

Korvin stared from the statue, and an icy shard sank through his chest. Amity was howling for victory, but Korvin found no lust for war within him.

I fought a war once, he thought. He had invaded Terra from the north, and he had faced the Horde upon the coast, and the scars still covered his body. Thirty years ago, when Amity had still been suckling at the teat, he had faced an enemy on the beaches, he too had shouted for victory.

Yet now I'm old, and now I know that war has no winners--only pain, only blood, only ruin.

How could he stop this tide? How could he stop the woman he loved--a woman he saw descending into madness, into bloodlust?

Korvin gritted his teeth, and his chest constricted.

I once loved another woman. I once loved a young priestess named Beatrix, an idealistic soul, her faith in righteousness strong.

That woman too had sent Korvin to war. That woman too had let bloodlust consume her. That woman had become a tyrant.

Standing on the gilded hoof, Korvin stared at Amity, at this new woman he loved, at the red dragon who flew and shouted ahead.

"I can lose my land, and I can lose my life," Korvin whispered. "But I cannot lose you, Amity. Do not lose yourself."

The thousand ships of the Horde set sail, heading north, leaving the coast of Terra behind. Finally Korvin leaped from the gilded hoof, spread his wings, and glided on the wind, flying with the fleet, flying to blood and fire, flying home.

CADE

He stood at the prow of the *Kor Taran*, a sprawling baghlah ship with many sails, and he stared north across the water. Many miles beyond the blue horizon, past sunsets and sunrises and waves, lay the northern continent, lay an empire called the Commonwealth, lay a memory of a fallen land called Requiem, lay a dream of a Requiem reborn, lay a stolen sister, lay all Cade's hopes and fears.

"Requiem," he whispered--the beat of his heart. "Eliana," he whispered--the fear and love in his chest.

For Requiem and Eliana, Cade vowed to fight. To kill. To give his life if he had to. He would liberate both the land of his forebears and the babe Mercy had stolen from him.

All around him, hundreds of ships sailed, griffins and salvanae flew, and warriors roared and brandished their weapons. Cade had seen the ships of the Commonwealth sailing in the northern waters, stern vessels, spotless, clinging to rigid formations. The Horde's fleet was like its army of warriors; a hodgepodge, scratched and dented and grimy, a swarm, a mass of metal, wood, and leather like flotsam spilled across the water. Drums beat and horns blared. Griffins and salvanae streamed overhead, screeching and bugling, riders on their backs, and thousands of banners streamed in the wind.

Scales clanked, wings thudded, and blasts of air ruffled Cade's hair. He looked up to see a dragon flying down toward the ship, her scales a mosaic of red, orange, and yellow of every shade. The fiery beast descended to hover above the deck, wings blasting the sails, then shifted into human form. Domi landed before Cade, her bare feet thumping against the deck.

"Hullo, Cade," she said.

For the first time since Cade had known her, Domi seemed . . . happy. Her orange hair was tucked behind her ears, not covering her face, and she smiled. Her nose and cheeks were turning red in the southern sun, and her freckles were seeming to multiply, but she was beautiful to Cade, the most beautiful woman he had ever seen.

And I fight for you, Domi, he thought. *So that I can see you smile more often. So that I can see you happy, free, no hair covering your face, not a firedrake forever hiding your human form.*

"Are you ready to roast Beatrix's backside?" he asked her.

She grinned. "We're going to roast it together--roast it until it falls off as ashes."

A grin stretched across Cade's own cheeks. "And don't forget about Mercy. I'm going to burn off her backside too. Burn it to ash. Burn it like she burned so many people. I'm going to burn her like she burned them." Suddenly he found that his eyes were stinging, that he was clenching his fists. "Like she . . . like she burned my . . ." He swallowed, looked away, and loosened his fists, the joke no longer funny, the pain too real, the memory too vivid.

She burned you, Derin and Tisha. I'll never forget you. I will avenge you.

Domi's smile faded, and she stepped closer and leaned her head against his shoulder. Then she looked up, kissed his cheek, and pinched his nose.

"I'm with you, Goldy," she said. "Always."

He raised his eyebrows. "Goldy?"

She nodded and her grin returned. "Your scales are gold when you're a dragon. Bit of a girl's color, if you ask me. Sort of like the legendary Queen Gloriae's scales. Or Princess Mori from the old stories. Or Laira, the first Queen of Requiem." Domi's grin widened and she hopped about. "Goldy! Pretty pretty Goldy!"

Cade grumbled. "At least I have a proper color. You don't even have one color, just all sorts of yellows and reds and such. Do you turn into a dragon or a quilt?"

She froze and gasped. Then a snort left her mouth, and she doubled over laughing. "A quilt? A flying magic quilt that blows fire?"

He nodded. "Yes. That's your new name now. Quilty."

She shoved him. "Shut it, Goldy."

He shook his head. "Getting angry, Quilty?"

She nodded and snarled, playfully pummeling his chest with her fists. Then she sighed and embraced him, her body warm against his. She wore only a cotton tunic, and Cade could feel her breasts press against his chest, her thighs against his. He closed his eyes, holding her close, never wanting to let go. He would be happy to live the rest of his life like this, on the open sea, the air fresh around him, Domi pressed against him. He thought back to the time she had first embraced him, had whispered "Requiem" into his ear.

He kissed her head, and he whispered to her, "Thank you, Domi."

She looked up at him. "For what?"

He cupped her cheek in his palm. "For a long time, I was confused. Sometimes I hated you, blaming you for what happened to my village, for how you bore Mercy on your back. But you tried to protect me. I realize that now. Without you, I'd never know about Requiem, never be standing here, sailing toward our home. And . . . it's not just about Requiem. I . . ."

I love you, he wanted to say. *I love you more than Requiem, more than my life, more than anything. I've loved you since the moment you whispered into my ear.*

Yet he could say none of these things; he dared not. So he only leaned down and kissed her cheek, his lips brushing the corner of her mouth.

She stared at him, eyes wide and huge, surprised perhaps at his audacity. But then she laughed, kissed his mouth with a quick peck, and pinched his cheek.

"Goldy," she said, stepped back, and shifted into a dragon. She flew off, heading toward Fidelity and Roen who glided above.

Cade remained standing at the prow of the ship. He walked across the deck, moving between many soldiers of the Horde: swordsmen, archers, gunners, and wild men and women bearing spears. When he reached the stern, he stood and stared south. Hundreds of ships sailed there, and beyond them stretched the coast of Terra, the southern continent. He stood for a long time, watching as the land grew distant and faded.

GEMINI

The red dragon flew above Gemini, circling the fleet, blasting fire and crying out words that chilled him.

"The Commonwealth will crumble! The Cured Temple will crash down! The bounty of the north will be ours!"

All across the fleet of the Horde, a thousand ships large and small, warriors roared for glory. Hundreds of beasts flew above the ships, just as mighty--griffins, salvanae, and weredragons. Greatest of all, Behemoth swam in their midst, back in the sea whence it had first risen, only its nostrils and horns thrusting up from the water. The coast of Terra grew distant behind them and faded to nothing but a strip, then a haze, then a memory.

As Amity, Queen of the Horde, roared above, and as her soldiers cheered, Gemini stood on the deck of a dhow ship and shivered.

"No," he whispered to himself. "No. No. It's not supposed to be this way."

Gemini paced the deck, shoving his way between warriors of the Horde--primitive men and women who stank of sweat and cheap wine. They didn't wear proper armor like paladins of the north, and their armor didn't even match, just random scraps of iron and metal scales sewn onto leather. It was disgusting. This was no army, this was a mob, a swarm of barbarians, a menace to the lands of Gemini's family and heritage.

"Domi!" he shouted, elbowing his way between the brutes. "Spirit damn it, Domi, where are you?"

The barbarians around him snorted and jeered. One man spat, and another wouldn't even move aside as Gemini tried to shove by. Gemini elbowed the bearded brute.

"Move!"

The barbarian stared down at Gemini and burst out laughing. Gemini was a tall man but thin. This brute stood several inches taller and must have weighed twice as much. His beard looked flea ridden, and his armor was a crude coat of rusty iron rings. Rather than a proper sword like the one Gemini had lost in the north, the barbarian held a heavy axe that looked more suited for chopping down trees than dueling an enemy.

"I'm warning you," Gemini said, glaring at the thug. "Move out of my way. Do you even know who I am?"

The brute grabbed Gemini's collar and sneered. "You're a maggot I'm about to squash."

Across the deck, other barbarians burst out laughing. One brute laughed so hard he sprayed spit onto Gemini, and a wild woman--her hair a great curly mane and her body barely covered--reached out to pat his cheek.

Gemini trembled with rage, shoving them aside. "I am Gemini Deus!" he screamed. "*Lord* Gemini Deus. This is my campaign. This is my army!" His voice cracked. "You fight for me. You serve me! This is my quest to redeem my home and--"

Roaring with laugher, several of the brutes grabbed Gemini and lifted him over their heads. They began to carry him across the deck, singing hoarsely.

"Put me down!" Gemini screamed. "I am your lord! We travel north to put me on the throne. I will kill you all! I order you to put me down!"

The bearded brute in iron mail laughed. "Very well."

The warriors swung Gemini backward, then thrust him forth. He flew through the air, screaming, tumbled off the deck, and--with horror and a strangled scream--crashed into the sea.

He floundered in the water, shock pounding through him. He breached the surface, gulped down air, and screamed.

"This is mutiny! I'll slay you all! I'll have your hides! I'm going to turn your skulls into chamber pots!"

Yet the dhow kept sailing away, leaving him behind. Hundreds of other ships sailed all around, more barbarians atop them, and the flying creatures kept gliding above. Nobody even glanced his way.

A shadow fell upon Gemini, and he looked up to finally see her. Domi glided down toward him, wreathed in smoke, her scales chinking. She beat her wings powerfully, hovering over the water, blasting him with air. Her claws reached out, and he climbed onto her leg.

"Gemini, what are you going in the water?" Domi asked.

"Fly!" he shouted. "Take me to a ship, damn it!"

As the fiery dragon flew, Gemini tried to climb onto her back, but he couldn't reach it. He remained clinging to her leg like some amorous dog humping its master. He could hear the army below mocking him, laughing at his wretchedness.

Apes, he thought, trembling with rage. *Foul, flea-ridden apes.*

It wasn't supposed to be this way. He was supposed to attack the Cured Temple with Domi alone, just two souls sneaking in, slinking through the halls, then burning down the guards and slaying Beatrix and Mercy. Later on, Gemini had allowed the other weredragons--the boy Cade, the whore Fidelity, and that brute Roen--to join his mission. They would have done the job quickly and easily, killing the High Priestess, killing Mercy, and placing him--Lord Gemini Deus--in command of the Temple. Not this. Not this . . . this swarm of insects, this diseased stain upon the land. Calling this ragtag army a "Horde" was being too kind. It was a brood of cockroaches.

Finally Domi glided down toward a *sambuk* ship--a long sturdy vessel with two masts, massive lateen sails, and an ornately carved hull. She landed on the deck, and once Gemini had climbed off her leg, she shifted back into human form and faced him.

"Are you all right?" Her voice was soft, and she reached out to touch his hair.

He shoved her hand away. "Don't pat me like I'm your dog! Of course I'm all right. I'm the lord of this host. Those brutes attempted to overthrow me." He pointed a shaky finger ahead at the fleet, not sure where the ship of mutinous warriors sailed but knowing it was out there somewhere, that the brutes still mocked him. This whole damn fleet was full of traitors.

Domi sighed. "Gemini, things are different now. Amity rules our assault." She pointed upward. The Red Queen was still circling above the fleet, calling out for war. "Amity is leading us now."

Gemini sneered. "That red-arsed baboon of a reptile? She's nothing! Just a barbarian harlot." He grabbed Domi's arms and snarled at her. "I'm the heir to the Cured Temple. Me! I'm the son of the Deus family. Me! Not some . . . some unwashed weredragon from the islands."

Anger kindled in Domi's eyes. "Release me. You're making a fool of yourself."

"*I'm* making a fool of myself?" He brayed laughter. "You're the one following this horde of miscreants. Domi!" His eyes dampened, and his voice shook. "Domi, we were meant to do this together. To fight Beatrix together, side by side. To take over the Temple and . . . and be together again. Me in the Temple, you in Requiem, a king and a queen. Allies. Friends." A tear streamed down his cheek. "In love. But now all that might be lost. Spirit, Domi, you hear Amity. She wants to crush the Temple--my birthright! To destroy it!" He trembled. "What would become of me then?"

Domi stared at him, her eyes cold, her face hard. "Nothing," she whispered. "You will become nothing."

Rage exploded through Gemini. Pure, all-consuming rage, hotter than dragonfire, louder than the roars of beasts. He howled and swung his arm, and he backhanded Domi so hard she crashed down onto the deck. Her blood splattered.

Gemini stood over her, hands trembling. His eyes widened, and he felt the blood drain from his face.

"I'm sorry," he whispered. "I'm sorry, Domi, I didn't mean to . . . I didn't . . ."

A howl sounded behind him, and Gemini turned to see Cade running across the deck toward him.

The boy, face red with rage, leaped onto Gemini and swung his fists.

One fist slammed into Gemini's cheek, knocking his head back. He crashed to the ground, Cade's fists driving down again and again. Blood filled Gemini's mouth, and panic flooded him.

"Get off me!" Gemini shouted and kicked.

His knee drove into Cade's belly, knocking the air out of the boy. Gemini growled, bloodlust consuming him, shoved Cade off, and landed his own punch. He laughed, blood in his mouth, as he turned the tide, pummeling the boy.

"I'll teach you a lesson, rat!" Gemini shouted, laughing, blood dripping down his chin. He was taller and heavier than Cade, and he punched again, hitting the boy's chin.

Lying beneath him, Cade shifted.

The boy grew in size, scales hardening across him. Gemini screamed and fell back onto the wooden deck. The golden dragon stood up and snarled down at him, blasting smoke.

"Coward," Gemini said and spat onto the reptile. "Too weak to face me as a man?" He rose to his feet, marched to the balustrade, grabbed a sword from a rack, and pointed the blade at

Cade. "I can slay dragons. I'm going to cut you down, boy." He raised his sword, prepared to swing the blade.

"Enough!"

The voice rose from above. Beating wings blasted Gemini's hair. Across the deck, warriors stared up, gasped, and knelt. Gemini looked up and sneered.

Amity, the Red Queen of the Horde, came flying down toward him. The red dragon was larger than Cade's reptilian form, and fire blazed in her maw. Her wings billowed the sails. The red dragon landed on the deck and shifted into human form. She stood before Gemini as a woman--tall and tanned, clad in armor, her limbs long and lithe. Her yellow hair was just long enough to fall across her ears, and her eyes blazed with rage.

Gemini sneered at the woman. "Do you know who I am? Kneel!" He pointed at the deck. "Kneel, reptilian whore, before your true master. I am Gemini Deus, and you will kneel before me!"

Amity glanced aside at Domi and Cade; the boy had resumed human form and now stood by the redheaded traitor. Gemini would burn them both later.

The Red Queen turned her gaze back toward him. "I know you, Gemini Deus. I know you well. Domi thought to wrap you in the robes of a High Priest, to create a little puppet ruler and pull your strings. But we'll have no more need for your services. And you will be the one to kneel before me. You will kneel now, as you asked me to kneel, and you will pledge your loyalty to me. Do this and live. Refuse and you will die."

Gemini growled. The rage flowed across him. He raised his sword. "How dare you, woman?" He spat at Amity's feet. "How dare you, harlot? You're nothing but a barbarian, a brute not worthy of polishing my boots. When I'm High Priest, I'll have you shoveling dung in the capital, I--"

Before Gemini could complete his sentence, Amity leaped forward, knocked aside his sword with her own blade, and drove her fist into his face.

His legs turned to jelly.

He collapsed onto the deck, reeling.

Cade had fought like a wild dog, but Amity pummeled Gemini with the intensity and heartless efficiency of a blacksmith beating steel. Her knees pinned him down, and her punches rained, and he screamed.

He felt himself shatter.

She grabbed him, tugging him to his feet, leaving a deck stained with blood. She shoved him against the balustrade and placed her sword against his neck. She sneered at him over the blade, a wild beast, still in human form but no less monstrous than a dragon.

"Now you die, Gemini Deus, Paladin of the Temple."

"Domi!" Gemini cried, slumped against the balustrade, blood in his mouth. "Domi, please!" He reached out to her. "I'm sorry. I'm sorry. Please." He wept. "I'm sorry. Please don't let me die. Please."

As the blade shoved against his neck, he stared at Domi through her tears. She stood on the deck, wrapped in Cade's arms.

She gazed at him with those huge eyes, peering through her strands of wild hair. And he saw the pity in those eyes. He saw the love for him.

"I love you," Gemini whispered. "I'm sorry."

He took a deep, shuddering breath, ready for Amity to drive her blade forward, to end his life. He would die looking at Domi, at the most beautiful thing he'd ever seen, at the woman he loved. He could think of no better way to die.

Amity nodded once and took a deep breath.

"Wait." Domi stepped forward. "Wait, Amity." The young woman stared at Gemini. "Spare his life."

Amity turned toward her, still keeping her blade against Gemini's neck. "Do you pity this dog?"

"I do," Domi whispered. "I loved him once. Let him kneel before you. Let him serve you."

Amity snorted. "He's a son of the enemy. He must die."

"He's a son of the enemy," Domi agreed, "which is why he must live. He's worth more to us alive. Let him be our prisoner if not our servant. Let us bring him alive to the Temple so that Beatrix might see that we've captured her son." She looked back at Gemini. "Let him cling to whatever remains of his life. He saved me, Amity. He saved my life once. Let me save his."

Amity stared at Gemini for a moment longer, then at Domi. She seemed to be considering. Finally she grunted, stepped back, and sheathed her blade.

Gemini fell to his knees, trembling. Droplets of blood dripped from his nose to splash against the deck.

"Thank you," he whispered. He reached out to Domi. "Thank you. I--"

"Lift him up!" Amity shouted to a group of sailors. "Tie him onto the mast. He tried to slay the Red Queen. He will be punished. Tie him up and beat him! Ten lashes of the whip, then toss him into the brig."

Gemini gasped. "No! I . . . I'm kneeling! I serve you! I . . . I serve you, Red Queen, please!" His voice was hoarse. "Please!"

But Amity was already walking away, and the sailors stepped forth. They grabbed Gemini. They twisted his arms behind his back. He struggled but he was too weak to resist.

"Domi, please!" he cried.

They tied him to the mast, and Domi wept and covered her eyes, and they beat him. They lashed their whips, again and again, tearing into his back, ignoring his screams, ignoring his tears, his pleading. When they finally untied him, he collapsed onto the deck, and they dragged him, and darkness fell upon Gemini, darkness greater than the night, greater than the dungeons of the Temple, greater than the loss of Domi's love. He knew nothing but shadows and pain.

CADE

He was flying high above the Horde's fleet, a golden dragon in the wind, when Cade saw the white ships rise from the northern horizon.

He frowned.

"Ships?"

Cade soared higher, and he saw them more clearly now--hundreds of masts rising from the horizon, a great armada, its sails white.

He glanced below him. The fleet of the Horde sailed there, the ships small from this height. When Cade glanced behind him, he could just make out the coast of Terra, a faded line on the horizon. He stared back ahead.

Were these more ships of the Horde, allies come to join them, sent here from another garrison?

Cade narrowed his eyes, beat his wings, and darted ahead. He shot across the sky, leaving the Horde's fleet behind, moving closer toward the distant ships.

He sucked in breath.

"Stars," he whispered.

The distant vessels--hundreds sailed there--were brigantines, carracks, and caravels, ships of the north. Their hulls were painted white, and their square sails displayed golden tillvine blossoms. Above them flew hundreds of firedrakes, riders upon them.

"The Cured Temple's fleet." Cade could barely breathe. "Beatrix attacks."

He spun around in the sky and flew as fast as he could, heading back toward the Horde's ships.

"Enemy ahead!" Cade shouted, voice roaring across the sky. "The Cured Temple attacks! Enemy ships ahead!"

Across the fleet of the Horde, sailors stared his way. Griffins, salvanae, and dragons cried out, beat their wings, and soared higher.

Wings thudded, and Amity rose to fly beside Cade. The red dragon gave the invading fleet one glance, then roared out for all to hear, "Horde! Battle formations! Horde, prepare for war!" Amity glanced at Cade and puffed a spurt of flame his way. "With me, kid. We're going to kill some star-damn Templers."

The enemy fleet kept sailing closer, and Cade could hear their war drums now, their horns wailing like dying men, and the distant buzz of priests and warriors chanting for victory. Below Cade, the sailors in the Horde's crow's nests spotted the enemy masts, and they cried out their warnings and blew their own horns.

"Enemy ships! Enemy ships!"

Griffins took flight from decks and rose to fly to one side of the Horde's fleet, a great cloud of fur and feathers and gleaming yellow beaks. Salvanae rose too, uncoiling to form great serpents in the sky, as long as the ships, chinking and gleaming and bugling out their cries. Upon the ships, archers nocked arrows, gunners poured gunpowder into cannons, and warriors brandished their swords, axes, spears, and hammers.

With a flash of blue scales, Fidelity soared to fly by Cade. "What is it?" she said, squinting toward the distance. In her dragon form, she didn't even have one lens to see through. "I can't see! How many Temple ships?"

"All of them, I think." Cade beat his wings. "Fly, Fidelity! Let's burn the bastards."

The two dragons flew, following Amity. The red dragon roared ahead, blasting out fire, crying out for war. More wings thudded, and three more dragons soared to join them: Korvin, a burly charcoal beast, his scales like iron plates; Roen, a long green dragon, a creature like a fairy tale monster of moss and leaf, a dragon of the deep woods, roaring for the burning of his forest; and Domi, a wild dragon with scales in all the colors of flame, a creature that seemed woven of fire itself. Together, six dragons-- the last of their kind in the world--stormed forth, forming the spearhead of their army, and roared out their flame.

A thousand firedrakes of the Cured Temple stormed toward them across the sea. A thousand arrows and a thousand jets of flame flew their way.

Cade roared and charged into the inferno.

The sea roiled and the sky burned.

Cade blasted out his dragonfire. The jet screamed through the air, loud as cannon fire. Streams of flame crashed around him, and arrows clattered against his scales, and he soared through the blaze.

"Fidelity, with me!" he cried.

He rose higher and saw the enemy firedrakes shooting his way, hundreds of them, covering the sky, flying in groups of five, their formations a machine of deadly precision. They stormed toward Cade, and on their backs, paladins fired their arrows.

"I'm here!" Fidelity cried, rising up toward him.

More fire flowed their way, and the two dragons--gold and blue--shouted and swooped, blasting down their dragonfire.

Their twin jets of flame wreathed together, crackling, spewing out fountains of heat. The dragonfire crashed into a flight of firedrakes below. The flames washed over one paladin, melting his armor, melting the flesh beneath. The man screamed and tumbled from the saddle, and Cade and Fidelity kept swooping. With a roar, Cade landed on one firedrake and closed his jaws around the paladin in the saddle. He bit deep, his fangs punching through steel plates, and whipped his head backward, ripping the screaming man from the saddle. He tossed the corpse aside and lashed his claws, digging them into the firedrake's tenderspots, cutting deep into the flesh within, piercing the lungs, then sending the firedrake falling. Cade reared in the sky, roaring, covered in blood, blasting out fire.

He had never known such rage, such bloodlust. The enemies swarmed around him. Fidelity, Domi, and the others fought at his sides, blasting their heat in a ring, their claws lashing. Arrows whistled all around. One arrow cracked one of Cade's scales. Another cut through his wing, and he bellowed with pain. He soared toward a firedrake above him, dodged the beast's claws, and gored the animal with his horns. Blood spilled, and Cade tugged his head madly, ripping the firedrake's belly open, spilling its innards. He yanked his head back, flew forward, and roared out fire, bathing another firedrake with the inferno. The paladin in its saddle screamed and burned.

Cade bellowed in the sky, feeling like a firedrake himself, a mindless beast who knew nothing but the hunt, the kill, the heat of battle. His roar rang across the sky. It was a roar for his dead stepparents. For his kidnapped stepsister. For his burnt village. For all those the Cured Temple had killed, for all they had destroyed. It was the roar for a lost kingdom, a fallen people, a memory fading under the light of the Cured.

"Requiem!" he cried, voice hoarse, mouth full of blood. "Remember Requiem!"

"Requiem!" Fidelity shouted, rising to fly beside him, scales blue and fangs red.

"Requiem!" shouted Domi, rising to fly at his other side.

"Requiem!" cried Korvin and Roen, blasting out their fire, and Amity joined them, shouting out for their lost kingdom. "Remember Requiem!"

Flying here with them, fighting with them, Cade was not fighting for the Horde, not for conquest, not even for revenge. He fought for that word Domi had whispered into his ear, for that memory Fidelity had kept alive in her books, for that kingdom Korvin had fought for all his life. For a memory of dragons. For dragons reborn. For Requiem.

He dodged a volley of arrows, skirted beneath the claws of firedrakes, and dipped lower in the sky. Past smoke and fire, he beheld the battle below upon the sea, and he lost his breath.

Countless ships covered the roiling waters like flotsam, burning, firing cannons, bustling with sailors. Hundreds of Temple ships, vessels with white hulls and towering masts, sailed with deadly precision. Agile longships with many oars surrounded the looming carracks and brigantines, forming dozens of battle formations. Cannons blasted from the Templers' hulls, spraying out smoke and light. Archers in white robes fired from the bulwarks. Iron figureheads, shaped as rams, drove into the hulls of Horde ships, cracking the wood, and gangplanks slammed down from deck to deck. Holy warriors, all in white, leaped from the Temple's ships onto the Horde's decks, swinging swords, raising shields. And everywhere the cannonballs flew, shattering hulls, snapping masts, driving along decks to tear men into red mist. Corpses filled the water.

Cade could only spare the battle a glance. More firedrakes flew toward him, their dragonfire crashing down. Cade shot forward and soared again, blasting his flames.

The sky was a reflection of the sea, a battle of no less intensity. The thousand firedrakes flew everywhere, a tapestry of scales and fangs. From the east flew the griffins, screeching as they lashed their talons and snapped their beaks. On their backs, riders of the Horde fired arrows and thrust lances. The griffins were burlier than dragons, their wings wider, but they had no fire; the firedrakes blasted them with their flames, and the griffins' lion bodies and eagle wings blazed. Every moment, another griffin tumbled from the sky, a fiery comet, to crash into the sea.

From the west flew hundreds of salvanae. The ancient true dragons coiled across the sky like many streamers, long and thin serpents of the air, and their beards fluttered in the sky. They were thinner and weaker than griffins, but they shot lightning bolts from their jaws. The shards of electricity slammed into firedrakes, cracking scales, driving into the armor of paladins. The salvanae were mighty, but they too were falling fast; their scales were too thin, things of beauty rather than the thick armor of dragons. Firedrake claws tore off those scales and sent them showering down in a parti-colored hail. Blood rained. Arrows drove into the true dragons, and fire washed over them, and they too fell from the sky, twisting madly as they crashed into the waves, ancient creatures gone into the sea.

By the stars of Requiem, Cade thought, heart sinking. *We're only hours off the coast of Terra, still days away from the Commonwealth, and already we're shattering.*

Korvin plunged down from the fray, covered in burns and cuts. Several of his scales were missing, and the skin beneath bled.

"Cade, with me!" the charcoal dragon shouted. "We have to protect the ships below!"

"But the sky--"

"The sky is lost!" Korvin shouted. "We must protect the fleet."

Cade glanced down again. The Horde's fleet was twice the size of the Temple's armada, but most of its ships were smaller. Rather than sail in formation, the Horde fought in an unorganized mass. Rather than follow commanders into battle, the Horde's warriors fought as a mob. Dozens of their ships blazed, listed, and sank, and cannon fire kept pounding them. Firedrakes kept swooping from the sky, raining down fire, and sails blazed. Already a dozen Horde ships had been claimed by the enemy; paladins and Temple soldiers chanted atop them, tossing off the corpses of the Horde. A few of the surviving griffins and salvanae were attacking the Temple's ships, but cannonballs and arrows slammed into them, sending them crashing down into the water.

"Dragons of Requiem, with me!" Korvin shouted and dived, curving his flight to charge toward the Temple's fleet.

Cade flew with him, screaming in his rage. Roen flew at his side; the green dragon bellowed, scales charred, claws painted red. Amity still flew somewhere above, calling out for war, and Cade could no longer see Domi and Fidelity, but he kept flying with Korvin and Roen, kept roaring, and they flew closer toward the enemy fleet. Several griffins and salvanae joined their flight, archers of the Horde on their backs.

Several carracks swayed ahead in the water, lofty ships with many sails, and hundreds of Templers stood on the decks--paladins in white plate armor and common soldiers in chain mail and white robes. As the dragons charged, Templer gunners wheeled cannons toward them.

Cade roared and dipped in the sky, skimming the water, charging toward the vessels.

The cannons fired.

Smoke blasted out. The sound was deafening. The water around the ship was flattened and waves blasted forth. With flame and roaring noise, cannonballs flew through the air. One shrieked above Cade, nearly hitting his horns. At his side, another cannonball slammed into a griffin. The beast collapsed, ribs snapping, flesh flying out in gobbets, blood raining. It crashed down into the sea, torn apart. Another cannonball slammed into another griffin's rider, scattering the body into a shower of meat and blood.

"Burn them!" Korvin roared above. The iron dragon blasted forth his dragonfire. Beside him, Roen opened his jaws wide, and the green dragon sent forth an inferno of light and heat.

Cade roared and blew his dragonfire with them.

The jets streamed forth and slammed into the enemy ships.

The carracks caught fire. Sails blazed, tore free from the masts, and flew through the air to envelope other ships. Men screamed, burning, and jumped into the water. The cannons blasted again, and Cade dipped to dodge the iron balls. He plunged into the water, sinking into the cold sea.

He opened his eyes underwater to see men sinking, struggling in their armor but only descending deeper. Blood danced around Cade like red fairies. Beating his tail, he swam under one of the brigantines, then drove upward.

His horns pierced the bottom of the ship, and Cade roared and lashed his claws, tearing through the floor, ripping out wooden flanks. Water gushed into the ship.

Cade tugged himself free from the hull, swam, and soared up from the sea, wings raining water. The blazing ship sank beneath him, but hundreds more spread all around. In the south, ships of the Horde were sinking, collapsing, blazing. The sea itself seemed to burn.

We're losing our army, Cade realized in horror. *Our griffins and salvanae keep falling dead. Our ships keep sinking.* He trembled in the sky. *We'll never even reach the coast of the Commonwealth, never mind the Temple.*

As one of the Horde's baghlah ships sank before Cade, he heard a voice cry out behind him.

"Hello again, brother! Hello, Cade! I bring you a gift of fire, and I bring you the song of death!"

Cade growled. He knew that voice. He spun in the sky and he saw her there. She flew upon a white firedrake, her cape billowing, holding a lance and shield.

Mercy Deus. His sister.

Her firedrake charged toward him, and her lance thrust, its tip smeared with green ilbane.

Cade roared and flew toward her, blowing his dragonfire.

Her white firedrake opened its jaws wide, and its cry tore through the sky, tore at Cade's ears, high pitched, twanging, beastly. Flames gushed forth from the gullet and swept toward Cade.

Dragons Reborn

The two jets of fire crashed together and cast out great fountains like an exploding sun.

The two beasts--a golden dragon and a white firedrake--charged through the inferno and crashed together.

At once their claws lashed and their teeth snapped. The white firedrake was smaller than average--even smaller than Cade--but it was a wild thing, twisting, clawing, shrieking. Cade had the sudden vision of some rabid, flying ferret covered in scales, thrashing in the sky. Fangs drove into Cade's shoulder and he yowled. Atop the white firedrake, Mercy raised her spear, prepared to thrust down the poisoned blade.

Cade hissed and swooped, dodging the lance, and flew across the sky. He soared toward the sun through smoke and flame, weaving around battling griffins and firedrakes, then spun downward. As ships blazed below, Mercy and her firedrake soared toward him. A golden dragon and a white firedrake, they charged toward each other again.

Cade rained fire. The jet crashed into the white firedrake, spraying Mercy. The paladin raised her shield, protecting herself from the inferno. The white firedrake reached out its claws and crashed into Cade again.

Cade drove down his fangs, trying to rip out the firedrake's neck, but his teeth slammed into scales as hard as steel armor. He could not pierce them. The rabid beast grabbed Cade in its claws, digging into him, holding him in the air. Cade beat his wings madly but couldn't free himself.

On the firedrake's back, Mercy rose in her stirrups and hefted her lance, prepared to thrust it into Cade's neck. Cade kicked and whipped his tail and beat his wings, but the firedrake held him fast.

"Feel the poison!" Mercy laughed. "Feel my lance drive through your neck as it drove through the neck of the gray beast."

She thrust the lance.

Cade yowled and released his magic.

The lance thrust above his head as he shrank to human form. He slipped free from the firedrake's grip and tumbled down toward the sea.

He tried to summon his magic again, but he was so tired. He was bleeding from several cuts. The blazing ships spread below, many of them sinking. Corpses rained around him, both of men and beasts. Smoke filled Cade's lungs, and the sea rushed up to meet him, and Mercy shrieked above.

Shift!

Cade gritted his teeth, reaching for his magic, desperate to clutch it. It kept slipping from him. A ship burned beneath him, and smoke filled his nostrils, and--

Finally he grabbed the magic, shifted and soared.

He rose up, seeking Mercy, but found a hundred griffins, firedrakes, and salvanae now between him and his sister. The sky burned with the battle.

"Mercy!" he roared. "Mercy, where are you?"

Cade flew through the battle, trying to see her. Arrows rose from the ships below, and one skimmed along his scales, and another sank into one of the spikes on his tail. All around him, more ships of the Horde sank, and tens of thousands of men bustled through the water like flies in blood, crying out, silenced, sinking.

And ever the ships of the Temple advanced.

White, towering vessels, they plowed through the sinking fleet of the Horde. Their cannons carved out their path, and two firedrakes flew above each ship, blasting down fire to clear any advancing Horde vessel. Again and again, the paladins on their firedrakes descended, blasting fire. Again and again, ships of the Horde sank. For every Templer vessel burned, ten ships of the Horde vanished into the water, their warriors drowned, leaving nothing but the memory of screams.

The Temple's fleet tore through the Horde's armada like a spear through flesh. Even the prodigious Behemoth roared in agony, floundering in the water, unable to fly, unable to charge. It swam like some obese, furless dog, and a hundred firedrakes kept charging toward it, bathing it with fire, tearing at its skin with claws. Again and again, the paladins fired their arrows, piercing Behemoth, and its blood filled the water.

"Mercy!" Cade roared, flying through the battle, seeking her. He had to find her again. He had to kill her. He could end this battle. He could kill its general. He--

"Cade!"

Fidelity came flying toward him. Burns marred her blue scales, and she bled from several gashes on her arms.

"Fidelity!"

She reached him and hovered in the air, panting. Her eyes were red. "Cade, we have to fly back! Back to Terra!" The blue dragon looked down at the Templer armada; a hundred ships had already plowed through the Horde and were sailing south. "Mercy hasn't just sailed here to stop our fleet. She's going to land on the coast and slay every woman and child of the Horde she can find. We have to fly back! We have to save them."

Cade stared down at the Templer ships sailing south. He stared up at the firedrakes, salvanae, and griffins still fighting above. He stared at the Horde's sinking fleet, and his heart seemed to sink just as low, and fear washed over him, as cold and suffocating as the sea's embrace.

AMITY

"Burn the ships!" Amity shouted. "Horde, fight! Fight them! Griffins, to me! Salvanae, fight, burn the firedrakes!" She flew through the inferno, burnt, cut, screaming. "Vir Requis, rally here! Requiem, burn the ships!"

Amity couldn't even see the other dragons. Korvin had been flying at her side only moments ago, but he had vanished. Amity called out to him. She called out to Domi, to Roen, even to that snot-nosed boy Cade. They had vanished into the darkness and the fire. Amity flew, dodging cannonballs, roaring as arrows scraped against her. She soared, flying between firedrakes, holding them back with her dragonfire. She dived toward the black sea, coughing from the smoke that rose from her ships. Most of those ships were gone now, buried under the sea. Most of her warriors, valiant men and women of the Horde, had burned and drowned in the water. Most of her dreams of conquest, of triumph, of a mighty flight into the Cured Temple, burned with the devastation of her forces.

No.

Amity trembled. She could barely beat her wings. She could summon no more fire to breathe, only sparks and smoke.

This wasn't supposed to happen. She beat her wings, flying through the smoke, seeking the others, calling out for them, calling for the ships, for her warriors, for a shred of hope.

We were supposed to sail toward the beaches of the Commonwealth, to sweep across their land, to conquer the north.

Now all her army, all she had fought for, the hosts she had tamed Behemoth for, slain Shafel for, bled and killed for, all burned and screamed and drowned under the waves. The sun set across the battle, and the sun set upon her hope.

"Amity!" The roar rose from below, hoarse and rumbling. "Amity, we must return to the coast!"

She looked down. Her vision was hazy. Smoke, tears, and flying scraps of burning sails hid her world. It felt like flying underwater. Through the murkiness he rose, a great charcoal dragon: Korvin.

"This wasn't meant to happen . . .," Amity whispered as the gray dragon rose to hover before her. "Korvin, this wasn't meant to--"

Howls rose above, and heat bathed Amity as three firedrakes came diving toward her. She tried to roar fire, but only sparks left her jaws; she was too weak, drained of her flames. She soared, lashed her claws, and whipped her tail. Korvin fought at her side, biting into the enemies, sending them crashing down.

"Amity, we must return to Terra!" he shouted. "Hundreds of Templer ships broke through, and the Horde's women and children are on the beaches."

Amity yowled and spun back north. "We must fly to the Commonwealth--to Requiem, Korvin! To Requiem!" She dived down, roaring for whatever warriors of the Horde remained alive. "Fly with me, Horde! Sail forth! Charge ahead! To the north, to the north!"

Korvin grabbed her tail, growling. "Amity, the women and children! They'll die without us!"

Her eyes stung. "And what of the women and children in Requiem?" Tears flowed down her scaled cheeks. "What of the babies Mercy is murdering because they're born with dragon magic? What of them, Korvin?"

"We can no longer save them!" he shouted, lashing his tail at a swooping firedrake. "Not like this, not this night! Amity!" He tried to grab her. "You are Queen of the Horde. You must protect your women and children."

"I must protect Requiem!" she roared, tears in her eyes.

She charged through the battle, cutting through smoke, fire, raining blood. She flew across ships of her army, trying to save them, to steer than onward to the north. She flew among griffins and salvanae caught in a sky of firedrakes. She flew over the dark water, over thousands of drowning people, and she was there again, a child again, flying over the sea, trying to save her parents, watching them fall dead into the water, watching them vanish, watching her life shatter, fleeing, weeping, screaming, vanishing into long shadows that engulfed her for years.

Where are you, Mother? cried a voice deep inside her. *Father, where are you?*

The sea seemed to burn in the night, the sinking ships a thousand stars, blazing with red fire. All was darkness and light, shadows and smoke, terror and memory. Defeat. Grief. Death.

I lived then, Amity thought as she flew through the smoke. *I survived, a frightened little girl, a girl grown into a vanquished queen.* She turned to look south. Past smoke and light they were sailing: the ships of the Templars, driving out from the ruin they had left on the water. And beyond the miles, beyond the dark water and death, they waited: the women, children, and elders of the Horde. Children--like the child she had been. Children whose parents she, Amity, had led to death in fire and water. Children whose blood would be on her hands.

She wept.

Goodbye, Requiem. I will not forget you. I will never stop fighting for you. But now I must fight for them.

Amity wheeled around in the sky, wings churning the black smoke, and flew south. She flew over the blazing masts of the sinking ships, over the corpses of men and beasts, caught between fire and shadow, until she reached Korvin. Until she reached the other Vir Requis. They flew together, emerging from the inferno, the ruin of their fleet. They flew south, back to the continent of Terra, back to save whoever they could before the world burned in the light of the Cured Temple.

GEMINI

He stood in the brig, shouting and pounding against the door.

"Let me out! Spirit, let me out!"

The ship swayed madly around him. Gemini fell, banging his elbow, rose to his feet again, then swayed and banged his head against the wall. The sounds of battle sounded from above: roaring dragons, clanging swords, screaming men, crackling fire. The Temple was attacking the Horde, and he was trapped here in the bowels of a ship, a prisoner again. The lanterns swung madly on the walls, casting dancing shadows. Gemini banged again at the wooden door.

"Let me out!"

With every movement, his back blazed with pain, and blood dripped from his wounds. The weredragons had beaten him, then whipped him. He was weak, maybe dying. The ship kept rocking, banging him against the walls and floor, tossing him around like dice in a shaken cup. His wounds throbbed. His head spun as madly as the ship, and every breath sawed through his throat.

"Domi!" he shouted. "Domi, let me out!"

He knew she couldn't hear him. Countless men and beasts were roaring above, cannons blasted, wood creaked, a deafening din. Gemini could barely hear himself scream. Domi must be flying high above the battle now, blasting out her fire. Mercy would be flying there too; Gemini was sure of it. He had to get out. He had to face his sister. He had to kill her himself, to take her place, to rule both Horde and Temple.

"Anyone!" he shouted hoarsely, pounding against the door again and again. "I am Lord Gemini Deus! Let me out!"

For an instant, the battle seemed almost quiet. The shouts from above faded. Only a few distant griffins shrieked.

Then, with roaring, blazing, all-consuming wrath and sound, the fists of a god pounded against the ship.

Gemini shouted and covered his ears.

Wood cracked. A cannonball tore through the ceiling and slammed down behind him, shattering the floor. Slats of wood rose like the fangs of some mechanical beast. Water, cold and black, gushed into the brig.

Gemini stared around with horror. The water rose around his ankles, then rose to his knees. Streams of more water gushed in from the walls. No more men screamed above upon the deck, only the roar of fire. The walls creaked, more water gushed in, and the brig tilted madly. Gemini stumbled and banged against the wall. Around him, he knew, the ship was sinking.

Fear, cold and wet as the ocean, flooded Gemini.

I'm going to drown. I'm going to die here. He trembled as the water rose to his waist. *I'll never get to kill Mercy. I'll never see Domi again.*

He thought of Domi's green eyes, her beautiful presence, an angel lying beside him in his bed, draped in sunlight.

I cannot lose you.

Gemini took a deep, shuddering breath and slogged through the water. He slammed against the door again and again. Water raced in, and more wood cracked, slats slamming down and shattering. The water was so deep now Gemini was swimming, his feet no longer touching the floor. He grabbed a slat of wood that thrust out from the wall and tugged, screaming, tearing it aside. He grabbed another slat. He pulled and widened the hole. More water raced in, mixed with blood. The lamps in the brig shattered and fell into the water, plunging him into darkness.

Gemini gritted his teeth and shoved himself through the hole. The wooden slats scraped against the wounds on his back, and he yowled, nearly passing out from the pain. Water slammed down against him, filling his mouth, and he coughed, pulled himself forward, dragged himself out of the brig. Blindly he swam, climbed, tugged himself up the stairs, and finally shoved a hatch open and crawled onto the deck.

The gates of the Abyss seemed to have opened around him, spewing forth their evil.

A thousand ships burned in the night, shattered, and sank around him, most of them the vessels of the Horde. Countless men screamed in the water, burnt, drowning. Thousands of corpses floated or sank. The skies were a reflection of the terror below; griffins flew above, blazing. Salvanae roared, their scales dangling loose, their wounds dripping. Countless firedrakes screamed above, spewing flame, and in the distance, Gemini could make out the carracks of the Cured Temple.

Mercy is here somewhere.

"Sister!" he shouted. "Mer--"

The deck swayed beneath him, and he fell to his knees. He looked around him, and his heart sank. His ship's deck had shattered in two, and wooden slats rose like quills on a porcupine. A mast cracked and fell down beside him, shattering more planks. Only a few scattered men still lived on the ship; Cade watched a few leap into a rowboat and begin to row away, only for a firedrake to plunge from the sky and burn them.

Gemini stared around in terror. More cannonballs slammed into the sinking ship, and he fell back down. The sky burned. The sea raged. A wave soared, demonic and black, and crashed down onto him. He swallowed water and coughed, and when the wave subsided, he realized that the deck was now fully submerged.

I'm going to die here. I'm going to drown. He panted. *I'm going to die, oh Spirit, please don't let me die, please--*

He clenched his fists.

No.

He growled and rose to his feet on the submerged deck. The water rose to his knees.

No, I'm going to live. He shouted to the sky, arms tossed back.

"I am Gemini Deus, and I'm going to live!" He laughed, the world spinning around him. Burning scraps of human skin rained from the sky. "I'm going to live! Do you hear me, Mercy? Do you hear me, Domi? You cannot kill me! No one can kill me! I am Gemini and I will rule the Temple!"

The deck gave a *crack* underwater. Bubbles shot up, the last air fleeing the cabins below. The ship plunged down into the sea.

Laughing, Gemini vanished under the water with it.

The air fleeing the cabins roared up around him, millions of bubbles. He tried to kick and swim but could not in the froth. He kept sinking, and the air ached in his lungs. Men sank around him, heavy in their armor, kicking but finding no way to swim in the roiling bubbles.

One drowning man slammed against Gemini. He grabbed the man and shoved as powerfully as he could, pushing himself sideways, out of the froth escaping the sinking ship. He kicked, desperate for air, and rose in the water. Firelight blazed above, and Gemini had to breathe, had to open his mouth, to fill his lungs, even if it was seawater. Stars floated behind his eyes. He had to sink. He had to breathe. He--

No. I will live.

He kicked madly.

He breached the surface.

He gulped down hot, smoky, beautiful air.

He floated in the dark sea, the flames raging around him. Flotsam floated everywhere, most of it burning. Corpses were sinking in their armor, and more kept raining from the sky. Some ships listed and slowly sank; most were already gone. The only ships that still floated were the warships of the Cured Temple, white carracks and brigantines. They were distant, sailing away, leaving him here.

"Domi!" he shouted, but he could not see her. Above, the firedrakes were streaming south, leaving the debris behind.

The Templers had come here with ships and firedrakes and paladins, Gemini realized. Better armed, better organized, better trained, they had shattered the pathetic flotilla of the Horde, and now they moved on.

Leaving me.

The Temple's ships sailed away, growing more distant until they were only floating lights in the darkness like fireflies. The firedrakes flew above them, their shrieks only distant echoes, memories of their wrath. Gemini remained, bobbing in the rising and falling water, as all around him scraps of wood blazed, the last few masts sank into the dark depths, and men screamed as they slipped down, down, down into darkness and silence, leaving him too.

MERCY

She flew on her firedrake, hundreds more flying around her, hundreds of ships sailing below, and she saw it in the distance, a line of light upon the black horizon: the coast of Terra.

The land that tried to topple us. Mercy tightened her jaw and clutched her lance. *The land that harbored the weredragons. The land that sought to darken the light of my lord.* She bared her teeth. *The land I will destroy.*

Behind her rose the smoke and fire of the fleet she had drowned, the enemy she had vanquished. She had sent hundreds of ships down into the depths, slain myriads of warriors. She was a queen of conquest, a bringer of blood, a holy warrior of the Spirit, the vengeful blade of her faith. And still she flew onward.

"I will not allow the Horde to recover, to nurse their wounds and their hatred, to seek vengeance against me," she whispered to her firedrake. "When you fight an enemy, you must destroy him. You must hit him so hard he will never rise again. If you give your enemy a bloody nose, he will heal and strike back with more vengeance than before. If you shatter his head against the wall and slay his brothers and children, none will ever contest your might."

The white beast below her clattered and cawed, spurting out smoke. Mercy smiled thinly.

"And so we will slay their brothers, their children, their wives whose wombs would bear new warriors. It will be a night of blood, a dawn of fire, the hour of our greatest triumph."

She flew toward the coast--Lady Mercy Deus, Lady of Wrath, Lady of Dominion.

The coast grew closer, and Mercy saw countless lights of campfires. Two massive statues rose ahead, shaped as rearing stallions with gilded hoofs, the firelight reflecting off them. The horses were still distant, but even from miles away, she could see them clearly. They must have stood hundreds of feet tall, as tall as the Cured Temple back home. Beyond the statues, even as Mercy and her army approached, she saw no civilization. No buildings rose ahead, no towers, no streets, no fortresses, as if the Horde-- this massive mob of many nations--had spent all their effort and industry on raising two equine idols, then remained with nothing but poverty for the remains of their realm.

They live in tents, Mercy realized as she flew closer. She guffawed. *Tents in the dirt. Nomads. Barbarians.*

Dawn began to rise in the east, its red light falling upon the coast and the camp that sprawled toward the hills. This was nothing but a camp for refugees, for all those the Commonwealth had driven from their homes: the Tirans of the desert, the brutes from the swamps, the scattered remains of humanity that had somehow survived the slaughter in Osanna and the fall of the ancient Terran civilizations. The dregs of humanity. Heretics. Seaside scum, no more. Benighted barbarians who did not know the light of the Spirit.

"But they will see our light now," Mercy vowed. "And it will burn them. The dawn rises, and so does the Cured Temple."

She raised her banner high, letting the tillvine blossom shine in the dawn, and she shouted out for her army to hear.

"For the glory of the Temple! For the light of the Spirit! Slay the heathens! Slay every heretic in the name of our god."

Across the sky, hundreds of paladins raised their banners upon hundreds of firedrakes. Many of the firedrakes were missing scales, charred, cut from the battle over the sea. Many of the paladins were bleeding, their armor dented. But they were ready for more bloodshed, for more holy light. They cried out with her.

"For the Spirit! For the Temple!"

Their banners streamed. Their horns blared out their cry. Below in the water, hundreds of ships still sailed, the victors of the battle. Brigantines and carracks flowed forth, sails wide, and longboats oared between them like great centipedes. Horns wailed. Men cried out for glory. War drums beat. Cannons wheeled toward the coast.

"For the glory of the Spirit!" the warriors chanted across the hosts.

And on the coast, Mercy saw them: the women and children of the Horde. They were pointing. They were crying out. And they were fleeing.

Mercy allowed herself a thin smile. She stroked her firedrake, and she spoke softly to the beast. "Burn them all."

With the cries of firedrakes, the beating of drums, and the chanting of holy warriors, the Temple fleet reached the enemy coast.

"Cannons, fire!" Mercy shouted from above. "Tear them down!"

In the ocean, the white warships of the Temple turned their guns toward the coast. Men lit fuses. With smoke and roaring fire, with a sound that cracked the sky itself, hundreds of cannonballs flew toward the Horde.

Flying above on her firedrake, Mercy watched and smiled.

The cannonballs tore through the heretics. They drove through tents. They drove into fleeing women and children, scattering gobbets of flesh and bone, crushing people like melons. Screams rose across the camp, and the people began to flee. Thousands emerged from the remaining tents like ants from a disturbed burrow. Wailing, they began to race inland.

"Fire!" Mercy shouted.

The guns blasted again, shaking the ships, flattening the water, blasting out smoke, and the cannonballs flew toward the beaches. Tents shattered. Chunks of human flesh flew through the air. Some of the heathens survived; they crawled forward, missing limbs, spilling their entrails. Fires blazed across the camp. Cannonballs thudded against the great horse statues, chipping the stone, deforming the proud stone faces of the beasts.

Mercy reached down to stroke Talis's white scales.

"Burn them," she whispered to the firedrake. "Burn them all."

Talis spread his wings and flew higher, tossed back his scaly head, and roared to the sky. Mercy roared with him.

"Burn them all!" she cried. "Firedrakes, attack!"

With thudding wings and shrieks, hundreds of firedrakes flew across the water and swooped toward the heathen hive of Hakan Teer.

The people screamed, fled, cowered, prayed.

And Mercy burned them.

She burned all that she could.

She plunged from the sky, and her firedrake spewed down his fire. The blazing stream crashed into tents, consumed sheep and goats in their corrals, slammed into fleeing women and children. They screamed. They fell. Some ran to the beaches, burning. But mostly they died. Mercy laughed, dug her spurs into Talis's tenderspots, and they soared toward the sky, then dipped again, blasting down fire. More heathens burned.

All across the tent city, the firedrakes streamed. They shot down flames. Some women and children were running to the hills, and Mercy flew toward them, burned them down, then dived back toward the tents and burned some more. Smoke and fire enveloped the world. The screams of the dying filled the air. Hundreds of firedrakes flew all around, sending down their death.

Mercy laughed as she fought, as she conquered. Her banner streamed behind her, and she was a figure of light, of piety, of holy victory.

"For the Spirit!" she cried. "Burn them all! Burn the heathens!"

She gritted her teeth as she flew, as she burned, as her drake screamed beneath her.

I lost my child. She clenched her fists. *And so they will lose their children. They will lose everything they've had. In your name, my fallen daughter, I will conquer this world, and I will shine the light of the Spirit upon the Horde's skeletons.*

A group of children were running ahead, heading toward the hills. One among them, a little girl, was missing her legs; they ended with shattered, spurting stumps. Her brother carried her, and they all ran, wailing, seeking safety. Mercy swooped, prepared to burn them down, a goddess of wrath, when the roars rose from the north.

She tugged the reins, pulling Talis upward, and stared toward the sea.

A smile spread across her face.

Mercy laughed and raised her banner high as the city burned beneath her.

"Hello, weredragons!" she cried. "Welcome to the Abyss!"

They flew out from the dawn's light, six weredragons, a dozen griffins, a dozen salvanae. A ragtag group of bandits. A group she would burn.

Let the death of their Horde be the last thing they ever see. They will die knowing the depths of their failure.

"Burn them, Talis!" Mercy shouted, digging her spurs deep into the beast. "Slay the creatures! Paladins of the Spirit, rise! Rise and fly! Slay the weredragons!"

Mercy grinned as the firedrakes shot forward. She steadied her lance. The dawn rose upon her and her firedrakes, a dawn of glory, of holiness. She had defeated the Horde in one of the greatest victories of her faith, and now--on this very dawn, the dawn of Mercy's ascension--she would slay the last weredragons.

She would bring about the Falling.

This dawn the Horde falls, she thought as she streamed forward, the wind roaring around her. *This dawn King's Column will shatter. This dawn the Spirit himself will descend to the world, and I--Lady Mercy--will become a saint, a seraph, a daughter of the Spirit.*

"A dawn of light," she whispered. "A dawn of victory. A dawn of dominion and falling marble."

Roaring and blasting out fire, the weredragons flew over the beach and charged toward her. Laughing, Mercy and her hundreds of firedrakes stormed forth to meet them.

FIDELITY

She had never seen such destruction.

As Fidelity flew over the blazing city, this mass killing field, tears filled her eyes, and her breath died in her lungs, and her ribs seemed to wrap so tightly around her heart they could still its beat.

Thousands dead, she thought, the world a haze. Her eyes were weak, especially in dragon form with no spectacles to wear. But she did not need sharp eyesight to see the fire, the mountains of corpses, to smell the burning flesh, to hear the screams.

Mercy did not come here merely to conquer, to defeat an enemy, Fidelity realized. *She came here to kill every last man, woman, and child in Terra.*

And Mercy, eldest daughter of Beatrix, heiress to the Cured Temple, now flew toward Fidelity on a white firedrake, and a hundred other paladins and firedrakes flew with her.

Fidelity tossed back her head, spread her wings wide, and roared for battle, for rage, for fear, for hope. She roared the word forbidden in the north, the word she had always fought for, her battle cry, her never-ending dream.

"Requiem!"

She charged toward the enemy, and her family flew with her. Korvin, her father, a great gray dragon, the strongest and wisest man she knew. Roen, a green dragon of the forest, the man she loved, the man she had loved since her youth. Cade, a new hope for Requiem, a young golden dragon with light in his eyes. Amity, a red dragon, a great warrior, a heroine Fidelity admired. Domi, a spirit of fire, a living flame, her sister. They flew with her now; they would always fly together, the last survivors of Requiem, their ancient kingdom's warriors and torchbearers. They stormed across the beach, and they roared for their homeland, and they blasted out their flame.

Six streams of dragonfire shot across like the sky toward Mercy.

Mercy's white firedrake rose higher, then plunged down. Countless other firedrakes swooped with her, blasting forth their flame.

Fidelity screamed.

She flew through a blazing sun, through the death of a nation, through the burning of a world, the shattering of souls. All was fire, heat, sound, rage, pain, light. She screamed. She flew blindly. She shot out from the fire and smoke, spun in the sky, and saw endless fangs, claws, eyes. More fire rained upon her. She cried out. Her scales expanded and broke, a dozen *cracks* like splintering wood. All around the firedrakes attacked. She spun in rings, blowing her dragonfire, trying to hold them back. She lashed her tail. She snapped her teeth. She clawed at her enemies. The few griffins and salvanae who had survived the battle over the sea flew above and around her, falling, burning, crashing down.

And still the cannons boomed.

Still the firedrakes sent down their inferno.

Still the people below died by the thousands.

Fidelity spun through the sky, seeking Mercy again, but could no longer see the paladin, and other riders kept flying toward her, blasting fire her way, and Fidelity soared higher, dipped through the air, knowing she could not fight them all, knowing she would die here, knowing everyone below would burn.

I must save whoever I still can.

She clenched her teeth and dived down.

I must save the women and children of the Horde.

"Domi, Roen!" she shouted. She spotted the two fighting farther away. "We have to evacuate them! We have to gather whoever we can and fly!"

She pulled her wings closer to her body and dived.

A firedrake flew up toward her. Fidelity bathed it with fire. Another beast flew from her side, and she lashed her tail, whipping the firedrake's rider so hard she shattered his armor and tore off his arm.

She kept diving, heading down toward a group of running children. One among them had no legs; he ran on stumps, screaming, before falling and crawling onward.

A firedrake came flying from the other direction, ready to blast fire, to roast the fleeing children. Fidelity roared. She beat her wings, soaring above the children, almost knocking against them, and blasted forth dragonfire. She slammed into the firedrake an instant before it could burn the children, snapped her teeth, clawed at its rider. Her jaws closed around the firedrake's neck, tore out flesh, and she spat. Fidelity bellowed, blood in her mouth, and the firedrake crashed down dead.

She shot fire skyward, holding back other drakes, then landed on the earth.

One of the children already lay dead, flesh burning, legs gone. The others ran, fleeing Fidelity, wailing.

They don't know I'm Vir Requis, Fidelity realized. *They see the blue dragon and think I'm a firedrake.*

She leaped upward, knocked down another firedrake with her claws, and landed in front of the fleeing children.

"Wait!" she called out. "I'm a good dragon! Listen to me!" The children wept, screamed, and turned to flee again. Fidelity slammed down her tail, cutting off their retreat. "I'm here to help you."

Several firedrakes shrieked above, plunging toward her, and opened their jaws to blow fire. Fidelity grimaced, prepared to feel the heat, when Roen and Cade shot overhead. The two dragons, green and gold, roared and slammed into the firedrakes, knocking them down. They blew their dragonfire skyward, sealing Fidelity in a blazing shell.

She took a deep breath and released her magic. She stood before the children as a woman.

"See me?" she said. "See? I'm like you. You have to trust me." She looked up. "Cade! Cade, land here!"

The golden dragon nodded, swiped his tail against another firedrake, then landed beside her.

"Cade, get them out of here!" Fidelity shouted, still in human form. "Take them over the water, fly north! Fly over the sea."

"To where?" he shouted.

"Anywhere!" she cried out as firedrakes and dragons roared above, as blood rained. "Anywhere that's safe. Fly! I'll find you in the Commonwealth!"

Cade cursed. "It's a big place, Fidelity. Where will we meet?"

"Draco Murus!" she said, choosing a name from the old book. "Fly to the ruins of Draco Murus! You remember!"

He nodded and lowered his wing. The children still wept, and at first they resisted, but Fidelity urged them onward, goading them up Cade's wing. They sat on the gold dragon's back, fourteen in all, clinging together.

"Now fly!" Fidelity cried. "To Draco Murus!"

Cade nodded and took flight, wings churning smoke. He dipped, rose higher, blasted fire at a drake, and cut a way through. He vanished into the smoke.

Fidelity shifted back into a dragon and soared, joining Roen. She blew her fire skyward, ascended through the blaze, and crashed into a firedrake. As the beast bled, she grabbed its paladin in her jaws and bit deep, punching her fangs through the armor, tearing the man out of the saddle, and finally spat him out. Roen thrust his horns into the firedrake's neck, goring the reptile, sending it tumbling down.

Shrieks rose behind her, and Fidelity spun to see a hundred or more people fleeing, women and children and elders. Three firedrakes dived down, paladins on their backs, and blasted forth their fire. The fleeing people burned, fell, rolled, screamed as they died. Their skin peeled back like bark, falling from their flesh, and the flames dug deeper, eating down to the bone.

All across the blazing camp, people were fleeing only to be torched or cut down. Some firedrakes were swooping, lashing their claws, scooping up people and tossing them into the air. Other firedrakes pounced onto children, bit down, tore the little bodies apart, scattering limbs. Several firedrakes stood above hills of dead and wounded, feasting on human flesh. One girl wept, lying in the dirt, as a firedrake chewed on her severed arms. A firedrake above tossed its head around, and a foot pattered down onto Fidelity, then the head of a woman, mouth opened in a silent scream.

How can I stop such horror? she thought, eyes burning. *How can I stop this bloodshed, this killing, this theater of death?*

"We have to save more, Roen!" she cried, eyes damp. "They're burning them all!"

The green dragon nodded. "Fly with me."

They soared together, crashing through enemies, burning through a falling sky, a collapsing heaven descending into chaos and light and dancing shadows, a world of demons. Domi and Korvin flew in the distance, back to back, holding off the enemies. Far below, Fidelity saw more people racing across the land, heading to the hills, leaping over the corpses of those who had already failed to flee. Fidelity knew they wouldn't go far, not without help.

"Domi!" she shouted. "Korvin!"

They saw her and flew her way. A firedrake dived between them, and Fidelity shot forward. The paladin on its back fired an arrow, and Fidelity shouted as the missile scraped along her cheek, shattering a scale. She grabbed the man in her claws and pulled back hard, tearing off his head, exposing a gaping neck that sputtered blood. Korvin roared as he gored the firedrake, tugging his horns along its flank. Its organs spilled like a gutted fish, and the beast crashed down to the ground. Domi flew above, spurting fire upward, holding back other firedrakes, her flames so hot they melted the beasts' bellies. Chunks of charred blood pattered down.

"Korvin, Domi--the women and children!" Fidelity pointed at the group she had spotted fleeing. "We have to save them."

They nodded and charged. The four dragons blasted their fire together, cleaving a path through the enemy. Fidelity prayed that Cade still lived, that he had saved the children, that he now flew over the water.

She landed before the fleeing children. Korvin and Roen remained above, holding back the swarm of firedrakes, as Domi lowered her wing. Fidelity became a human again, herding the children onto Domi, one by one.

"Hurry! Onto Domi, go, and--"

Fidelity's voice died as a firedrake made its way past Korvin and Roen. The bronze beast slammed down onto the ground and shrieked, its cry so loud Fidelity covered her ears, and the children who stood closer screamed as their eardrums ruptured, as blood dripped from within. The firedrake lashed its jaws, so fast Fidelity barely saw it move, and tore a boy apart. It tossed back its head, guzzling down the top half of the boy. The child's stomach and legs collapsed onto the ground.

Fidelity screamed, shifted back into a dragon, and charged. She gored the creature's neck with her horns. It fell back, and Roen roasted it with dragonfire.

"Go, Domi!" Fidelity cried as another survivor climbed onto the fiery dragon. "Fly to the sea! Fly to Draco Murus!"

Domi nodded and took flight. Below in the blazing camp, other survivors cried out, reaching up to Domi, begging for their lives, begging to be carried away.

Korvin landed next. Ugly gashes bled on his side, and holes peppered his wings. One of his horns was cracked, and several of his scales were shattered. He lowered his wing, forming a ramp, and more survivors raced up. The gray dragon took flight, tearing through the enemy, rising into the clouds, vanishing into the shadows.

A roar pierced the killing field. Wreathed in fire, a figure of wrath and ruin, a red dragon swooped, a creature so beastly at first Fidelity thought it a firedrake. Then she recognized Amity. The Red Queen landed, covered in burns and cuts, her eyes wild.

"So many dead," she whispered, voice haunted.

"Grieve later!" Fidelity shouted. "We have to save who we can. Amity, help me!"

They took flight. Only three dragons remained now: Fidelity, Roen, and Amity. They crashed through enemies. There were barely any more survivors left, only corpses, thousands, hills of them burning. Finally they found a group of survivors who raced over the dead, seeking safety on the beaches, and loaded them onto Amity's back. The red dragon soared, barely able to blow any more fire, her wings creaking, her scales bleeding. Crying out in agony, Amity flew off across the sea, a score of firedrakes in pursuit.

Only Roen and Fidelity now remained on the coast, and hundreds of firedrakes still flew. Without the other dragons--the burly Korvin, the wild Amity, the fiery Domi--to hold them off, the firedrakes charged forth toward the beach, bloodlust in their eyes. Again Fidelity saw the white firedrake and the white paladin upon it--Mercy Deus.

A group of children came racing along the sand, fire clutching at their clothes.

"Help!" they cried, racing toward Fidelity. "Blue Queen, help us!"

Fidelity made to leap toward them when the fire rained from the sky.

An inferno.

A holocaust of heat and light.

A shattering world, collapsing heavens.

Fidelity yowled, flying through the pain, trying to reach the children. Several of them fell, burning.

"I'll hold off the drakes!" Roen shouted, soaring. "Fidelity, fly with the children!"

Fidelity wept, trying to reach them. A firedrake landed on the beach. She swiped her claws, knocking it down.

"Roen, fly with me! We have to leave, now!"

The green dragon growled, soaring higher. "Save them, Fidelity! Fly with them, go!"

Another firedrake landed on the beach, snapped its jaws, and tore a child apart. Fidelity screamed, leaped toward it, and cut it down. But more drakes kept landing. One landed on her back and bit into her shoulder. Fidelity screamed. Another landed before her and lashed its claws, slicing her face. She cried out in pain, desperate to cling to her magic, to remain a dragon.

Above she saw Roen battling dozens of the creatures. He whipped his tail around, blew his fire, sent paladins crashing down on their mounts.

Fidelity cried out, shook off the firedrake on her back, lashed her tail, and knocked down the drake ahead of her. Only a few children still lived.

"Onto my back!" she shouted. "Hurry!"

They raced forward. A firedrake landed, lifted one child in its jaws, and feasted. The other children screamed, raced up Fidelity's wing, and clung to her bleeding back.

She beat her wings. She took flight.

"Roen, let's go!" she shouted.

She flew off the beach, over the water, and looked back toward him. "Roen!"

A hundred firedrakes streamed toward Roen. Hundreds more rose from the camp, blood and flesh in their jaws, flying toward the green dragon.

He turned to look at Fidelity.

He whispered through the storm.

"Fly, Fidelity. Fly. I love you."

Then Roen roared and blasted out his fire, a torn roar, a great howl, and he charged toward the enemy.

"Roen, no!" Fidelity shouted. "Roen!"

She wanted to charge forward. She wanted to fight with Roen, to die with him if she must, but how could she sacrifice the children on her back? She watched, helpless, as the fire draped across the green dragon. She watched, screaming, as he slew firedrake after firedrake, burning them, cutting them, biting out their throats, lashing his tail at their riders. She watched, weeping, as hundreds of arrows slammed into his scales, as hundreds of flaming jets crashed against him, as he roared for her, as he called out her name in his pain. The corpses of firedrakes lay around him, victims of his wrath, until finally it was Mercy Deus upon her firedrake--Mercy, an angel of wrath and retribution--who rode toward him, who smiled, laughed, and thrust her lance.

Roen's roar died in the sky. His wings spread out, wreathed in fire. The lance drove into his chest, cut through him, and emerged from his back.

"Roen!" Fidelity screamed, weeping.

Above the beach, the green dragon lost his magic.

He tumbled down from the sky, a man again.

Mercy swooped and her firedrake caught Roen's human form before he could hit the beach. The white firedrake rose, holding Roen, cackling madly, and upon its back Mercy stared across the water toward Fidelity.

"This will be your fate too, Fidelity!" Mercy cried out. "I know your name, weredragon! I know who you are, and I will kill you all like I kill him."

Roen was still alive, Fidelity saw; he twitched in the firedrake's claws. He was so beautiful, so hurt, the kindest man Fidelity knew, the bravest, the noblest, the man she loved.

The white firedrake raised him higher, and Mercy drew her sword. The paladin leaned forward in her saddle and drove her blade into Roen's heart.

Fidelity wept.

She turned and flew across the water, the children on her back.

Roen . . . I'm sorry. I'm sorry. I love you. I love you.

She streamed across the water, those she had saved--those *he* had saved--upon her back. Her tears fell. She had seen her father fall, seen Amity burn, but this time there could be no doubt. Roen had given his life--to her, to them. To Requiem. Fidelity's tears fell as she flew, as behind the hundreds of firedrakes roared and followed.

I love you, Roen.

She thought of his warm eyes, his arms wrapped around her, his love, his strength, his wisdom, his kindness, and she could not stop weeping. The children clung to her, and she flew as fast as she could, fleeing the blaze, the crash of a kingdom, fleeing into the darkness. Perhaps there was no place left to flee to. Perhaps all the world was now ruin and above it the cruel light of the Cured Temple. Her hope faded to but a sliver, but a last grain of life like those she had saved, a dying hope in a dying world.

A few lights burned ahead; Fidelity did not know if they were her fellow Vir Requis or the husks of sinking ships. She flew onward, into despair, into darkness, as behind her the fire burned.

CADE

He crashed down onto the beach, scales cracked, wings whistling with holes, smoke puffing out of his nostrils. As soon as his claws hit the surface, he collapsed and slid across the sand, and his head fell onto its side.

He stared through narrowed eyes. The world was hazy. Cade could barely see through the veil of pain. A rocky beach. Barren hills.

"The Commonwealth," he whispered.

The women and children he had saved from the inferno in Terra climbed off his back. They huddled in the sand, lips parched, throats dry, wounded, burnt, shivering, barely alive. Cade shifted into human form and lay on the sand, too weak to cling to his dragon magic, too weak to rise.

Where are the others?

He pushed himself onto his wobbly elbows. He had flown for three days across the sea. Vaguely he remembered giving Amity--an Amity in human form, bruised and bleeding--a ride on his back, then shifting into human form and sleeping on the red dragon's back. He could not see the Red Queen now. He could not see Domi, Fidelity, Korvin, Roen.

"Where are you?" Cade whispered, and something tore and bled in his throat. He had not had water in three days aside from a few drops of rain.

A flame flickered across the sky, coiling under the clouds, flying nearer. A torn howl rose, and wings spread wide, and Cade could finally make out a red dragon over the gray sea. Amity flew closer, wobbling, and crashed down onto the beach. She lost her magic at once, spilling the refugees off her back. They landed in the sand, shivering, the burnt survivors of the camp. One child, a little girl still clutching her doll, was dead, her skin gray, saved from the fire but too wounded to survive the long flight.

Amity crawled across the sand toward Cade. Blood caked her short yellow hair. Her clothes were as tattered as his. Rents on her trousers revealed raw cuts, burn marks stretched across her arms, and bruises coated the left side of her face.

"Amity!" Cade managed to whisper, voice hoarse. "Have you seen the others? Have you seen Domi and Fidelity? Korvin?"

She reached him, shivering, and clutched his arms. Her fingers dug into him, hard and painful, almost tearing his skin. She stared at him, eyes wild, lips trembling, teeth bared.

"We . . . we have to go back." Amity shook wildly. "We have to fight. We have to kill Mercy. We have to attack the Temple. We . . ." She lowered her head, and her tears fell into the sand. "How did this happen? We should be here with an army. A great army that I lead."

Amity doubled over, shaking, sobbing. Cade wrapped his arms around her, holding her close. They sat together in the sand,

and Cade kept watching the horizon, waiting for the others to arrive: for Korvin, the strongest and wisest man Cade had ever known; for Fidelity, his dearest friend, the woman he had fought with for so long; for Roen, quiet and wise and strong, a great warrior of the forest; for Domi, precious and wild Domi, the woman he loved.

Yet no more dragons flew from the sea.

No more survivors reached the beach.

Domi . . .

Cade turned toward the survivors. He walked among them. A young woman, no older than him, holding her babe. A boy and his sister, younger than ten, their limbs burnt. An old man, weeping, whispering of his lost sons. A handful of others, remnants of life.

"We saved them," Cade whispered. "We failed Requiem. We failed the world. But we saved a few. We saved some life." He turned toward Amity. "We have to find them water, food, shelter, we . . ."

But Amity did not seem to hear him. She stood with her back to him, facing the sea. Her fists trembled at her sides, and her head was lowered. The wind ruffled her hair. Cade approached slowly.

"Amity?"

Ignoring him, she tossed back her head, and she howled to the sky. A torn howl. A roar of rage, of fallen nations, of broken dreams, of genocide and death in fire. Her entire body went into her roar, arms stretched out, a cry that tore through her limbs, belly, lungs, soul. When finally her cry died, cracking into a faded rasp, Amity fell to her knees and her head slumped.

Cade stood beside her. He placed a hand on her shoulder, not knowing what to do, how to comfort her, how to comfort himself, how to find any hope in a fallen world.

When Domi whispered in my ear, I dared to dream of Requiem. I dared to hope we could revive our kingdom, save babes from the tillvine . . . yet now those babes are dead, and now all our armies are laid to waste. He looked at Amity. The warrior's eyes were clenched shut, her lips tightened, her face a mask of grief. *Now perhaps Amity and I are all that remain of our fallen nation.*

"I'm sorry, Amity," Cade said softly. "I don't know what to do. I don't know how we can keep fighting. I'm not strong like Korvin or Roen, not wise like Fidelity, not brave like Domi. But for whatever it's worth, I'm here with you. You're not alone."

Amity rose to her feet and tugged him toward her, and at first Cade thought she would attack him, scratch him, gouge out his eyes in her rage, but she only crushed him between her arms, her body shaking against his, clinging to him.

Are you out there? Cade thought, staring at the sea and the veiled sky. The clouds roiled above like smoke, and a drizzle began to fall, pattering against the sea and sand, washing the dirt from his hair, streaming down his face like tears. He stood for a long time, holding Amity close, staring into a horizon of shadows, of memories of fire . . . and of dying hope.

The story continues in . . .

DRAGONS RISING

REQUIEM FOR DRAGONS, BOOK 3

NOVELS BY DANIEL ARENSON

Dawn of Dragons:
Requiem's Song
Requiem's Hope
Requiem's Prayer

Song of Dragons:
Blood of Requiem
Tears of Requiem
Light of Requiem

Dragonlore:
A Dawn of Dragonfire
A Day of Dragon Blood
A Night of Dragon Wings

The Dragon War:
A Legacy of Light
A Birthright of Blood
A Memory of Fire

Requiem for Dragons:
Dragons Lost
Dragons Reborn
Dragons Rising

The Moth Saga:
Moth
Empires of Moth
Secrets of Moth
Daughter of Moth
Shadows of Moth
Legacy of Moth

Alien Hunters:
Alien Hunters
Alien Sky
Alien Shadows

KEEP IN TOUCH

www.DanielArenson.com
Daniel@DanielArenson.com
Facebook.com/DanielArenson
Twitter.com/DanielArenson

Printed in Great Britain
by Amazon